QUICKSAND

QUICKSAND

A NORA KHALIL NOVEL

CAROLYN BAUGH

A TOM DOHERTY ASSOCIATES BOOK | NEW YORK

This is a work of fiction. All of the characters, organizations, and events portrayed in this novel are either products of the author's imagination or are used fictitiously.

QUICKSAND

Copyright © 2015 by Carolyn Baugh

A Forge Book
Published by Tom Doherty Associates, LLC
175 Fifth Avenue
New York, NY 10010

www.tor-forge.com

Forge® is a registered trademark of Tom Doherty Associates, LLC.

The Library of Congress Cataloging-in-Publication Data is available upon request.

ISBN 978-0-7653-7560-5 (hardcover)
ISBN 978-1-4668-4780-4 (e-book)

Our books may be purchased in bulk for promotional, educational, or business use. Please contact your local bookseller or the Macmillan Corporate and Premium Sales Department at (800) 221-7945, extension 5442, or by e-mail at MacmillanSpecialMarkets@macmillan.com.

First Edition: September 2015

Printed in the United States of America

0 9 8 7 6 5 4 3 2 1

For Aya

ACKNOWLEDGMENTS

An opinion piece by LZ Granderson ("Treat Chicago Gangs as Terrorists") helped shape my thinking about gang violence in the United States and the definition of terror; meanwhile, Nick Kristof and Sheryl WuDunn awakened me to the terrors of sex trafficking. Many people helped bring Nora Khalil to life, in particular my daughters, who I expect to always be as badass and sweet as Nora, in that order, and my mom, my biggest fan. I want to thank my cousin Mary Lowry, who inspired me by being in the first generation of female FBI agents and who dropped everything to "be there" when she was most needed. Finally, special thanks to Angela Bell, FBI, who was patient enough to share her knowledge with me and purge some of my biggest mistakes.

QUICKSAND

PROLOGUE

Her bare feet smacked against the cold, slick grass. She ran fast, faster than she ever thought she could, and the sharp, crisp air could not keep up with her; she gasped, trying hard to pull enough air into her body to propel it faster, faster, faster. She could not stop, must not stop, she must run, and this time she must get away, away, away, where they couldn't get her, couldn't touch her, couldn't take her back, never go back, never, never, never . . .

She saw the curling, intertwined letters, out of place, it seemed to her, on a neon sign with a deep gash in one corner. She focused on the sign, and her feet left the littered lawns that stretched out in front of tall, tired houses and she ran across cement, and then onto jagged gravel. She looked for the side door and found it, and, as she doubled over in pain, everything within her shocked at having run so fast, it was all she could do to push open that door and stumble inside.

Scarved heads jerked up immediately at the sound of her entrance. Eyes widened.

But she could not speak, could barely breathe. Somehow, her thin legs took her near the circle of women, and then she sank down, down, onto the soft carpet, knowing she could go no further.

Shocked murmurs floated above her head, and she felt some of the circle pull away, but then one face came into view, and she saw clear, honey-colored eyes filled with concern, with care. She felt a hand touch hers, and the skin was warm and soft.

"Are you alright, Sister?"

Rahma's chest was still heaving, and she could not speak to answer.

The words were incomprehensible, but the woman's voice was so gentle, so gentle . . . she found tears flooding her eyes. She had not cried in a very, very long time.

"Sister?"

This second time she could understand: the woman had spoken in Arabic.

When had anyone last spoken to her so gently? It was not since her mother had clutched at her, parting tears tumbling down her sunstained cheeks. Rahma fought to focus her eyes on the woman's face, searching hard for the words to tell her that they would be coming soon, that they would have their guns, that they would try to take her back.

The words formed so slowly on her tongue! "There are six of us," she whispered at last, hoping that her dialect would be intelligible.

The woman leaned down, and Rahma saw the intent look in her eyes, knew with relief that she had gotten the right words out.

"I am the oldest," she continued. "Help us. Please . . . "

It was then that the door burst open and the shouting began.

PART **ONE**

CHAPTER 1

Nora Khalil had just reached the river path when an incoming text vibrated against her upper arm. She came to a quick halt, wiped sweaty hands against her leggings, then yanked her phone off her armband, read the text, and called her partner.

He picked up immediately. "You jogging?"

"Running, yeah," she corrected him, trying not to pant into the mic.

"We found him. Where can I pick you up?"

Nora squinted at the early-morning traffic inching tortuously across the bridge, then back in the direction she had come. "I'm at the river. Looks like you should stay off the expressway. I'll come up Cherry 'til I meet you."

"Ten minutes."

The *tabla*-heavy beats of a Nancy Ajram track overtook Nora's earbuds. Nora stood for a regretful moment, watching the quiet, olive-green water. The skinny Schuylkill River wound its way along the western edge of Philadelphia's Center City. To Nora, it looked like it flowed directly from the Art Museum, which sat imperiously atop Fairmount Hill. Cliché or not, running the museum's steps was her favorite workout, and she frowned, annoyed, as she turned and headed away from the river, in among the stately town houses of Cherry Street. She let her sneakers fall into rhythm once again with the music. It was much less than ten minutes before John Wansbrough's black Suburban intercepted her at the densely congested Benjamin Franklin Parkway. He pulled up, and she climbed in.

"Good morning," she said, yanking the door shut and then tugging gently on her earbuds.

"Don't sweat on my leather, now."

Chest heaving, she narrowed her eyes at him.

"You have your piece and badge?" he asked.

She nodded. The 9 mm Glock was strapped to the small of her back in a sweat-stained velcro-and-elastic carrier that also held her ID. All of this was neatly concealed under her long, loose tee with the words TEMPLE UNIVERSITY emblazoned across the front. She arched her back slightly as she buckled her seat belt, shifting the gun slightly left so that it wouldn't dig into her spine as she sat. "So what's the story?"

"The lead from little miss gangster turned out to be right on. Good work, by the way." Nora had spent most of the previous day with a young Junior Black Mafia recruit, such that she'd memorized her every tattoo. Progress had come only after a trip to the basement of the FBI building. Furious, Nora herself had pulled out the long, refrigerated drawer, and then sank her long fingers into Daniella Miller's braids and held the young woman's face six inches from the cold, knife-slashed body of fourteen-year-old Kylie Baker.

Soon afterward, Daniella was willing to tell what she knew about Dewayne hiding out in a loft apartment in Northern Liberties with a high-priced white hooker.

"Calder and Burton staked them out and finally spotted Dewayne when he passed by a window. Took a while to nail down the warrant." He waved a folded white piece of paper at her, then tucked it back into his navy-blue blazer.

Nora checked her watch. It was almost seven thirty. "Calder still there?"

"Yeah, waiting for the cavalry."

"He'll be tired. He always ends up shooting stuff when he's tired."

"That's why you get to go in first. Rookie's privilege."

Nora flinched. "Didn't you promise to stop calling me that after I'd been with you guys for six months? You do know that I went through all this with PD. I've paid my dues."

John Wansbrough snorted. "Are you suggesting that being a rookie with the Philly PD is anything like being a rookie with the Federal Bureau of Investigation?" Her partner gave her a patronizing smile born of twenty-six years of active duty.

Nora responded with a small groan. "Right. What was I thinking?"

Traffic was bad. Wansbrough flicked on the red and blue lights embedded in the front grille and window, and Nora watched as early morning commuters grudgingly pulled to each side to make way for the SUV. Wansbrough navigated the snarls with great efficiency, and Nora envied him his cool. Although she'd passed the necessary driving tests for the police academy, she still hated driving. There had been no real need, growing up in the city. She had walked everywhere, or ridden the subways and buses.

When the Philadelphia Police Department had tapped her to join the FBI's Safe Streets Violent Gang Task Force, she ended up working full-time with the FBI, and got a desk and a navy-blue Ford. But it was almost always parked in the garage under the field office at 6th and Arch. Nora was a competent but nervous driver and always felt better with the pavement under her feet. She sighed, still regretting the abrupt end to her run along the river. She had just paid far more than she should have for a pair of pink and gray Adidas Energy Boosts, and she admired them as she sat waiting for her pulse to slow.

For Nora, being locked in the interview room with Daniella Miller yesterday evening had been like living through a five-hour assault. Nora had learned at least seven new swear words. Running it off this morning was all she had wanted to do. It had taken every ounce of her strength to keep from throat-punching that woman. Even just going over it in her head now enraged her.

Wansbrough glanced at her, noting the deep V that had settled between her eyebrows.

"What?"

Nora shrugged.

"Come on, what? Nervous? You're a pro at this now."

"What, oh, the bust? Nah. Well, a little."

"Daniella the gangbanger??" Wansbrough guessed correctly as Nora laughed. "She was somethin' else."

Nora nodded.

"You kept it together, though. Except in the basement, maybe."

"I just . . . do you know that's the first time somebody called me a 'white bitch'?"

Her partner raised his eyebrows.

"No one has ever called me white before. Do I look white to you?"

Wansbrough laughed out loud. "Well, girl, you don't look black. Did you think you were black or something?"

"I always got 'sand nigger.'"

John's wide forehead creased into a scowl. "I'm gonna have a long, long talk with you about using that word in my presence. After we get Fulton into custody."

He switched off the flashing lights, indicating to Nora that they were near. She sat up a little in the seat, taking in the neighborhood. Northern Liberties had undergone a series of gentrification efforts, and rehabbed buildings and town houses preened under the muted early morning light. Nora spotted Calder's car parked across from a former factory; long fire escapes snaked along the building's sides, linking the cramped, wrought-iron balconies. Just beyond Calder's car was that of Agent Lin. His partner Jacobs sat up front, with two sergeants from the sheriff's office rounding out the task force group in the back. Nora struggled for their names and came up blank. "Looks kinda conspicuous, don't you think?" she observed as they pulled closer.

"Too early in the morning for anyone to be paying attention," Wansbrough said. "Difference between us and the bad guys is the bad guys get to sleep in."

At Wansbrough's suggestion, she called Calder.

"Hi, Nora."

"You awake?"

"For you, always."

"You're on speaker, Ben."

Wansbrough tsk-tsk'd as he began parallel parking the Suburban, then said loudly: "Focus on this arrest, Calder, and keep your mind off my rookie."

Nora glared at her partner and tapped the mute button. "What did we just talk about?"

He waved away her glare. "Never mind. I also told your dad that, as a father, I would keep you safe from young men with bad intentions."

Nora's nostrils flared. She opened her mouth and then shut it again, speechless.

"Plus," John added, "Ben's so obvious. He needs to tone down his flirting a little. Or at least do something original." He tapped the mute button, opening the line, and grinned at Nora. "What do you have, Ben?"

The Suburban's dashboard screen flashed with two photos. One was a face she'd memorized by now, Dewayne Fulton. The other was of a thin white woman with a curtain of chestnut-colored hair. Special Agent Calder cleared his throat loudly and said, "Apartment 4-F is a corner unit. Two occupants: Fulton, Dewayne, male, a.k.a. 'Reality,' boss of the Junior Black Mafia, aged twenty-one, and the lessee, Halston, Lisa, female, aged twenty-six. John, you want us to cover the balcony by sealing off the fire escape?"

"You read my mind," Wansbrough said. "Two with Ben, four with me. Burton—you there?"

Eric Burton's voice floated through the speaker, succinct as always. "Yes, John."

"Burton, you come with me and Nora. Calder, try not to shoot anyone today."

"I hardly ever shoot anyone on Fridays," came the response.

Nora strapped on the bulletproof vest John handed her, then accepted the task force raid jacket.

She looked at John. "Crowbar?"

He shook his head, pulling off his sunglasses and tucking them carefully into the visor clip. Gesturing at the building, he said, as though stating the obvious, "Nice building. Doorman. *Key*."

They slid quickly out of the car and jogged toward the building. Eric Burton and Lin and Jacobs materialized behind them, all looking grim and unshaven. Eric was shoving his arm into a black Windbreaker that matched the one John had given Nora. She saw Ben Calder leading the rest of the arrest team toward the fire escape. She wished that Ben was with them. Ben's flirting made her uncomfortable, but Eric's icy cold shoulder always left her disconcerted.

Nora pressed her badge against the glass door. The concierge stared at the group in confusion, then hesitantly released the lock. They watched her closely, but she did not seem to be reaching for a cell phone or any buttons that might function to warn Unit 4-F. She wore a name tag reading JUANITA, and she stared at them with fearful eyes.

Wansbrough advanced on the woman quickly, showing his badge and smoothing out the warrant for her perusal. "Federal officers. I need the spare key for 4-F."

She began in heavily accented English, "We do not . . ."

John leaned in close. "Now."

The concierge leapt out of her seat and unlocked a cabinet set against the wall. Her hand shook slightly as she handed over the key. "Shut down the elevator and let no one up the stairs," Nora said over her shoulder, as the five of them started the climb.

Juanita did not need to be told twice.

Unit 4-F was clearly marked. Wansbrough plunged the key into the lock and turned it quickly. The door was chained from the inside. He gave his team a mirthless smile, then motioned at Eric to join him. The two leaned against the door and shoved hard. The chain snapped immediately, and as the door swung open, the five of them darted into the spacious loft apartment as Wansbrough shouted, "Federal officers! Come out with your hands up!"

The door crashed against the inside wall, and Nora heard shouts of surprise from behind a low divider wall that demarcated the bedroom area in the otherwise entirely open space. Billowing, gauzy curtains dangled from the tall ceiling down to the low wall, concealing what lay within; beyond these, a woman's voice began screaming and did not stop.

With fierce, abbreviated motions, Wansbrough waved Burton and Lin into position in front of the door they'd just entered, and directed Nora and Jacobs toward the open kitchen area. They hunkered down by a set of cabinets, a position that still afforded them a sweeping view of the loft. Nora worked to breathe deeply in order to slow her thumping heart. Wansbrough darted to the low wall, crouching, waiting, and called again for Dewayne to come out and surrender himself.

It was only a moment before Dewayne Fulton pushed aside the curtains and burst out from behind the half wall, wearing nothing but boxer shorts and a dark web of tattoos. He was waving a heavy pistol, what looked like a .44 Magnum, and stumbled slightly. He saw Burton and pointed the gun at him, but Wansbrough landed a sweeping kick to Dewayne's knees from behind. Dewayne thudded to the floor, the gun discharging. The bullet plowed into the exposed brick of the wall, and a shower of shards rained down on the polished hardwood. In an instant, Wansbrough had his knee in Dewayne's back and was twisting his gun arm up behind him as Dewayne unleashed a hail of expletives.

Nora and Jacobs leapt in unison over the dividing wall, seeking the source of the uninterrupted screaming. They saw a mostly naked woman, her long, brown hair a disheveled mess, sitting upright in the middle of a king-sized bed. "Shut up," Jacobs yelled at her, aiming his gun in her direction. The screaming stopped. Nora trained her own gun on the woman as she scanned the bedroom area. She called out to Wansbrough, "We've located Lisa Halston!"

Nora found that her back was to the one solid retaining wall and what looked like a bathroom door, and it flashed through her mind that her position wasn't secure. The woman on the bed raised her hands as if in slow-motion, and Nora saw immediately that her pupils were wide and dilated. The bedside table was piled high with more ice methamphetamine than Nora had ever seen in one place.

Nora began edging back toward Wansbrough and Burton, and was about to tell the woman to get slowly off the bed, when the bathroom door behind her flew open, and Nora felt steel at the base of her neck. She froze, not breathing, her eyes holding Jacobs's alarmed gaze. Jacobs immediately began shouting, "Federal officers! Lower your weapon!"

The gun rested just below Nora's tightly wound chignon. The weapon was at least as heavy as the .44 Dewayne had been wielding.

A woman's voice shrieked in Nora's ear, drowning out Jacobs's. "I've got your girl! Now get the hell out of here or I'll kill her!"

Nora could feel the woman's breath in her hair. Nora had not stopped pointing her gun at the woman in the bed, who watched the scene in detached, but mercifully silent, terror. Nora was rigid, waiting breathlessly for what would happen next. She heard no voices or movement from the next room, though she strained for any hint of Calder and his team. From the corner of her eye, she saw Wansbrough peek around the divider wall. Nora knew he didn't have a clean shot. They exchanged a quick glance, then his low voice called out, "Drop your weapon. You got nowhere to go here."

The woman's voice seemed to climb an entire register higher. "You drop your goddam weapon or I will kill this bitch, so help me God . . . "

Nora called out in as calm a voice as she could muster, "We've got some drugs in play here, John, so we may not all be thinking clearly . . . "

The gun dug more deeply into Nora's neck. "Shut up, just shut the fuck up!" In the living room, Nora heard Dewayne Fulton begin laughing almost hysterically.

Nora fought for breath and found her gun arm starting to shake. She thought about plunging her elbow backward into the woman's sternum, but she was too scared that the heavy gun would go off.

Suddenly the sound of a gunshot thundered through the loft, and Nora found herself tumbling to the floor, as the nearly naked woman resumed her screams.

The wait was interminable. It was rush hour, and the medical examiner, the EMTs, and the evidence techs from the field office had all been slow in coming.

The very blood-soaked Nora could only seem to focus on her shoes. And her partial hearing loss, for which none of the support crews had any remedy. The tech team was busy photographing the scene within the loft apartment and cataloging the weapons in preparation for transporting them to the office. The two men and one woman would wait for Nora and Calder to carefully collect the meth and its accompanying paraphernalia; Benjamin Calder was an expert on street drugs—how they looked, how they were made, and the intricate silk roads of production and distribution that entangled the city. He had logged endless hours on this case. They all had.

But it was Nora and John who had been on the scene shortly after Kylie Baker's body was discovered. They had found her mother shrieking with grief on the bloodstained grass of her Kingsessing home, refusing to leave her daughter's fast-cooling, knife-slashed body. It was the first time since Nora had entered law enforcement that she wished she'd listened to Baba and picked a different career.

Not that being murdered at fourteen had made Kylie Baker at all remarkable. It was Philly, after all. And Kingsessing was . . . well, Kingsessing was boarded-up buildings that somehow still seethed with listless energy. It was the sound of daytime screaming. It was head wounds that left indelible, forever-stains on gappy, stumbling sidewalks.

Nora had had no reason to wander that far into Southwest Philly before joining the force. She had grown used to Kingsessing, the domestic violence calls and small-time drug busts and even the occasional corpse with a bullet wound or two. But this task force work found her looking at a little girl whose neck was slashed so deeply that her trachea lay exposed. Nora had knelt beside Kylie's thin, naked frame. She was charged with counting knife wounds for the preliminary report, but she found herself counting other things as well. She counted the number of piercings arching up along the cartilage of Kylie's right ear (six). She counted the dusting of freckles along the bridge of her nose and across her smooth cheeks (eighteen). She counted the shards of brown bottle glass that lay on the sidewalk, just beyond the girl's jarringly fuchsia toenails (seven large shards, three small).

Apart from its extreme violence, Kylie Baker's murder had drawn the task force's attention as an act of vengeance. Her brother Kevin's gang trafficked in meth and heroin—not only in Kingsessing, West Philly, and Northeast Philly, but over the Delaware River in angry, dilapidated Camden. Kevin's gang, the A&As, had engineered a drive-by shooting that took out a member of the Junior Black Mafia.

Dewayne Fulton led the Junior Black Mafia. But rather than take revenge for the shooting by killing a member of Kevin's gang, he had killed a member of Kevin's family. *Kylie.*

Everyone knew the story. Everyone was talking about it. The two gangs ran strong in Kingsessing, where crack houses outnumbered grocery stores, and there were more pawnshops than schools or parks.

But something had broken in Kylie's mother as she had watched the task force begin work on her little girl's corpse. She had turned to Agent John Wansbrough and said, plain as day and loud enough for all the neighbors to hear, that she would talk. She would tell him everything she knew about every gang member she had ever known. From her own son Kevin and his gangbangers to Dewayne Fulton and his. Nora had looked up, her latex gloves damp with Kylie's blood, listening to the girl's mother in open-mouthed astonishment.

John, stunned, had had the presence of mind to coax her into the Suburban and take her with him to the William J. Green, Jr. Federal Building. There, he recorded a detailed statement before the shock of Kylie's death wore off and the fear of the gangs reasserted itself. The Safe Streets Task Force acquired more information on Philadelphia gang members from Mrs. Baker than they had from all sources in the entire previous year.

It was Mrs. Baker who had told them where to locate Daniella Miller, and Daniella Miller who had given them Dewayne himself. And now, Ben and Nora sat on the small balcony, watching the swirl of activity inside and down below in the street. Nora had peeled off the task force Windbreaker, drenched with the blood and tissue of Halston, Lisa, aged twenty-six, and she sat now in her T-shirt that had never quite dried from her morning run. Nora had asked for a large glass of water, then demanded that Calder pour it over the back of her head. She was grateful her hair had been tied in its customary knot. Still, both of them had stared as the pinkened run-off dripped through four floors of wrought-iron balconies to tumble down to the street below. Calder went back to the kitchen to refill the glass three times before the improvised shower ran clear. Nora kept resisting the urge to pat the back of her head. Finally, she wrapped her arms hard around her knees.

"They're ruined, Ben."

Calder put an arm around her shoulder. "I will get you new ones. I promise."

She pushed his arm off. "I really, really liked these."

He tilted his head, regarding the blood-soaked sneakers. "They are pretty fly."

"*Were* pretty fly."

"Yes, were pretty fly. Now, they're pretty nasty."

She turned her head to look at him. "What if you had missed?"

He grinned at her, green eyes flashing. "But I didn't miss."

"But what if you had missed? You were on stakeout all night. You were a wreck. You're always a wreck after stakeouts. How could you trust yourself with that shot?"

"Nora, I couldn't miss. With all that shouting, no one heard us come in the balcony door. I was, like, four feet away. And . . . it was *you.*"

She tilted her head slightly, realizing suddenly how much she liked the way he had said that. Then, to make sure he didn't sense her feelings, she pointed at her ear. "What? I can't hear you because I'm actually deaf now."

"I'm sorry, Nora. We didn't know there was a third person in the apartment."

"How long had you been watching the place?"

"Hey, as soon as we got the information from Daniella Miller we started watching the place."

She went back to staring at the commotion four flights down, willing herself not to think about the life snuffed out to save her own. Below them, Wansbrough was overseeing the bag that contained Lisa Halston's nude and mostly headless corpse as it was bundled away by the medical examiner. The third in the threesome, apparently a working colleague of Lisa's, had been turned over to the police for prosecution. They had found no identification for her in the loft, and once she had stopped screaming, she could not be coerced to speak.

John had wanted Nora to come down so the EMTs could check her out, but she wasn't budging. Irritated, he finally stopped motioning up to her and called her cell phone.

"Nora, just let them see you," he said.

She switched the phone to her good ear. "John. It's okay. I'm okay. I just want to go home and take a shower."

"Nora, come down now . . . it will take five minutes."

"I can't . . . Calder and I are bonding over how he almost killed me."

Calder waved down at him.

Wansbrough was frustrated. "Look," he said, "Like it or not, I know you're shaken up. Burton and I will take Fulton downtown, and Calder can drive you home after you secure the scene up there. Take it easy the rest of the day, and we'll meet up to talk to Dewayne tomorrow morning at nine, when the meth is out of his system." He hung up without saying good-bye, and went back to sorting through the controlled chaos around him. Dewayne was the last to go, and Nora watched curiously as Eric Burton ushered him into the back of Wansbrough's Suburban.

Nora and Calder walked through the crime scene together, stopping at the bathroom out of which Lisa Halston had pounced on Nora. They stared at a laptop computer. It sat next to an empty condom wrapper on the tiled floor. The darkened screen gaped up at the ceiling.

"Why is there a laptop in the bathroom?" asked Nora.

Ben took a pair of latex gloves from an evidence tech. He pulled on the gloves and then tapped the screen.

"Password?"

"*Grumpy hooker?*" Nora suggested.

"Nice," said Ben. He tried a few entries, then shrugged. "We'll take it to Jonas and Libby."

They catalogued it with the techs and then made their way out of the building, passing Juanita, who appeared in the midst of a classic concierge-breakdown as she fielded frantic inquiries from tenants and neighbors. Nora nodded at her as they passed out into what was left of the cool autumn morning.

Traffic was light on the way back to Center City. Calder was quiet, and Nora observed him carefully. His auburn hair was thick and close-cropped, and his features were strong. His pointed chin was covered with stubble after his night in the car. The green eyes had dark shadows under them. "Hey, you okay there?" she asked.

He nodded.

"How many people you killed so far?"

Calder glanced over at her. "Total? In the past four years of service?"

"Yes. Total."

"One."

Despite herself, Nora laughed out loud. "All that shooting—?"

"I try to aim for like, legs and thighs . . . I wasn't a college track star like you, so I have to get the advantage somehow."

"Very savvy," she admitted. "What's next?"

Ben shrugged. "I'll take this laptop to Jonas and Libby. I'll write up my report about what happened with Halston, Lisa, twenty-six, and hope it matches what the medical examiner finds so that Internal Affairs doesn't make a big deal about it. I'll go home and play a violent video game and hope we get to do it all again tomorrow."

Nora smiled. "I'm not even gonna worry about you . . . "

"No, no worries," he said, pulling up in front of the Cairo Café. "Okay, Nora. If you need anything, call."

She nodded. "Thanks, Ben." She opened the car door, then paused. "Ben."

"Yeah?"

"Thanks for saving my life."

His eyes locked with her wide, brown ones, and she watched him exhale slowly, looking for words. She slipped out of the car before he said anything she might want to hear.

She was careful not to watch him drive away as she pushed open the door to her father's restaurant.

The Cairo Café sat quietly in the midst of the Logan Square neighborhood, only a few blocks from the river and the Market Street skyscrapers—just out of the way enough, it seemed to Nora, to be doomed to constant struggle. It was small but spare, with simple two-top tables and long leather benches running along each wall. It could seat about fifty people comfortably and, in its twenty-seven years of business, it had never departed from the staid, pressed, beige tablecloths and primly folded cloth napkins. The requisite Quranic verse warding off envy hung over the hostess's stand (although there was never a need for an actual hostess), and various Egyptian relics were rather randomly placed throughout the dining area.

The electronic bell announced her, echoing through the empty restaurant, lancing through the soft strains of an old Abd al-Wahhab tune that spun from the CD player. It was ten thirty, and they opened for lunch at eleven. *"As-salaam alaykum,"* she said into the dimness.

Baba set down his glass of tea and hastily stubbed out his ciga-rette. *"Wa alaykum as-salaam, ya Noooora!"* He was sitting at his customary table near the cash register, enjoying a quiet moment before dealing with the first customers of the day. He offered her a rough cheek. *"Inti fayn?"* Where have you been? "I didn't think you were home at breakfast."

She bent to kiss him, waving away the remaining cloud of smoke, then sank into the chair across from him. "Working," she answered in English.

"In that?" he asked, taking in her running clothes. He didn't no-tice her blood-soaked shoes in the muted light, and she hurriedly pulled her feet under her seat.

"Casual Friday," she said. "And you know you shouldn't be smok-ing inside the restaurant. Your employees can sue you."

"I'll never do it again," he said contritely. This was Ragab's latest strategy for dealing with his daughter's many "don'ts."

She narrowed her eyes, recognizing the strategy for what it was, and moved on. "Did you get Ahmad his breakfast?"

"He can't get his own breakfast?"

Nora frowned at her father. "He can but he won't, he's spoiled. You have to lay something out for him or he won't eat. You know this."

Her father made a disapproving noise and patted his own girth where it strained against his button-down shirt, as though to say that that was certainly not his own approach. "I think he's become more spoiled since he's started studying for this test."

Nora sighed. "Well, he's entitled, he's studying hard." The SATs were two weeks away, and Ahmad had been haunting the Kaplan sessions.

Her father shrugged, then regarded her. "What can I make you to eat?" he asked. "You want a foule sandwich?"

"Nothing now, not hungry." Nora wondered if the writhing in her stomach would ever ease, or if she would ever stop feeling the gun at her head or the sticky heat of Lisa Halston's life splashed across the back of her neck and hair.

"Eat with me. Don't be rude."

"You're not eating," she observed.

"I'll have Katie make you some tea," he said, gesturing at the straggly ponytailed server hunched over her phone, thumbs a blur.

But not even tea sounded good to Nora today. She stared distractedly at the Egyptian newspaper splayed out across the table, open to the sports section; Arabic headlines shrieked the footballers' latest triumphs. "You could get that paper for free on your phone, by the way."

"Phone, phone. Phones are for calling. Everything is on the phone now, you lose the phone, you lose your whole world," Ragab said. "Anyway, what can I do to the phone when I read that Zamalek has lost again to the Ahly bastards. I can't smack it, like this," he gave the page a dismissive slap with the back of his palm. "What, I'm going to throw my phone across the room? I didn't buy the insurance."

She smiled at him, shaking her head. Ragab was a born extrovert who knew almost all of his customers by their first names. His booming laugh always seemed to fill the small restaurant and spill out onto the street beyond. He had only shouted at Nora once: when Zack Gray from the boy's track team had had the audacity to try to ask her to prom. Apart from that, she had only really seen Baba enraged and explosive when Zamalek lost to the Ahly club in the Egyptian national championships. He had actually punched his fist through the living room's drywall.

He leaned in. "What are you working on, anything interesting?"

"Nothing I can tell you about," she whispered; this was their routine, and she gamely responded the same way every time. Nora rose. "I'm going up to take a shower, Baba. And maybe a nap."

He squinted at her. "What is this, are you okay?"

She nodded. "I finished a project at work, and my boss gave me the rest of the day off." Simple.

Ragab smiled, his features relaxing. "Good, good. You can go to Friday prayer for once!"

"Maybe," she said. She quickly kissed the top of his head and headed through the kitchen to the back stairs leading to their apartment. She tried not to think of the health code violations attached to her bloody sneakers.

Nora stood for a long time under the shower with all of her clothes on. Even the shoes. Especially the shoes. The water swirling into the drain was at first tinged slightly pink. Little by little Nora had begun peeling off layers and pushing them into the far end of the tub. She shampooed and rinsed no less than ten times before emerging to wrap herself in a fraying green towel.

She rubbed a circle in the fogged mirror and stared at herself. Her facial features were her mother's, the brown eyes, the caramel skin and high cheekbones, the prominent nose that was the legacy of her mother's father. After the long, hot shower her hair had reverted to its unrepentant curl, and it fell in inky coils to her shoulders.

Nora liked to tell other people that her mother had asked her to join the force—that it had been her dying wish. It had great shock value, and wasn't exactly a lie. *Nora,* habibti, *you are so strong, so smart. Fast feet and fast mind,* ma sha Allah. *I'm depending on you. Your father is a good man. But he is not wise. You need to help him. Help him take care of Ahmad. Protect Ahmad for me, and make sure he can grow to be a good and wise man.*

Her mother had asked her to take care of her family, and this turned out to be the way that made the most sense to Nora. "I know today wasn't what you had in mind, Mama. I'm sorry," she said softly.

She transferred a load of Baba and Ahmad's things from the washer into the dryer to make room for her bundle of sopping clothes, wishing—as always—for her own place, her own space. Then she slid under her blanket, and the quiet tears that came had slightly less to do with dead hookers and rather more to do with wishing her mother's voice could suddenly break the stillness with an old Arabic love song, or that her warm hand was there to rub Nora's back and stroke her hair until she slept.

He was waiting. In the same room from which she'd fled, he was standing, his face dark and angry.

The tall one with the dark glasses did not disentwine his coarse hands from her hair until he shoved her into the shabby room, cursing her.

It won't happen again, *he said, by way of apology to the waiting man. Tonight she's learning the consequences of running. Isn't that right, whore? Isn't that right? If you didn't have a customer waiting, I would have taken that bitch who tried to help you and cut her up right in front of you. But I'll deal with her later . . .*

Rahma cowered, terrified for the stranger she had now endangered.

He leaned close to her face, and she saw through the dark glasses the blank, shriveled skin where his eye had been. His breath was hot against her face. You and the others will learn what it is to defy us.

As the tall one's footsteps echoed on the stairway, Rahma watched in terror as the man crossed to her. She whimpered, hating the scent of him, hating him, hating him. He had something cupped in his clenched fist, something she couldn't see, and it scared her that he was hiding it from her. Could there be something worse or more fearsome than what had gone on in that room the night before?

He sank on one knee onto the mattress and clamped his free hand over her mouth, a sure sign that he was going to rape her again. But suddenly his clenched other hand opened and he wiped his palm under her nostrils, pushing hard against her nose—she struggled for

*air, trying hard not to inhale through her nose, but she was gasping
and choking, and then she felt the powder shoot up into her nose,
exploding behind her eyes, boring into her brain, and she was overcome.*

It will be better for you now, *he was saying, and his voice seemed
distant and detached from his body.* It will feel better, you'll see.

*As she felt her muscles relaxing, and her body sliding away from
her, she was aware that he was on top of her again, pushing apart
her legs and pulling down her camisole to expose her just-budding
breasts.*

This time she did not scream.

CHAPTER 2

"Nora?"

She turned over and squinted into the dimness. "Hammudi?"

"You okay?" She felt the mattress sink as her brother sat down on the edge of her bed.

Nora sat up, disoriented. "*Ya habibi*, Ahmad. I'm sorry, I meant to stop by your school. I had the afternoon off."

"Nora, I'm not ten, you don't have to walk me home anymore."

Her eyes adjusted, and she took in Ahmad's rimless glasses and the dimple on his left cheek. His hair was raw black silk that framed his features in soft layers. She stretched her hand and ruffled it, even as he ducked away. "Yes, I know you're not ten," she said, smiling. "How was your day?"

He shrugged. "It was a day. How was yours?"

Nora shrugged back.

"Shoot anybody?"

She groaned and pulled a pillow against her face.

"Did you?" he pressed.

Ahmad was the only one in the world she talked to about her job. She spoke low and swiftly, even though she knew that her father couldn't possibly hear her from the restaurant's cramped kitchen downstairs. She told Ahmad about Dewayne and about Kylie Baker's angry mother. She told him about the screaming woman and the gun at her neck and finally about Calder's shot from four feet away and all that blood.

When she finished speaking, Ahmad surprised her by folding her into a hard hug. "Nora, that's really scary."

"Oh, Hammudi, it was my own fault. It didn't occur to me there might be anyone else there, even though we're always supposed to assume that. It was stupid not to wait for John, and stupid not to open that bathroom door as soon as I realized it was there. I'm gonna get lectured tomorrow."

"Tomorrow's Saturday!" he protested, holding her at arm's length. "You said you were gonna help me study."

Nora grinned. "Come on, we'll study now. Did Baba bring up some food?"

Ahmad nodded. "Kofta and rice. Some salad."

The small, open kitchen was more like a wide corner of the living room, and was rarely used for actual cooking anymore. Their mother had insisted on painting it yellow, and it was a warm, inviting space. They ate food brought up from the restaurant there, and Ahmad always studied there, never in his room. Nora usually sat with him at night, her laptop open, researching and reading and attending to any reports she had to produce. Now the computer and books were shoved to one side, and they sat, not bothering with plates, eating out of the aluminum catering pan their father had filled with food and sipping from twin cans of Coke.

Nora started drilling Ahmad on the tall stack of vocabulary flash cards. In his practice tests for the SAT, Ahmad always aced the math sections. But the vocabulary and essay sections were torture for him.

"Ubiquitous." Nora said, chewing a mouthful of spiced beef and rice.

"Huh?"

She swallowed, then said again, more clearly, "Ubiquitous."

"That isn't even a word."

She shoved the card at him as proof.

"I have no idea."

"*Being everywhere at once. Constantly encountered. Widespread,*" she read, then stuck her fork in a slice of cucumber.

"Okay." He thought, swishing Coke in his mouth, swallowing, burping softly, then said: "Homeless people are ubiquitous on the streets of Philadelphia."

Nora nodded. "Yessss. Can you think of an antonym?"

Ahmad shrugged. "Rare?"

"Sounds good to me." She pulled out the next card. "Exegesis."

"Exegesis?" he repeated.

"Yep."

"Sheeez . . . Nora, I never—"

"*Critical explanation of a text, especially a biblical text,*" she read.

"Okay, what would be an antonym?" he demanded.

Nora shrugged. "Obfuscation? Try a synonym first."

He thought. "Clarification."

"Good." Nora cut off another chunk of the kofta.

The phone vibrated where she'd left it on the table, and Ahmad motioned to it. "You're getting a call."

Nora reached swiftly for the phone. "Hello?"

"Just calling to check on you," she heard Calder saying.

She pushed back her chair and stood up, then walked over to the living room window. "Thanks. I'm good."

"Good, good . . . You should know that Jonas and Libby opened the laptop. It was totally empty. They are guessing that this Lisa Halston had just ejected a flash drive."

Nora struggled to focus. "A flash drive?"

"A flash drive."

"Was there a flash drive on her? Or collected by the evidence techs?"

"Nope," he answered. "So. Something to think about."

"Yep, I'm thinking about it alright. Maybe we should go back and double check the loft?"

"Eric and I already went. Nothing. But we're a little more interested in Lisa Halston at this point than we were this morning when she was just a hooker hanging out with Dewayne." Ben was silent for an awkward moment, then said in a rush, "Do you want to go out for a while tonight? Get some coffee? Process stuff?"

Nora cast an eye at Ahmad who was studying her intently. "I can't, but thanks for asking."

"Other plans?"

"Yes. Unbreakable. Sorry. But we can catch up tomorrow—you're coming in, right? Even though it's a Saturday?"

"Of course. So we can get Dewayne's statement." Calder was quiet, as though waiting for her to say something. Then, with what sounded like resolve, said, "Okay, Nora. I'll get on your calendar earlier next time."

She felt her cheeks flush. "See you tomorrow, then. Good night."

"'Night."

She sat down again and pulled out the next card.

Ahmad stared at her. "You have a boyfriend."

"Ahmad! I do not have a boyfriend," she spluttered.

"You *so* have a boyfriend."

"Oh my God, I swear that you are the reason I need my own place. Benjamin Calder is an agent, a *colleague*."

Ahmad pointed his fork at her. "But he likes you."

"Maybe. Probably. But I've never encouraged him. And also he saved my life today, okay? So he called to check up on me. Both of those are nice things to do."

Ahmad was smiling. "Thank youuuuu, Agent Colleague!"

Nora rolled her eyes.

"Are you dating him? Oooh, you remember what happened when Ayesha got caught dating that white boy . . . "

Nora remembered. Her friend Ayesha's father had kicked her out, her mother had stood up for her daughter, and the parents actually divorced over it. "I don't date, okay? You know that. *You* are my only date. Ever." She went back to eating.

Ahmad regarded her for a long while. "I wouldn't tell him, you know."

Nora looked up. "Huh?"

"Baba. I would never tell him. If you want to date, you should date. You're an adult."

She shook her head at him. "I'm glad I have your *permission*," she said sarcastically. "But it's not an issue."

"I will totally cover for you," Ahmad pressed. He imitated his father's heavy accent. "*Ya Hammudi, it's three A.M. Where is your sister?* and I'll be like, 'Saving the world, ya Baba, she's saving the world,' and you'll be, like, gettin' your groove on with Special Agent Colleague . . . "

Nora waved a flash card at him. "I'm touched. Now study. The word is, '*ambivalent.*'"

"Ha, I know that one. *Nora is ambivalent about her commitment to Egyptian traditions!*"

The punch she landed on his shoulder produced exactly the howl of pain she had hoped for.

The William J. Green, Jr. Federal Building sat heavily on the corner of Sixth and Arch Streets. The ten floors of black steel and dark glass had always seemed a bit menacing to Nora. Yet most in the city seemed to pass it by unseeingly. Taxi drivers and their fares were focused only on the impossibly congested four lanes along Sixth Street, jockeying with brave bicyclists for position. School kids in navy pants and polo shirts lugged overstuffed backpacks as they ambled toward one of the many charter schools crammed into converted office buildings. Early morning tourists would soon descend on the massive Constitution Center just across the street from William J. Green, or the Liberty Bell complex, with the clock tower of Independence Hall presiding over the expansive mall beyond it.

Nora had arrived at the office early. She was panting slightly as she entered; it was her habit to jog up the eight flights of stairs, especially if she hadn't had time to run before work. She had hoped to settle in early, before Jonas and Libby, both of whom worked Computer Forensics in the next cubicle, started bickering. Their nasty jabs at each other seeped toxically through the vinyl wall.

She nodded to two or three agents who looked up from their BlackBerries to murmur greetings. Special Agent Laurie Cruz paused to speak with her, shifting a fat file from side to side as she asked her about the shooting. It was the longest conversation Nora had had with Laurie, but she was grateful for—and a little embarrassed by—her concern.

When Nora finally rounded the corner, she found that Wansbrough had beaten her by a few minutes. He was holding a white Dunkin' Donuts cup and had just switched on his laptop. The anticipated lecture was fast in coming.

"You okay?"

She nodded. "I'm good. Hearing's a little off, but other than that, it's all good."

"Good. You messed up. I already spoke with Jacobs yesterday, but now I'm talking to you." Wansbrough spoke softly, so that his voice would not carry. His face was kind but grave.

Nora agreed quickly. "I know, I'm sorry."

"Tell me what went wrong."

She sat on the edge of her rolling chair, back straight. She took a deep breath. She had been over it all so many times in her head. "I should never have put my back to that wall. I should never have assumed that the woman I saw was Lisa Halston just because her hair was brown. I should have waited for you to fully secure Dewayne and leave him with Burton, and then we could have all entered the unknown room together and you could have covered us and vice versa."

John was nodding, watching her carefully.

"Is Ben going to be in trouble?"

He shook his head. "No, Nora. They've taken the body so that the medical examiner can look into what happened, but only as a matter of procedure. It isn't urgent, and there are no accusations of impropriety against him, so they won't even get to it until next week or the week after. He'll have to file a report, I'll file a report." John shrugged. "He did exactly what he was supposed to, given the situation. He'll be fine."

Nora let out a jagged exhalation, remembering.

John smiled at her. "Okay, lesson learned the hard way. I'm about to type up my report now, I'll expect yours later this afternoon."

"I e-mailed it to you this morning, sir, along with a copy to my lieutenant in the PPD."

Wansbrough smiled. "Overachiever. Any thoughts on the empty laptop?"

Nora shook her head. "I have no idea, John. I sure didn't see any flash drives or anything. Lisa Halston had both hands on her gun, as far as I could tell. And she wasn't wearing much that had pockets. Maybe she just wiped its memory. Or put it on a microdot or something."

John Wansbrough nodded pensively. "I wonder if whatever information's gone missing was related to her business or Dewayne's?"

"I guess we can ask Dewayne."

"I guess we can. Now: we aren't seeing Dewayne for another hour, what are you up to so early?"

Nora looked at her hands, then up again. "I thought I'd spend some time at the range. I started worrying about having to take that shot Calder took for me. If, you know, I needed to do it for you or Calder or Burton . . . I want to be sure I wouldn't have missed."

He got that fatherly look that made Nora feel like a gradeschooler. "Good idea. Go on, Nora. Just be back at nine." She was surprised he didn't pat her on the head.

"Okay," she said, starting to walk away.

Wansbrough immediately called her back, though. "Nora, one more thing."

She returned to stand in front of him. "Yes?"

"About that word . . . "

She was quiet, waiting.

"I've been working hard all my life to fight that label. My whole life, you understand? And I won't let any human being call me that to my face. I particularly hate it coming from other black men. Even when they use it to mean 'friend.' 'My nigger!' Saying it aloud *means* something, something ugly, and even turning it around, as they say, *appropriating* it does not mean empowerment. Just the opposite. It's more like . . . internalization."

Nora shifted from foot to foot under Wansbrough's gaze. She would rather he chastised her for poor performance.

"What was it, bullying in school? You wanna tell me about it?" he asked her.

"Yes I do. Someday. It's . . . not my favorite subject."

He nodded. "Look, Nora, I understand that. But you have to decide what your own labels are. You pick them out, every day. And you live up to them or you don't. And you have to decide if they have to do with surface or substance. But I can't have you sticking to one like 'sand nigger' or any other kind of 'nigger' on my time."

Nora listened intently.

"You know that Schacht assigned you to me because I've got so many years under my belt. I'm the best one here to train you, toughen you up. This is at least as important as how to fight bad guys."

Nora raised her chin and held his eyes.

His voice was gentler: "Nora, I've lived through more racism than you will ever know. I guarantee it. You can trust me."

She nodded, feeling something release inside of her, grateful for the sense of recognition, the familiar, she found in his eyes. "I trust you, John. Thank you." The fatherly look she'd chafed under just a moment earlier suddenly felt warm and calming. Nora gave him a half smile. "I'm gonna go shoot stuff now."

He waved her off, shaking his head.

She was grateful to find the firing range empty except for a dull-eyed young man signing out ammunition from behind a heavy glass partition.

The firing range occupied the back third of the basement. Nora hated it. She hated the long, dank hall she had to walk down, almost always alone. She especially hated that to get there she had to pass by Monty Watt's forensic lab, and she knew now all that it contained. She hated the angry crack of a firing gun and the acrid smell of a discharged weapon. But she also hated reeling in her target and finding a smattering of bullet holes everywhere but dead center.

She pulled the heavy plastic earmuffs over her ears and stood steadily in place. She slowly pulled her Glock out of its armpit holster under her navy suit jacket. It was a weight she'd grown used to; Nora knew her gun well. In her police academy training she had learned how to disassemble and reassemble it from the ground up. She knew the trigger mechanism housing from the magazine spring and floor plate, the locking block pin from the extractor depressor plunger spring. She understood what made the gun work, but it still felt alien and deadly in her hand.

She aimed carefully at the target. Slowly and methodically she emptied her clip.

The tap on her shoulder took her by complete surprise, and she whirled, her gun still raised.

Calder had his hands up.

She pulled off her ear protection.

"I was afraid of that," he said, hands still in the air. "That's why I waited for you to empty your piece."

"I think there's a shooting range etiquette, approaching from the *next* stall, not from behind."

"I'll make a note of it."

She waited for him to say something, and when he didn't, she turned and reeled in her target. The left side of the target bore the majority of the hits.

Ben looked over her shoulder. He looked bemused as he asked, "Did you pass firearms at the police academy?"

Nora was indignant. "Of course I passed." She thought for a moment, then added, "But just barely."

"And Nora Khalil doesn't like coming in anything but first," he surmised.

She looked sheepish. "Something like that. Also I guess I'd like to feel competent to take the important shots."

"Hmm. Okay, can I offer two suggestions?"

She nodded.

"First, I think you're not there yet mentally."

"Meaning?"

"You have to really believe you need to shoot this person."

Nora was silent, frowning.

"You have to stop thinking that you can run down the person and tackle him, or talk him out of it. There is no other way to deal with him than to shoot him dead. You have to be clear in your head that your partner or the victim or whoever—they need you more than the perp needs to live." His face was very close to hers as he said, "Yesterday, I knew that I had no other option than to shoot that woman."

She tilted her head, regarding him, aware again of the enormity of the life taken for her own. "Are you okay?" she whispered.

"Nora, I'd do it over a thousand times. It was absolutely the right thing to do." His voice was strong. It looked like he meant every word.

"Even if it was my mistake for getting myself in that situation?" she said, her voice heavy with regret.

He gripped her arm, and his touch shot through her, electric. "Nora, you didn't hand her the gun!"

She nodded, taking a small step backward so that he was forced to release her. She fought to make her voice steady. "Okay, what's the other thing?"

He sighed, smiling. "You're tightening your elbow and upper arm on discharge. You have to relax."

Nora narrowed her eyes. "How can I get all this clarity about the need to shoot someone and still . . . relax?!"

"Well . . . " Ben Calder scratched his head for a moment. "Would it make sense if I said that the clarity should let you relax? When there's no other choice whatsoever, your body should just submit to that and function in a way that lets your actions become really smooth and true."

She blinked a few times, skeptical. "Okay. Show me."

Calder stepped into the next stall, and they both pulled earmuffs over their ears. He extracted his weapon from its holster and extended his right arm, resting his wrist in the palm of his left hand. He looked at her, then spoke loudly enough so she would be sure to hear. "Your neck muscles have to be soft, relaxed—it's an easy way to tell if your upper arm is gonna be tense or not." She watched him pat the tendons in his own neck by way of demonstration.

He took a visible breath, centering himself, and then unloaded a round of bullets.

Nora waited 'til he had reeled in his target to walk into his stall. "Impressive."

The target's head was gaping with bullet holes.

"Try again?"

She nodded. "Okay." She had another full magazine.

"Show me your stance."

She faced the target, cradling her gun hand in her open palm.

He shook his head. "Try turning your right side—you are right-handed, yes?—turn slightly toward the target."

She turned obediently. She felt his palm against her neck, as his other hand tugged the left side of the ear protection away from her ear. "Relax," he said, softly, before replacing the plastic. When he withdrew his hand from her neck, he left traces of his scent on her skin. She inhaled deeply, then leveled the gun and depressed the trigger as she exhaled. One, two, three, four . . . she stopped at ten, reluctant to waste all seventeen rounds again.

"Better," he said, as they both pulled off their earmuffs to pore over the target. "Stick with me, you'll own the range in no time."

She nodded, noting the improvement. "Thanks. Thanks, Ben. I'll spend some more time this afternoon, after we're done with Dewayne Fulton."

"Good." He took a breath, and the now-familiar flirtatious glint came back to his eye. "Now, why won't you go out with me?"

"Oh, man . . . " Nora forced herself to look away. She made her voice cool. "If I'd known you'd start hounding me, I'd never have let you save my life."

"Come on, Nora. I'm a really nice guy. Ask Burton."

Nora laughed. "Burton hates me. I'm not Ivy League enough. Or too PD—not FBI material. Or too brown."

Calder couldn't disagree with her. "I think it's because you run so much faster than he does. Makes his manhood feel all threatened and stuff."

She gave a half smile, disappointed that Calder didn't refute what she had guessed about his partner's dislike for her.

"BUT!" Ben continued, "But he's brilliant, so he'd be a good character witness, right?" As she shook her head, he added, "Okay, look, ask Wansbrough. Hey, you can do a background check on me and everything."

"Look, Ben . . . " she sank onto the bench at the shooting stall's edge. "What you're up against here is . . . complicated."

"Complicated how?" he demanded.

"I just—look, I just don't date. That's not how we do things."

"Who? How who does things?"

"Egyptians. Muslims. It's just not done."

Ben holstered his gun and sat down on the bench across from her, frowning. "Are you seriously telling me you can't date me because I'm not Muslim?"

"I don't . . . "

He leaned forward, then, eyes intense. "Wait. Are you seriously telling me that this kick-ass, fast-as-lightning, proud officer of the Philadephia Police Department has *never* been on a date before, *ever*?"

"Oh, for . . . " Nora sighed. "Yes, okay. I've never dated. I don't see how that affects my ability to kick ass."

"Never gone to prom?"

"Never gone to prom," she affirmed. "So?"

He tilted his head to regard her. "Never been kissed?"

Nora rose. "Okay, this conversation is over. Come on, it's almost nine."

"Nora, have you ever kissed a guy?"

With her left hand, she pointed at the Glock. "Benjamin Calder, I have seven bullets left in this thing. Do not push me." She made for the door.

He stood too, then placed himself between her and the door. "You would prefer shooting me to kissing me?"

Nora swallowed hard, inhaling the scent of his aftershave again. "Yes," she answered curtly.

"Why won't you date me?"

"Are you sexually harassing me?"

He put his hands up again. "No, I'm asking a perfectly valid question."

Nora met his green eyes, then carefully holstered her weapon. She sighed. "Because . . . our relationship has nowhere it can possibly go. Girls like me don't date just to date, for entertainment. And guys like you, no matter how nice, are not interested in going where girls like me want to go."

"Which is?" he asked softly.

"Home to meet my dad," she answered. This time, when she moved for the exit, Calder let her pass.

Dewayne Fulton was defiant. He did not look like he had appreciated the night in the holding tank where he'd come down off his high. His lawyer exuded *slick*—expensive suit, mauve tie, chunky gold watch. From her position on the other side of the two-way glass, Nora felt queasy. Dewayne was not scrimping on legal fees. What sort of defense could he possibly be planning?

Calder and Burton took the lead on the questioning. Nora stood with John, listening to the tinny sound of the voices as they were piped through the hidden speakers. She was relieved to be able to stand on the sidelines this time and watch the scene unfold. Dewayne was by turns hostile and silent. His attorney kept repeating like a mantra, "I advise you not to answer that, I advise you not to answer that." The agents worked hard to establish Dewayne's whereabouts on the night Kylie was murdered, and they came up against wall after wall.

Finally, Eric Burton asked about Kylie. "How long had you been following her before you got her alone?"

Silence.

"How did you get her into your car?"

Silence.

"How did you muffle her screams?"

This set him off. Dewayne sprang out of his chair, twisting his cuffed wrists in frustration. "I didn't rape that raggedy girl. And I sure as hell didn't kill her!"

"Isn't it true that you raped and stabbed Kylie out of revenge? Wasn't one of your Junior Black Mafia brothers killed by Kylie's brother Kevin?"

"Nobody messes with my crew. Nobody!" Dewayne Fulton shouted furiously.

His lawyer was on his feet, "That's enough, Dewayne, just calm down!"

"Exactly," Burton was saying, ignoring the lawyer, his voice the picture of Princeton calm. "That's exactly right. Nobody messes with the Junior Black Mafia. So you taught the A&As a lesson they wouldn't forget."

"Shiiiit," Dewayne said, shoving his chair aside with his foot. It careened across the room, toppling when it hit the wall.

"Sit down, Dewayne," Calder said, retrieving the chair. "Why don't you tell me about the meth we found."

"I don't know shit about no meth."

"Dewayne. Are you still buying from New York?"

Dewayne looked up contemptuously. "You don't know shit."

"Okay, enlighten me," Calder replied, perching on the edge of the table.

But Dewayne Fulton had lapsed back into silence.

Calder said softly, "We found a laptop at the scene."

Dewayne looked up sharply, but said nothing.

"Do you want to tell me about it?"

"You're fishing, Agent Calder," the lawyer observed. "I doubt you have anything at all."

Nora watched as Dewayne's features relaxed. Dammit.

Burton leaned in, practically hissing at the lawyer, "At this point, you should know there's a ninety percent chance that Dewayne will be looking at the death penalty. I give no guarantees, but your client has intimate knowledge of the meth trade here in Philly. Might be a smart legal strategy to convince him to tell us what he knows. The more information he can give us, and the more meth labs we can shut down and supply chains we can disrupt, the more likely it is that he will be looking at a life sentence instead of death."

The lawyer actually rolled his eyes. "You're in no position to offer life or death at this point. You have no crime scene to place him in, and no murder weapon. Do you have anything concrete to link him to drug trafficking? Not that you've offered. What are you planning, to convict him on hearsay? The word on the street? You have *nothing* at this point—except a dead hooker."

Calder gave the lawyer a cursory look, then spoke while staring down Dewayne. "Dewayne knows what we have. Ask *him*."

He and Burton exited and joined Nora and John in the next room.

"There's one other thing we do have," Nora said immediately.

"What's that?" demanded Burton, still irritated from the interview.

"The not-dead hooker. The hysterical one."

Wansbrough was nodding, his face pinched. "I got reports that she had a tough night in the hold. The methamphetamine levels in her system were apparently much higher than Dewayne's."

"Do we have a name on her yet?" Calder asked.

"No name. Prints show nothing, no priors. She won't talk. Still in shock." Wansbrough sighed.

"Well, we can see her, right?"

"Tomorrow. Maybe Monday," Wansbrough said dismissively, clearly uninterested. "Now, I hate to admit it, but that lawyer has some points. Any updates on the search for the murder weapon?"

"Montgomery Watt is trying to get us an exact description of the knife, make and model," Burton said.

Wansbrough shook his head.

Nora said, "But I thought it was open and shut. The CODIS database had confirmed that the semen on Kylie's body was Dewayne's."

"Yes, but that doesn't mean he killed her, especially if we don't have an exact crime scene or a weapon."

"We found Kylie's hair in his car . . . "

"But no blood. And we can't find the knife. It isn't enough. The Assistant U.S. Attorney is going to complain."

"You don't think Dewayne could ever make bail, do you?" Nora asked.

"If it were only on the murder-rape charges, he could at this point. We're focusing on possession and firing at a federal agent with intent to kill until we can sew up these other things. I have a call in to Judge Rippin. I think I can trust him to be reasonable, but I'm going to try to cover all the bases." He looked at Calder and Burton. "After you two are done with him, take Watt's description of the knife and flip Fulton's car and home upside down. And gentlemen, if there was some pertinent information on that computer, you had better bring me some pertinent information."

"But we already . . . "

"I know. Do it all again. Go sweet-talk Libby and Jonas. They are already pissed they are here on a Saturday. Piss them off more."

Nora fought off a fierce wave of anxiety, envisioning Dewayne out on the street. "We need Mrs. Baker to consent to protective custody."

"She's already refused," Burton said. "Some of your brothers from the PPD were there only yesterday, and they didn't get anywhere with her."

Nora looked at Wansbrough. "Let's go ask her again."

Nora stared mutely out the window as the landscape began its rapid transformation. As they crossed over the Schuylkill at Market Street, they passed the gritty splendor of 30th Street Station and entered in among the erudite brick high-rises of University City. Every other block had a dust-caked construction crew coaxing another harsh-angled building into its place in the skyline. It was here that Drexel and Penn fought for turf as viciously as any street gangs. Nora gazed at a group of young women waiting for the pedestrian crossing signal. Each wore a slight variation of the same uniform: leather boots, long sleek hair, nubby sweater, skinny jeans, oversized bag. They laughed in unison, and Nora tried to remember if she had ever made quite the same sound.

At 38th Street, the landscape changed again. The lumbering blocks of mega-labs and research centers gave way to pawnshops and check-cashing storefronts, grimy restaurants that offered both Chinese food *and* hot wings, and small groceries with crippled neon signs and tense metal gratings that seemed ready to be yanked down at a moment's notice.

As Wansbrough guided the car into Southwest Philly, they passed residential areas with wide-shouldered twins and Queen Anne-style houses with wraparound porches, but at 50th Street these became slimmer, wan-looking houses, crowding in on each other with matching cases of peeling paint and partially collapsing rooftops. Block after block fanned out beyond the Suburban's bulletproof glass. Old men sat empty-handed on front stoops, tired eyes looking out from gaunt, stubbly faces. Boarded-up storefronts wore the bold, defiant marks of gang artists.

Mrs. Lenora Baker answered the door. She wore an apron and held an oven mitt in her hand, suggesting she had been in the middle of preparing lunch. She regarded them steadily, took a deep breath, then invited them in. With a slow, pained shuffle, she led them into an immaculate sitting room, coughing slightly, and the agents took their seats on a sofa that looked as though no human had actually sat there before.

"I'm sure you have some reason for being here," she said, laying the oven mitt on her lap. "But first I need to know when you'll be giving me back my Kylie."

John and Nora looked at each other. John, at least, seemed prepared for the question. "Mrs. Baker, I know it would be far more difficult for you to bury Kylie and then have to submit to an exhumation if some issue comes up. Please give our forensic scientist just a little more time to make sure he has everything he needs in order to put Dewayne Fulton away forever."

"*Away?* Shouldn't he get the death penalty?" she demanded, clutching the gold cross that dangled from her neck as though to steady herself.

John answered, "We're threatening him with that given the heinous nature of the crime . . . "

"Because she was *little*, my Kylie. Just a *little* girl . . . "

Nora cleared her throat softly. "Twelve, actually. When a murder victim's age is twelve or less, it's considered an aggravating circumstance warranting the death penalty in Pennsylvania."

Mrs. Baker looked as though she wanted to spit at her, and Nora looked quickly away. Her eyes fell on a tall black man with a long, heavy beard who was emerging from what looked to be the basement. He wore flip-flops and a carefully pressed long white gelabiyya.

"My son, Rashid," Mrs. Baker said, by way of explanation.

Nora and John rose and extended their hands. Rashid shook Wansbrough's but not Nora's. Instead, he let his gaze slide quickly over her and then focused on the floor.

Mrs. Baker's voice was anguished. "They won't give us Kylie yet." She pressed a tissue to her mouth to cover a fit of coughing.

Her son patted her back as he stood next to his mother's wing-backed chair, his black eyes glittering with emotion. "It's time we buried my sister," he said. "Your people have had enough time."

"Mrs. Baker," Wansbrough was saying. "We owe you a debt of gratitude. Your information led us to Daniella Miller, and without her, we would have had a far more difficult time finding Dewayne Fulton. He's in our custody now. What you did was a remarkable act of courage . . . "

Lenora Baker interrupted him, her tone even. "It wasn't courage, Agent Wansbrough. It was pain."

John and Nora shared a look. John continued, "Mrs. Baker, a very powerful link in the East Coast drug trade has been brought in. Dewayne has links to drug trafficking organizations all over the Delaware Valley and into New York. The Junior Black Mafia have been distributing throughout our area—Camden and south Jersey, and out in the suburbs. He's part of something very dangerous."

"Dewayne . . . and my boy, too, right? My boy, Kevin?" The grief was evident in Mrs. Baker's voice. "You'll be going after him next, right?"

Rashid spoke, and Nora noticed again how measured and calm his voice sounded. He lay his hand on her shoulder as if to steady her. "My mother felt that no more kids should die for the cycle of violence my brother and his gangbangers have perpetrated. That's why she is willing to testify against him and against . . . his rival." He looked as though his every word was a careful choice, a massive effort at self-control.

Nora answered, "And we are so grateful for her willingness. But we are also extremely concerned about her safety. This is why we want to enter her into protective custody until the trial is over."

Mrs. Baker shook her head, mirrored by Rashid. "No," she said.

"No?" Nora asked, surprised at the woman's clarity.

Rashid leaned forward as though translating, then said gently, "My mother refuses your offer of protection."

Nora's mouth felt dry. "But why? I'm sure you know that Dewayne's crew all want vengeance for their leader, and the A&As think you sold them out."

Wansbrough added, "We believe that there is a possibility your own son could . . . exert pressure to keep you from testifying."

Mrs. Baker shook her head, then coughed lightly again. "Kevin? No. You don't know my son."

Rashid said, "My brother fears God, Agent Wansbrough. Maybe not in all things, but when it comes to our mother . . . "

Nora shook her head. "I'm sorry, but I have to disagree. Kevin hasn't 'feared God' enough to keep from dumping cocaine and methamphetamines on the streets of Philly. Whether or not he was the shooter, it was his car that was used in the drive-by that started all this."

Wansbrough was nodding. "My partner is right. Mrs. Baker, I don't believe that we can guarantee your safety unless we can take you out of your daily routine, and get you somewhere that neither gang knows exists."

Lenora Baker inhaled deeply. "I will not back down, and I will not run from these young fools." She tapped the coffee table in front of her, accentuating every few words as she spoke. "I have lost much more than I ever had to give, you understand? There is nothing left. What's the worst they can do? Put a bullet in me? So be it. I'll just be with my baby sooner."

Nora took in the deep creases around Mrs. Baker's mocha-colored eyes, and the bright streaks of silver that adorned her precisely curled hair. This woman had seen a lot in her time, too much. She was not scared. "Mrs. Baker—" she began, the agitation visible on her face.

The woman interrupted her. "Child, I know you want to protect me. Thank you. I don't take that lightly."

Rashid addressed both agents, "We know that you are responsible for tracking down the man who raped and murdered my—" his voice slowed, then resumed, wracked with emotion. "So it is we who are grateful. But my mother is getting on in years, and she does not want to leave her home. Surely you can't blame her for this." He stifled a cough, then laid his hand again on his mother's back, very gently, very tenderly. "I will take good care of her," he added, and his mother smiled wearily, resting her head against his arm.

Nora watched, as John nodded gravely. "Mrs. Baker, if you change your mind at any time, please know that we will do everything in our power to keep you and the rest of your family safe. All you have to do is call."

"Yes, Agent Wansbrough. I have your card." Mrs. Baker rose. "Please notify me when I'm to appear in court," she said, turning to go. "And please—when you find my Kevin, be gentle with him. He must be very scared by now."

Rashid walked them to the door. As the two agents descended to the front porch, Rashid stood and surveyed the neighborhood. Angry voices, one a woman's near-hysterical shriek, cut through the cool afternoon air. The sound of shattering glass made both agents reach automatically for their weapons. Rashid said, in his slow, calm voice, "This neighborhood . . . Look, you need to know that my brother is a good man. But he never had a chance here, nobody does."

John Wansbrough seemed about to respond, but he let Rashid talk.

"Kevin got sucked into this thing because he needed to help take care of Mama when I was gone. I know he never meant to hurt anybody."

John said, "Your brother will be well-treated, Rashid. Just make sure to contact us if he calls you. And advise him to turn himself in. It will be much, much better for him."

Rashid shook John's hand, flicked his eyes over Nora and gave a slight nod before returning to his home.

Wansbrough looked at Nora as they walked to the Suburban. "What do we have on the brother?"

She shook her head, opening the file. "Nothing. I'm guessing Rashid is a name he adopted after converting to Islam. He looks a lot older . . . Maybe he's a half brother or something. Do you think 'gone' means he was in prison?"

"I assume nothing. Check him out for us, Nora. See what his involvement is, if any, in the A&As."

She jotted this down on the file as she slid into the passenger seat. "Why wouldn't he shake your hand?"

Nora shrugged. "Some pious Muslims think touching a woman disrupts your state of ritual purity—you would have to perform ablutions with water before you can pray again. Some won't touch any woman not related to them."

John raised his eyebrows. "Does it insult you?"

She hadn't considered it before. "To think I could wreck someone's state of purity with my touch?"

He nodded.

"Nah. Makes me feel kinda brawny," she answered.

"That's my girl."

Calder straightened when she walked into their office.

"How'd it go?" he asked.

Nora shook her head. "No go. She refused our protection."

"Imagine wanting to stay home instead of holing up at the Comfort Inn in Norristown."

"You've seen the neighborhood. The Comfort Inn is paradise." She nodded at the sheaf of papers on his desk. "How did it go at Fulton's?"

"Eric is still there with some techs. No knife. No knife in the Beemer. No flash drive anywhere. Had to ask Libby again to try to find traces of the information on the hard drive itself."

Libby's voice floated over the vinyl wall. "Didn't ask very nicely . . ."

"Thank you, Libby! You are the best computer geek ever!" Ben called out.

"Yes! Yes I am!" she called back.

He continued, "I came back to finish these task force reports for the D.E.A about yesterday's haul—I'm supposed to file within thirty-six hours, or they get irritable."

"Didn't you just submit your report to the medical examiner about Lisa Halston? Why do you have to write all the reports? Where are the sheriff's office guys, anyway? They should have to do something around here."

Calder shrugged. "You know it's dicey, Nora, since the FBI is investigating the sheriff's office because of that tax thing—so they are making themselves scarce around the office here."

She actually hadn't known, but she nodded as though hearing old news.

Calder seemed unconcerned, continuing, "Anyway, now that we have most of the real names of the gang members from Mrs. Baker, Eric is actually making a statistical model that he says will allow us to find most of the A&As. He's basing it on prior arrests and known activity, a certain radius from their homes, and I don't know, coordinates for the mothership or something."

Nora was impressed. "A statistical model?"

"You heard it here first. But Nora, we think there's an all-out gang war brewing."

"How so?" she asked.

"A Mike Cook from Philly PD just called about a lower-level JBM kid who had been jumped by a group of A&As late last night. Knife wound. He'll live. But his statement was they were screaming at him about Kylie Baker."

"Mike's a good cop—a good guy," Nora said. "This could get out of hand really fast." She frowned, thinking. "What does it even mean, the name 'A&As'?"

Ben leaned forward and said in a low whisper, "I happen to have that information. If I tell you, will you drink coffee with me?"

She flared her nostrils slightly and laid Mrs. Baker's file on her desk. "Nope."

He frowned. "Why not?" he demanded.

"I hate coffee."

"*Nobody* hates coffee. Six-year-olds drink frappuccinos."

"Yah, well, I'm just that uncool." She sank into her roller chair.

"What do you drink?"

She opened her laptop and powered it on. "Calder, I don't think—"

Wansbrough appeared behind her, answering for her as he entered: "Mint tea. One package of Splenda. Preferably fresh mint leaves added to black tea, but dried leaves will do. She'll settle for packaged mint tea, but she'll have to complain the entire time she's drinking it."

Nora's face flushed as she turned to stare at her partner. "What about protecting me from guys with bad intentions?"

Wansbrough smiled. "After yesterday's performance, I've decided Ben's intentions are honorable." He explained to Calder, "When they bumped her up to work with us, and Nora's dad first started giving me food, I made him a promise to look out for her . . . "

Ben shuddered. "Why does this man scare me when I've never met him?"

Nora was glaring at John. "Why don't you tell him my sign, too?"

Ben grinned. "Cancer. I looked it up. So. Mint tea?"

"I've got some work to do," she said, focusing on the computer screen.

Ben circled her desk to stand over her. "Tea's good. Tea's just fine. We can talk about gang history. The whole time. It will be a working tea."

Libby's voice ripped through the cubicle divider. "Just drink some tea with the man and put us out of our misery!"

All three laughed despite themselves. "There are way too many people working Saturdays lately." Nora said. She sighed, shook her head at both men, then spoke in hushed tones. "You realize that you're taking advantage of me by withholding information I actually need. I think I have my harassment case after all."

Calder rose and offered her his arm as though to escort her out of their cubicle and into the bustling hall. "Now, now, it would be very shabby to sue a man who saved your life. Come on, then. I know this out-of-the-way granola-y coffee shop . . . "

She refused his arm, then pointed toward the floors below. "Cafeteria."

"There is no way they have mint tea in the cafeteria!" he protested.

She smiled, opening her bottom drawer. "I keep a stash for emergencies."

It was Saturday afternoon, and the cafeteria was nearly deserted. Calder watched as Nora placed a Lipton tea bag and then a few spoonsful of dried mint into the bottom of the paper cup. She opened the spigot on the canister of hot water, filled her cup, then poured a small yellow package of Splenda into the mix. She stirred carefully, sealed the cup with the plastic lid, replaced the baggie full of mint leaves in her drawstring backpack, and walked to the cash register.

Ben Calder held his cup of black coffee rather self-righteously.

She caught the look in his eye. "You think I'm high maintenance?"

"You think you're not?" He didn't wait for a response. The gray-haired woman at the cash register opened her palm to accept his payment. "I'll get both of these," he said.

"Will not," objected Nora, waving a dollar at the woman.

The woman, whose name tag declared that she was "Lois," glared at both of them. "Work it out, kids."

"Ben. Come on. We agreed."

"Nora. It's called being polite. Besides, you brought your own weeds. Let me buy you a tea bag."

Nora appealed to Lois, who was still glaring, unmoved. "Fine," she said at last, appending a muttered "Thank you."

"Don't worry. You won't upset the cosmic order," Ben whispered.

Lois took Ben's money, still scowling.

Nora followed him to a table by the window. "Don't you diss my mint tea again, though," she said, sinking into her seat.

"What's the story with the mint tea?" he asked.

Nora toyed with the string that dangled over the side of the cup. "My mom always drank mint tea."

Ben regarded her, his gaze softening. "I'm sorry."

"Thanks," Nora said simply.

"Is her passing part of why your dad is so protective of you?"

Nora smiled wistfully. "I . . . yah, I guess it is." She met his eyes and found them to be greener than she'd realized. She was lost in them for a moment, before she said, "Okay, you were gonna tell me about the A&As."

Ben sighed. "Yes, yes I was. The A&As used to be called African Annihilation."

"That's a mouthful for anyone."

"Yes. Started as a black power group, actually, in the late sixties. Man named Hugo Jack. They called him Black Jack. Lot of antipolice activity, taking out a few officers as revenge for police brutality in Kingsessing."

"They killed officers?"

"Black Jack got the death penalty for it. But the group lived on. Got into drugs. Very hierarchical organization, so succession lines were always clear, which kept them together." Ben stopped to take a long sip of his coffee. "The Junior Black Mafia were Jamaican-based—really had nothing to do with the Philadelphia Black Mafia, despite the similar names. They are way more recent, born from the crack cocaine boom."

"And the rivalry?"

Ben shrugged. "Turf. Plain and simple. Through some divine irony they both fight over the worst patch of it we have—Kingsessing. The A&As favored heroin. They originally got some product from New York just like the JBM did, and even some stuff from Pittsburgh of all places. But now it seems Mexico is their primary source. A cartel known as Los Zetas. Very scary guys. The JBM and Dewayne have been left behind in this respect. It's been good for the A&As, but I know that some of their guys have disappeared. Permanently."

Nora blew across the surface of her tea, then observed, "Kevin Baker is young. He and Dewayne both are. How did they get so much power?"

"Murder. They are both really good at that."

Nora nodded, considering this.

Ben said wryly, "It's a far cry from—what was your first case again? Lebanese Ponzi schemes?"

She laughed out loud. "Not a Ponzi scheme. This idiot—well, the simplicity of it wasn't really idiotic, I guess. He would pay new immigrants, mainly Mexicans actually, to swipe merchandise from Walmarts and Targets, then he'd resell it to the wholesalers."

"You got to put your special skills to work?"

"Yeah. He kept all his records in Arabic, which he thought would keep him off the grid somehow."

"Little did he know . . . " Ben grinned, then tilted his head. "You speak all the different dialects?"

"Of Arabic?" She shrugged. "No, but I can understand. Thing about growing up here is the mosque communities are really diverse. Kids'll try to speak English together, but your four hundred aunties and uncles will speak to you in Iraqi Arabic, Yemeni Arabic, Palestinian Arabic. So, yeah, I knew enough Lebanese dialect to understand him, and I can read and write it just fine."

"I heard you chased him down."

"Well, most Arab guys smoke. It wasn't that hard."

"I heard he was on a motorcycle."

Nora looked away. "Well. That part was hard."

She ignored the look Ben gave her and glanced at her watch. "Look, I should go shoot some more before I head home . . . "

Ben leaned in, "Come on, Nora. Talk to me a little. I want to know how you got here. John said you had a shot at the Olympics. He said your team at Temple University crushed the competition at the Penn Relays. What made you join the police force? How did you get tapped for the task force?"

Nora leaned back in her chair and folded her arms. "Why is any of that important?"

"Come on. We work together, right, so it helps to know each other better. You never know when you'll be held hostage and I'll need to know the deep dark details of your life in order to think like you think and help you outwit your captors."

She stared at him, then took a long sip of tea. "You watch too many movies."

"I'm single. We do that."

Nora hesitated, feeling like she couldn't catch a deep enough breath. Then she leaned in. "Okay, but you can't tell Burton. He's such a snob."

"Yes, yes he is," Ben agreed. "I promise."

"Well, I really wanted to join the FBI, but there were two reasons why I couldn't even try."

Ben cocked his head, listening closely.

"One, the stay at Quantico. My dad shot that down straight out. I had to commute to college, no dorm, so he was never gonna agree to going away on my own. Two, they assign you somewhere besides your hometown. And I needed to be here for now. For Ahmad— and for my dad too. He's sort of a bear, but he needs me."

Ben opened his mouth to say something when John Wansbrough burst through the cafeteria doors. He crossed rapidly to their table.

"Believe me, I hate to break up this scene. But we've got another corpse."

Even through the fog in her mind, she could see the body with perfect clarity. Cold, gray light poured across the alley, falling on exposed skin, on an untamed mass of hair, on big ugly gashes mottling face and body.

Rahma stood, peering out through the dirty glass. The curving metal bars were meant to keep others out but that now kept her in. She stared down, knowing the body had been placed there so she and the other girls could see it. She felt a tidal wave of tears surging, pulsing, begging to explode out of her. She placed her hand against the glass, imagining that it touched the woman's hand, remembering through the fog how warm and soft her hand had felt when it held hers, so briefly. Rahma imagined that her own hand could close the holes in the body, could warm the cooling flesh, could bring her
back,
back,
back . . .
A dog ambled into view and began to sniff at the corpse.

She slammed her hand against the window, trying to find the words to shout, but forgetting what they might be. Don't touch her! She tried to help me . . . please let her be, let her be . . .

She looked desperately around the room and finally found a small, silent clock. She pounded it against the glass—it took an infinitely long time for a corner of the window to finally shatter, but before she could shout at the dog she heard heavy footsteps pounding up the stairs. She scrambled backward, her heart racing, racing. She cringed as she heard his key in the lock, and the door swung open. He paused for a moment, surveying the broken window, as everything inside her writhed in fear. His face clouded, and he entered swiftly, moving so fast she could barely track his movements, and he

swung at her, landing his blows on her back and her arms that now
clutched her knees as she tucked herself into a ball,
   made herself small,
   made herself into stillness, into nothingness,
   and gave herself over to the fog.

CHAPTER 3

The office she shared with Wansbrough, Burton, and Calder was overly bright and smelled of a collision of aftershaves. They had a visitor, she saw. Special Agent-in-Charge Joseph Schacht. He was tall with a wide girth, a thick crop of gray hair, and pale pink skin that always seemed a bit flushed. He was famous for some of the ugliest ties Nora had ever seen, and today's was no different. Burgundy, with a smattering of silver paisleys. Schacht looked up from the file folder he was reading over Burton's shoulder. He nodded to Ben, Nora, and John as they entered, then he sat on the edge of John Wansbrough's desk.

"Okay," Schacht said. "Possible gang killing in an alley behind a residential area. Not far from 55th and Chester. Busy area. Very mutilated, very naked female body; very nervous locals."

"Who called this in?" Wansbrough asked.

"Neighbor." Schacht handed Nora a printout bearing the logo of the Philadelphia Police Department. "Elderly woman. She has already been questioned extensively but didn't have much to tell, apparently . . ."

"That's in the heart of Junior Black Mafia territory," Burton observed.

"Is the stabbing similar to Kylie's?" Nora asked, feeling an anxious sort of clutching in the pit of her stomach. She and John exchanged glances.

Schacht answered, "In addition to multiple stab wounds, her throat was slit. Much like the Kylie Baker case. Only this time we add to the mix that her eyes have been cut out. So if there's a connection, it looks like they're doing Kylie one better. The natural assumption, then, is that this crime could be an act of revenge for Kylie's murder."

All four frowned. It was a gang war after all. But it was being played out on female bodies.

Schacht shrugged. "Like Kylie's murder, the crime is very open, very brazen. But Kylie's body was basically tossed on the lawn of her family home so that Kevin could find her. We knew immediately who she was and what her death meant. This is in JBM territory, yes, but doesn't seem directed at anyone in particular. We need to find out who the victim is, and if she's linked in any way to the Junior Black Mafia. Or the A&As for that matter."

Wansbrough nodded as he listened. "At this point, I think we also need to prioritize the arrest of Kevin Baker."

Schacht nodded. "I agree. Calder and Burton: I want you guys to lift every rock in the city. Find Kevin Baker. Maybe if both Kevin and Dewayne are in our custody their respective crews will take it down a notch and we won't have any new bodies for a while. Wansbrough and Khalil: Philly PD is holding down the fort on our most recent stabbing 'til you guys get there. Work closely with Watt and the forensic team on this one, and find out if these killings are linked. Keep me up to date."

All four watched as Schacht left the room. Nora stared at the address of the witness in her hand. She looked at Wansbrough. "I guess we're going back to Kingsessing, then?"

A bicycle race on the parkway had snarled Saturday traffic on the 676. John didn't bother with the lights. They sat quietly a while in a crawl, Billie Holiday filling the silence with a protracted, throaty complaint; sometimes being stuck in traffic was their downtime before being "on." After Kylie Baker, Nora wasn't eager to see another stabbing victim up close. Instead of merging onto the Schuylkill

Expressway, though, John pulled onto Market Street behind the 30th Street Station, and wove his way through University City.

"Wait, stop for a minute. Coffee break." She was pointing at a Dunkin' Donuts.

John looked at her. "You're drinking coffee now? What has Calder done to you?"

"Just . . . give me a minute," she said, getting out of the car. She poked her head through the still-open door. "Thirty seconds. You want something?"

"Were you gonna go into a Dunkin' Donuts and *not* get me something?"

Nora shut her door and ran into the store, returning a long five minutes later with a carrier containing three cappuccinos.

She handed one to John and kept the other two on her lap.

He stared at her, then shifted the car into drive. "What kind of fool goes into a Dunkin' Donuts and comes back with only coffee?"

She ignored the question, responding simply, "I learned something last time we found ourselves in a situation like this."

They emerged from the car on a side street just beyond a battered Ethiopian restaurant. Scarlet and gold leaves dusted the trash-strewn sidewalks and the yards of tightly packed homes. Gang symbols peppered the landscape. The Junior Black Mafia's upside-down crown with two intersecting pitchforks was spray-painted on the sides of abandoned buildings, on stop signs, and on corner mailboxes. The crime scene lay in a wide alleyway that fell in the center of a block of shabby duplexes marked by their peeling paint and bowed wooden porches. A Philly PD car was parked at an awkward angle. More yellow crime scene tape decorated the area than Nora had seen in recent memory.

Mike Cook and Pat Crone were two of Nora's fellow officers. They looked cold and irritable, but they greeted her warmly, and she introduced John.

"How they treatin' you, Nora? I need to rough somebody up for you?" Mike asked, looking pointedly at Wansbrough.

Nora laughed as she handed over the cappuccinos. "It's pretty posh with the feds, guys. This is just a token of our appreciation. Thanks for all your hard work on this case so far."

Mike chuckled, looking Nora over. "Oh, I know exactly what this is. And yeah, it's probably gonna work, too."

"Nora's always giving people food or tea or something in order to get them to help her out," Crone said to John. He sniffed the small opening, then took a tentative sip. "That's why we miss her," he added.

Nora grinned. "So? What do you think? Anything you can tell us about the initial canvassing of the neighborhood?"

Crone shrugged. "Went to the old lady's house. She saw the body when she came out to feed the pigeons or some dumb-ass old lady thing. Houses here, here, and here wouldn't answer." He pointed at the surrounding homes that backed up to the alley.

"Gawkers?" Wansbrough asked.

"Plenty. We started tellin' 'em that anyone standing around would be questioned by the police. They dispersed pretty quick after that."

"Press?" Nora asked.

"Nah. Must have sounded too much like just another Philly gang killing. Gangs don't get press anymore unless they're called al-Qaeda." Mike Cook said all this through gritted teeth that showed how cold he was. He took a long sip of his cappuccino.

"You got any sense that the A&As are owning up to this one?" Wansbrough asked them.

Both shrugged. "Didn't hear anything about that," Crone answered.

Nora let her eyes wander across the landscape. She could feel the questions pouring out of the upstairs windows of the surrounding homes, imagined the fearful curiosity of the neighbors. She slowly took in the entrance to the alleyway, the long, dark passage between two tall row homes.

What brought you out here? She questioned the woman where she lay, an opaque beige tarp covering all but her toes and some strands of dark hair. It was then that Watt drove up with the van.

"Well, that looks like it for us," Crone said, pulling out the security log for the crime scene and handing it over to Wansbrough. He glanced over it and signed it.

The two cops extended their hands to shake John's, then fist-bumped Nora. "Don't be such a stranger, Nora," Mike Cook said, his gaze taking her in from head to toe. "Don't go forgetting where the good guys hang out."

Nora smiled. "Just don't you guys get in the way of any bullets, okay?" She watched them walk off toward their car.

"Sly," John was murmuring. "I think Officer Cook was especially grateful."

Nora glanced over just in time to see Cook staring at her from the passenger seat as his partner guided the car toward Chestnut Street. "Not my type," she said, even as she gave him a small wave.

Pale and paunchy, Montgomery Watt emerged from the crime scene van and shrugged into his heavy field jacket. He had started a scruffy beard since last Nora had seen him. He carefully draped a high-speed digital camera around his neck, then rifled about for a moment before grasping his kit. He had a shine in his eyes that made Nora smile despite herself. He was unapologetic about how good he was at his job. His bedside manner was a little dry, but he made up for it in unflinching competence. Now he was trailed by two evidence technicians, each of whom carried small video cameras. "Shall we?" he said brightly.

Watt and his small team signed the security log and then started digitizing every inch of the scene as they walked carefully around the perimeter that the Philadelphia Police Department had outlined with their bright yellow tape. Watt placed booties over his shoes and then ducked gingerly under the yellow tape and squatted next to the corpse. He lifted the tarp from the body, and Nora first saw a mass of thick, black hair, some spilling across the dark and bloodied brick. The body was covered with deep, dark gashes; very little remained of the victim's facial features. Both eyes had been cut out, leaving gaping burgundy holes.

John directed the technicians to include in their video work the back of the home of the woman who had made the call, Elfreda Chambers, 5501 Chester. Nora watched as the camera lenses swept along the alleyway and the tilting chain-link fences that lined it. There was little to obstruct the view of this stretch of cement from the windows and back balconies of the surrounding homes. Not all of the homes were inhabited; some had broken windows and roofs in a state of near-collapse. Mike Cook had made clear his opinion that those that were inhabited would produce little information.

The evidence truck had brought a crowd with it, and John quickly called for more agents to help keep the crime scene off-limits.

Watt dug in the technician's box for his gloves and began passing them out.

"She looks pretty messed up," he said to no one in particular. When he got to Nora, he withheld the gloves as he studied her face. "You good? You didn't do so well last time."

She took the gloves, frowning at him. "Watt, come on. I'm all jaded and experienced now."

"Cool." He returned to squat next to the corpse, gently placing his fingers to her flesh. "Time of death maybe twelve hours ago. She's about twenty years old."

Nora and John pulled booties over their shoes and stepped under the yellow tape. They gave Watt his space, but squatted near him. Leaning in, Nora peered at the texture of the dead woman's hair and found it slightly coarse. The skin along the woman's arms and legs, though, looked smooth and hairless. Nora looked closely at what was left of the cheeks and upper lip. Also smooth. She peered at the fingers of the left hand. There was no telltale indentation on the ring finger.

"She has your coloring, Nora," John observed.

Nora had been thinking the same thing.

Watt nodded, glancing up at Nora. "So, probably Arab. Or Hispanic maybe." He was running his gloved fingers gently along the woman's wounds. There were small gashes up and down her torso. Monty was pointing toward her neck. "Long, flat blade." The woman's throat had been ripped open, leaving her with a wide, dark streak under her thin, pointed chin. "The neck wound is what killed her; I can't tell yet if it preceded the other wounds."

"How different are the wounds from Kylie Baker's?" Nora asked.

"At first glance? Different. Kylie was killed with one blade. And there were several wounds, but she wasn't mutilated, and her face wasn't touched. The eye thing . . . it's pretty intense. It's not an easy thing to cut someone's eyes out like this. You have to really deliberately intend it. But her cheeks are also slashed. The neck wound is almost . . . well, it's pretty clean. Kylie Baker's was pretty deep. Unnecessarily so. From here it looks like a copycat. But given the eyes, they were amping it up a bit. Whoever did it has done it before."

Despite herself, Nora felt her fingers climb to her own throat.

Watt looked back at the corpse. "There's a lot of something under her nails, here. I'm thinking . . . carpet, maybe. Like she was clawing a carpeted surface."

John nodded, then said to Watt, "What do you think of the splatter-pattern?"

He stared thoughtfully for a while at the bloodstains. "I don't *see* splatter, do you?" He stood, frowning; crouched, then stood again, pointing. "Dog prints." He pointed until they all saw them, and could follow with their eyes the trail that led off toward 55th Street.

Nora and John joined Monty in staring long and hard at the ground around the body. Nora noted the way the blood had gathered in the crevices between the uneven brick of the alley.

Watt finally said, "It really looks to me like she was left here to bleed, but not attacked here. Look, there's nothing on the fences, nothing even right here." He pointed at the ground just a few inches from the blood. "No dots, no splatters. It's all localized, from directly beneath her. The Baker murder had a trail of blood leading to the street, indicating she'd been taken out of a car before being dumped."

John stood, his gaze taking in the entire surrounding area. "Then, they would have had to wrap her in something. It would have been a very messy project to transport a body with that many holes in it," John said.

Watt nodded. "Much messier than the trail at the Baker scene."

"And why here?" Nora was demanding. "If it's some sort of message, who's the intended audience *here*?" She looked again at the backs of the houses along the alley. "Do we have JBM kids here, or their families?"

Wansbrough said, "We may get more details on that from Burton. He's working something up on all the known members now."

Watt sat on his haunches and then put his head up. "How's the wind?"

Wansbrough understood. "It hasn't been too windy."

"I want a hair, guys," he said to his techs, who were covering their shoes. "There's just no surface that could retain any prints. I need to find some perp hair here."

Nora was shaking her head. "No, it's been windy enough. You're never gonna find anything."

Watt was handing the assistants plastic gloves, a couple pairs of tweezers and some baggies. "Never say never."

The three men pored over the scene, with Watt occasionally stopping to photograph something.

"Could she have been wrapped tightly in plastic, or a tarp? She could have been placed here and then, like, unrolled?" Nora asked.

"I don't see why the plastic wouldn't have dripped when it was opened," Watt answered. "No, if that's the case, then it had to be something absorbent, like a carpet. So we're looking for traces of a vehicle that could have transported her, and also for fibers." The techs nodded when they heard this, and one headed over to look for tire prints in the mucky mix of leaves and dirt that rimmed the gutters and sidewalks near the alley.

John Wansbrough had seen enough for now. "Nora, let's go see the neighbor lady."

That sounded great to Nora; the lack of movement in the autumn chill was starting to get to her.

As they started out, John paused. "I just got one more question," he said. Watt nodded, focused intently on his tweezers.

"What about this woman's missing parts?"

Watt rested his elbows on his bent knees, looking to Nora rather like a Bedouin. He surveyed his surroundings quite intently, as though seeking a previously overlooked eyeball. Finally he said, "Same issue. I don't think they messed her up here, so they probably kept them or disposed of them before dumping her."

Nora couldn't help shivering. "Nice."

The other agents had finally arrived, and she waited for John to hand over control of the crime scene, then followed him gingerly along the alleyway heading away from the street. They walked slowly, aware of each step, looking for signs that the terrain had been disturbed in any noticeable way.

"So, like Kylie's, we're looking here at a secondary crime scene," Nora said as they walked.

John nodded, his eyes scanning this other entrance to the alley, then looking up and down the street. "Yeah, let's hope we have better luck finding the primary crime scene this time."

"Probably not a car, like we'd postulated for Kylie."

"That was Eric Burton's idea, not mine. No black man kills anybody *in* his ride."

Nora said, "Well, it would be impractical in this case, right? Messy. And she would have had to make a lot of noise, don't you think? Unless they drugged her first?" They bent under the outer perimeter of yellow tape and slipped out of their booties. John thought for a moment, then answered, "Sounds too merciful. It looks like they wanted to cause her a lot of pain."

They continued along the sidewalk. "I wonder what she saw to make them wanna cut out her eyes," Nora said.

"Or who," John countered. They had arrived at Elfreda Chambers's home. Iron bars wove impenetrable webs across the windows and storm door, always evidence that the homeowner had been frustrated by more than one break-in. "Ready?"

Nora motioned at the doorbell. "Go for it."

He punched it, and they waited. John was not good at waiting.

"*Patience is beautiful*," Nora quoted, as John sighed in irritation and was about to punch the doorbell again. Just as he let his hand fall to his side, they heard a slow, shuffling step approaching.

No less than three bolts creaked open before Elfreda Chambers pulled open the door, leaving the agents on the other side of the security storm door. Looking at least eighty, she was erect but battle-weary. She added a perturbed frown to the landscape of wrinkles on her face. "I've already spoken to the police."

Nora and John offered up their badges for scrutiny. "Mrs. Chambers," Nora said, "we're with the Violent Gang Safe Streets Task Force. We are so grateful for all the help you've provided already today, and we hate to bother you. But we would really appreciate getting a chance to stand on your balcony as part of the investigation of this crime."

Elfreda Chambers regarded them steadily, then pulled open the iron door and stepped aside to usher them both in. "You can go straight upstairs. The balcony is off my bedroom, at the end of the hall." Mrs. Chambers was sharp and her diction was perfect. Nora pegged her for a former English teacher.

John walked straight toward the stairs; Nora hesitated, her instinct being to await their hostess. But Mrs. Chambers waved her on. "It takes me awhile, dear. I'll join you, but you get started." Indeed, although she could walk, her gait was slow and it seemed that the left leg dragged slightly. Nora nodded, offered Mrs. Chambers a smile, and followed John.

They walked up a steep stairway that was lined with family photographs. It looked as though Elfreda Chambers was the matriarch of a large family. From the stillness and total order in the house, however, it seemed that she lived alone. They passed two tidy bedrooms with perfectly made beds. No traces of clutter, nothing out of place. The woman's bedroom had high ceilings and a queen-sized bed that stood regally under a handmade quilt. A pair of reading glasses sat like a tiara upon the stack of books on the bedside table. Powder-blue curtains were primly tied on both sides of a bank of windows and the door leading to the balcony; all of the glass was secured with a framework of iron. John tugged at the locks and then led Nora out onto the balcony. They could see Watt and his techs still bent over the scene. A tech noticed them and must have said something to Watt, who looked up and acknowledged them by raising his chin in greeting. Mrs. Chambers's balcony afforded a view of the alley that was clear enough; Watt and the corpse could not have been more than one hundred feet away. The tall fence lining the alley was chain-link, with occasional viney weeds braiding themselves along the twisted wire.

Nora regarded the balcony. It was neatly arranged and held several planters; a few were empty, while others contained small evergreen shrubs. Mrs. Chambers maintained four bird feeders. Nora noted a wide metal scoop sitting on a large plastic lidded tub. The floor around the tub was littered with strewn birdseed. This balcony stood in stark contrast to the ones around it. To the left, most of the balcony wall had tumbled into the yard below, revealing a rotting floor; the whole house looked abandoned, and Nora spied a few old tires and a discarded commode in among the weeds. The balcony on the right was cluttered with junk, including a rusted ironing board, a child's plastic basketball backboard, and a collection of scum-encrusted chairs piled atop one another.

Nora glanced behind her to make sure that Mrs. Chambers had not appeared behind them, then said. "So . . . my friend and I have just brutally murdered a twenty-five-year-old woman. We roll her up in a carpet, toss her in our . . . "

John filled in, "Van. Or truck. I'll ask Watt to spend some time on trying to find us some tire impressions."

Nora continued, " . . . And we pull up at the entrance of this alley. Probably if we back up between the two houses, we can slip our package out the back with little chance of anyone seeing us."

He nodded, staring down at Watt's bent form. "It just doesn't sound like gangbanger MO to me."

"Yeah, me neither. Someone was meant to see her, John. Probably not Mrs. Chambers. Let's figure out whose houses these are," Nora said. "There's only like, what, ten possible candidates in eyeshot here. And a couple are vacant," she added, gesturing at the house to their left.

Elfreda Chambers pulled open the door and walked out onto the balcony as she wrapped a heavy shawl around her shoulders. She cast a long look at the crew down at the crime scene, and the truck just visible beyond the houses that bordered the alley's entrance.

"Mrs. Chambers," began John slowly. "Do you know anything about gang activity around here?" John asked.

She tightened her shawl around herself. "Young fools. Selling their drugs. My hairdresser says that the A&A gang is trying to take over the territory here." Nora's and John's eyes met, as Mrs. Chambers continued: "I lost many young students to these gangs over the years, but somehow it seems much uglier now. Much uglier."

Wansbrough quizzed her on some names, but she shook her head each time.

"Have gang members ever threatened you in any way?"

Mrs. Chambers shook her head. "No threats. Maybe I'm just too old of an old lady. But just . . . rudeness, you see. Rudeness is just as bad, in my book."

"Do any gang members live in your immediate neighborhood?"

She shook her head again. "No one I know of. But the one who will know is my hairdresser, down at the Tress It Up. Cheryl."

"Thank you, Mrs. Chambers. Just a couple more quick questions." Nora said. "What about the makeup of the neighborhood?"

"With regard to what, exactly?"

John clarified: "Your impressions. Black folks, immigrants? Who are your neighbors?"

The elderly woman looked thoughtfully from home to home. "Used to be just black folks. Many more immigrants now, lots of Hispanics. Some Africans. Some of the Black Muslims, those men in the gowns and the beards, women in the . . . " she paused, frowning, as though searching for a word that eluded her, then came up with, "burkas—No," interrupting herself. "That's what they call it in Afghanistan, isn't it. What is it here?"

"Niqab?" Nora offered.

Mrs. Chambers nodded. "Yes. Niqab. So . . . oh, yes, lots of renters, I think. I can always tell because they don't really take care of their homes the way they would if they owned them."

"Is there violence that isn't gang-related?" Nora asked.

Elfreda Chambers exhaled in disdain. "Of course. Always. Gunshots, here, screams there." She sighed, gesturing with a small nod of her head to the balcony with the basketball hoop. "The white man next door, when he is around, beats his wife mercilessly," she said.

She shivered, and Nora realized it was as much from the cold as anything else.

"Perhaps we could continue inside?" she suggested gently.

Mrs. Chambers nodded and entered. The agents cast last glances over the alley and the surrounding area, then followed her in.

John and Nora emerged into the fast-waning afternoon.

"I like her," said Nora, scribbling the name of Mrs. Chambers's hairdresser into her file as they walked back to the crime scene.

"What's not to like? She looks just like my grandma but without the crazy. I kept waiting for her to give me some pie."

"It's always food with you."

"I've been married twenty-four years. It's all about the pie now."

Nora rolled her eyes at him.

He said, "Okay, look, I can tell you want to keep asking questions here. But I also know that Cook and Crone already questioned a lot of these neighbors, and I guarantee the rest aren't gonna be sweet old ladies like Mrs. Chambers. I think we should check in with Watt, get that report that Burton's working on, and start here in the morning. Nobody's gonna open the door to us in the dark anyway."

Nora was nodding her assent as she huddled deeper into her jacket. "I can work on some demographics from my laptop tonight."

But Watt was motioning to them. "There's one more thing I want to show you before we go ahead and transfer her to the lab," he said. He gestured toward the woman's toes. "Look here."

Nora and John dug two more pairs of booties out of the box and crossed over the tape again. They squinted in the fading light.

The woman's toenails, like her fingernails, were unpainted. It looked like they had been scraped and torn, and the tips of her toes were bloody. John said, "Digging in with her toes. . . . Or, she's been dragged over gravel. Both, maybe?"

Watt nodded. "Yes, but that's not what I wanted to show you." He tapped the skin on the top of her right foot. "Here, and here, above the talus."

Nora squatted and peered closely at the woman's flesh, then swallowed hard.

Watt was saying, "Calluses, but I've never seen calluses quite like that, as though she. . . ."

"Prayer calluses," she said, not meeting his eyes.

"Hmm?"

Nora said softly, "She's sat on the floor for long periods of time with her feet tucked under her. Probably on a mat, maybe straw, or just a rough rug or Berber carpet. From sitting to prostrating and back again. Not much of a shift for the foot, but just enough friction that, if repeated, will roughen this part of the skin."

She straightened and looked at John. "Muslim woman. The pious kind."

PART **TWO**

CHAPTER 4

Wansbrough drove in silence for several minutes before a stoplight allowed him to turn and regard her. "What makes you so sure about those calluses?"

Nora took a long breath and looked out the window. "Mmm. If I tell my secrets, you guys won't keep me on as the token Muslim chick."

He snorted, "There are lines of them, as you know, waiting to fill your position." He went back to navigating the crush of traffic on Market Street as they put Kingsessing behind them.

She waited a moment. "My mom had them. She . . . was really good about all that, the five daily prayers, the reciting Qur'an in the night. Her dad had a passion for the written word, and taught her to love reading everything from old Arabic poetry to law books. So she was like an encyclopedia. As for the calluses, she always had them. She usually prayed on a mat instead of a soft rug." Nora was still, remembering the feel of her mother's skin under her fingertips, her warmth.

She watched John as he nodded meditatively. She was grateful that he didn't ask about her mother. It was one of his best traits; he seemed to know when she couldn't talk about things any further.

"You see them on guys's foreheads sometimes," she added, after a while.

"Huh?"

"Calluses." She was tapping the center of her own forehead. "They look sorta like bruises. Sometimes I think they bang their heads on the floor in order to look, you know . . . pious or something."

"Your dad got one?" he asked.

"Nope," she said. "He thinks he's supposed to pray, and feels guilty for not praying, but doesn't quite muster enough energy to actually do it. He'd like to go to the mosque on Friday afternoons, but always has the excuse of not being able to leave the restaurant, so he never, ever goes."

Wansbrough smiled. "Good intentions thwarted."

Nora nodded. "Well, he'll always quote at you, 'Work is worship.' He's worked really, really hard his whole life."

"Noble work," John said earnestly.

She looked over at him. "You talking about all the free kabob you get?"

Wansbrough laughed, patting his stomach. "Girl, being your partner has been the high point of my career."

"Thank God," she said. "I knew I was here for some sort of higher good."

"So why would a gang killing—with two gangs who have no known Muslim members—involve a nice, praying Muslim woman?"

"Well," Nora said, "now we have Rashid, Kevin's brother."

"You were working on him, right?"

"Yes. His real name is Roland Baker. When he said he'd been 'gone, ' it was because he was doing five years of a seven-year sentence for grand larceny."

"Larceny? Nothing gang-related?"

Nora shook her head. "Class D felony larceny. He'd been working for some kind of warehouse in South Philly on the docks, and was caught swiping merchandise stored there. There's no record of him ever being in a gang."

"But he could have gotten involved after his return?"

Nora shrugged. "It occurred to me. Maybe all his concern with gang violence was a sham, and he's busy trying to pick up where Kevin left off?"

"Hmm." Wansbrough lapsed into silence. "We would need to connect this woman somehow to the JBM for it to be a possible act of vengeance for Kylie. Does Dewayne have any siblings we don't know about?"

Nora shrugged, then jotted the question into the file.

He said, "What if I told you I think there's something about these killings that's connected."

Nora shrugged again. "I'm just the PPD interloper."

"Okay, PPD interloper," he said, pulling the Suburban onto the rim of the curb that ran in front of the Cairo Café. He turned to look at her. "Then see what you can find out about all the houses in the neighborhood there. Who owns them, who inhabits them . . . If she was dumped there for a reason, let's see who might have been meant to see her. We can meet up Monday morning early."

"I want to try to talk to the other hooker tomorrow," she said, opening the car door but not yet descending.

John shrugged. "I got an e-mail last night that she's still not talking."

"But I can try, right? Nothing says I can't try."

"Nothing says you can't try, Nora. It's your Sunday."

As he said these words, Ragab emerged from the Cairo Café with a plastic bag filled with to-go boxes. Nora sighed as she watched her father make his way to the driver's side of the Suburban.

John winked at her, then descended to greet him.

She watched the two men shaking hands warmly. In twenty-five years of dealing with Americans, Ragab had learned not to embrace men and kiss them on both cheeks. But she could tell he still had to remind himself.

She gathered her stuff and got out of the car as John was accepting the bag full of rice and kabob.

"Only reason I give you to-go is I know Mrs. John Wansbrough loves my cooking. Otherwise I insist you stay and eat with me," Ragab was saying.

"You're a good man, Ragab. I don't know how to thank you," John replied, grinning.

"You do enough, keeping my Nora safe," Ragab said sincerely.

John nodded gravely. "I do my best," he replied.

Nora rolled her eyes at him, and Ragab caught her. "You giving that look to John Wansbrough? Your expert FBI partner, and you just a police officer?"

John laughed loudly, winking at Nora again as he got into the Suburban. "Exactly my point, Ragab. You keep her in line, now."

Ragab held the front door of the café as he shooed his daughter inside. "*Yalla*, learn some manners, Girl," he was saying in an exaggerated tone so John could hear him.

Nora fantasized about a roundhouse kick that would take out both of them simultaneously, but entered the café in silence.

"Hey, Nora," she heard Ahmad call out, as her eyes adjusted to the dimness of the restaurant. Her brother and father had been sitting together at the dessert bar, tasting; Amr Diab was singing over the stereo system.

It was a ritual with them. Every few months, Ragab would order in three or four new cakes, and the two of them would sit and taste. It was Ragab's concession to the fact that not all of his customers had the refined palate necessary to appreciate his konaffa or baklava. He could satisfy his sweet tooth while bonding with Ahmad, not that Ragab would ever have used the word "bonding."

Nora just wanted to walk up the stairs and vanish, but she sank down into the chair next to Ahmad. "What's the best one so far?" she asked, trying not to sound tired or shell-shocked.

Ahmad dinged his fork a few times against a plate holding a layer cake. "This one," he said enthusiastically. "It's *sick*."

Nora peered at a vanilla cake with about six layers of what looked like buttercream interspersed with raspberry ganache.

Ragab rejoined the tasting session and pushed a fork in her direction, but she pushed it back.

"No cake? Nora, you aren't eating. I'm worried about you."

"Baba, I eat all the time. But I was just snacking at work," she lied.

Ragab tsk-tsk'd anyway. "No, you look thin. Doesn't she look thin, *ya Hammudi*?"

Ahmad made a show of looking at Nora, then grinned at her. "Hmmm—thin . . . dark circles under her eyes . . . Perhaps she's in *love!*"

Nora slapped the top of his head. "I have a *gun*, boy. When are you gonna figure that out?"

Baba chewed on a mouthful of cake. "*Ya Noora*, you know, your aunt Madiha called me last week. Her coworker at the ministry has a son who just finished medical school here in the States. In Dallas."

"Really?" Nora said, feeling queasy. "Tell her I said, '*Mabrouk*, Congratulations.'"

"Sarcastic, always. He saw your picture—"

"Baba!"

He threw up his hands, without releasing his fork. "—I didn't give it to him, Aunt Madiha gave it to his mother."

"With your permission?"

"She didn't ask me! She worries about you—"

Nora put her head on the tiled surface of the bar. "*Ya Hammudi*, please tell Baba something . . . "

"*Ya Baba* . . . Nora has a gun," Ahmad offered.

"Your gun doesn't scare me, girl. Not having grandchildren scares me."

Nora rose, kissed her brother's cheek and then her father's. "I'm going upstairs," she said. "Neither one of you is allowed to follow."

Both were too busy chewing to respond.

Google Maps was one of the most convenient and dastardly pro-grams ever invented, as far as she could tell. Nora stayed up most of that night, printing up detailed close-ups of the alley, and she began charting the row houses and twins that clustered around it. She hated the feeling that they could be way off, that the body left on the weedy bricks was only thrown there randomly. But trying to determine who lived there was the only good direction they could go in at this point.

A total of ten homes were in eyeshot of the corpse that had been left there. Mrs. Chambers's house was one of four single-family homes, and three twins rounded out the number. Nora drew in the body's location and figured the angles relative to each home. She got current names for the owners of each place, and made a chart with whatever demographics she could locate in the municipal da-tabases to which she had access.

The next morning she struck out early, before Baba and Ahmad had arisen.

Nora showed her badge to three separate sets of security guards, and then sat waiting for more than thirty minutes. Finally, "Jane Doe"—Nora forced herself to stop mentally referring to her as "the not-dead hooker"—was brought into the interview room of the Al-ternative Detention Center.

Nora regarded her curiously. In her orange jumpsuit, and with an elastic tying back her hair, she looked very different from the hysterical, mostly naked girl Nora had first seen next to a pile of meth.

The girl did not look at Nora.

Nora intercepted the guard, asking if the cuffs could be removed, but the guard shook her head. "We're used to the drugs here, but this one has an extra measure of instability somewhere in the mix. Lot of hair-pulling, self-abuse. The cuffs are as much for her own safety as for yours."

Left on her own with Jane Doe, Nora found herself unsure of

how to begin. "I'm Officer Nora Khalil," she said. "We've been trying to find out your name, but it seems you aren't talking."

The girl shrunk in on herself, not looking up.

Nora studied her. She realized Jane Doe was much younger
than they had thought. Perhaps she was no more than sixteen, and
Nora's stomach immediately began to twist anxiously. "I know we
found you in a difficult situation." Nora paused, carefully watching the girl's expression. "But I'm going to recommend you be
transferred out of here, to a hospital. We can help you, if you'll let
us. Get you medical help. Rehab. Help you get back on your
feet . . . "

Nora started doubting if the girl even understood what she was
saying. "You do speak English, right?" She squatted, looking up at
the girl where she sat. "Right?"

Jane Doe glanced at Nora, then looked away. It seemed to Nora
that the girl's whole body was trembling.

"Yes? Is that a yes?"

Silence.

Nora sighed. "We are trying to find out information about Dewayne Fulton. Can you tell me how you ended up in that loft with
him and Lisa Halston?"

Silence.

Nora rose to standing again. "How about if you just tell me your
name? How old you are? We can try to find your family."

Silence.

"How about . . . " she backed away from Jane Doe and went to
sit on the bench across from her. "How about if I just sit here with
you for a little bit then. And maybe . . . maybe you'll talk if you feel
like it?"

The girl flicked a glance at Nora again, in what she was starting
to accept as acknowledgment. And so they sat.

It was very, very still; almost immediately, Nora became hyper-
aware of her own breathing. Only seven minutes passed before she

choked on her own silence and started chattering. "I bet the food is pretty nasty here. My dad has a restaurant, you know."

The girl was unmoved. She would not surrender over food.

"Really good stuff," Nora continued, undaunted. "Chicken kabob and lamb curry and these giant Greek salads with his own secret dressing. And then there's the baklava. He has an awesome baklava. Kill you straight up if you have a nut allergy."

No reaction. Nora went on, trying to make her voice sound chatty and friendly instead of pestering. "He came from Egypt before I was born. He didn't know a thing about cooking before he came. Used to call his mother from the kitchen, asking her how to do things. When my mom moved over from Egypt to marry him, he'd call her at work." Nora stopped and tried hard to get the girl to meet her eyes.

But Jane Doe closed her eyes as if to shut Nora out. She leaned her head against the wall. Nora sank into a sitting position in front of the girl, and remained there in silence another few minutes.

Finally she stood and fished a card out of her Windbreaker's breast pocket. She left it on the bench next to the girl. "You can ask them to call me when you change your mind. We can help you."

Nora walked to the door and rapped on the glass, angry at herself for having come all this way without a solid idea of what to say or how to say it. The guard appeared and escorted her through the maze of hallways and back down to the lobby.

The air on 7th Street was biting. She quickly walked the single block over to the field office, determined to match Jane Doe's face to a missing persons report.

It was midafternoon when she made her way back to the apartment over the Cairo Café. Ahmad was seriously angry with her.

"You have studied with me, like, not at *all*. Not even a little. What the heck, Nora? How many times did I help you train for a race? You made me ride my bike all over this city with you. Made me hurl insults at you so you'd run faster. You warped my entire childhood. And now you can't even ask me a few terms from some flash cards?"

Nora kissed his head, then sat down at the kitchen table. "I'm sorry. Forgive me. Hand over the flash cards."

"What was so important?" he demanded.

"Nothing is more important. I'm sorry, *habibi. Dissimulation.*"

He put his head down on the kitchen table. "I have no idea."

"False appearances. Pretense."

He jerked his head up, still irritated with her. "Yeah, you know the worst part, is that I totally couldn't concentrate because Baba was on the phone with Aunt Madiha for like an hour this morning talking about this doctor from Dallas. Like, talking all loud the way he does."

Nora felt queasy. *"What* about the doctor from Dallas?"

Ahmad shrugged, "I don't know, Nora. What his father does in Egypt, and where they live in Cairo and all that stuff. How many bedrooms his apartment has and what part of town *that's* in. How he feels about his wife working. If he could come here for a weekend, and where he would stay. . . ."

Nora shot back in her chair and took the stairs down to the restaurant by twos. As the door closed behind her, she heard Ahmad shouting, "I thought we were studying!"

Her father was standing over a huge pot that bubbled with rice pudding.

"What is going on with this kid from Dallas?" she asked, working to keep her voice low. "I thought this was just some joke, that you were teasing me."

He looked up, startled, then he frowned and went back to stirring. "I'm pretty sure when someone enters a room he or she should say, *As-salaam alaykum*. That's what I know about that."

Nora said, "Are you really thinking I'm going to marry some man I don't know from Dallas?"

"He's from Cairo," her father corrected calmly.

Fifteen different faces flashed before her, girlfriends saying the same sentence, voices swimming in and out of unison: "A suitor came last night for dinner . . . "

She searched for words she could not even formulate. She'd known this conversation was coming, known it to be inevitable, but had somehow been sure it was far off in some murky future, not now, today, here, in front of a pot of rice pudding. Her brain flailed about for words that refused to emerge in either language.

Her father spoke gently. "Nora, this is the way we marry. This is how I met your mother, God rest her beautiful soul," he took a moment to mop at his brow, in what seemed to Nora like a purely dramatic pause. "This is what works. You know it works better than the system here—look at the divorce rate in America." He gestured to the kitchen, as though it encompassed the entire country.

Javier the dishwasher walked by, carrying a still-steaming plastic tray full of dishes out to the server's station. He nodded to Nora, and she nodded back before whispering, "I don't want to marry that way, Baba."

Her father looked up sharply, then set down his spoon, extinguishing the flame beneath the rice pudding. "Listen to me, Nora Khalil. If you think I let you go off to be a big bad police officer in order to have you forget who you are, you are very wrong. You are still my daughter. And it is my job to see you happily married. That. Is. My. *Job*."

He watched her digest his words. "When Dr. Dallas comes, you will meet him. Because I wish it. And I'm your father. And I. Still. *Matter*."

———

The November sun rose coolly over an already bustling Monday. The thirty-three bus ground to a screeching halt under her window, and car horns echoed irritably through the streets as Nora donned her running gear. She had been tossing and turning most of the night, partially because she was so angry with her father, partially because she was so angry with herself for being angry. Of course he wanted her to marry an Egyptian doctor. Every Egyptian father wanted his daughter to marry an Egyptian doctor. Didn't every father on the planet want his daughter to marry a doctor?

It was all completely normal.

She stared at herself for a long time in the bathroom mirror, then began to laugh. *You're only upset because you've gone and fallen in love with Ben Calder.*

She laughed for a while, felt tears spring to her eyes, then determined that she would run it all off. She packed her drawstring backpack full of maps and print-ups of Kingsessing (all of Saturday night's research), and every missing persons report that looked vaguely like Jane Doe (all of Sunday's research), and she headed out into the Monday morning swirl. Her backpack flopping against her back, and Haifa Wehbe singing in her ears, she sprinted along 21st Street and over the train tracks to the river. She passed faces she recognized—serious runners could always pick each other out of the group on the Schuylkill Banks. She watched as a few Canada geese feinted at a swanky stroller. A demonic shout from the speed-walking mother scattered them.

Nora emerged by the Spring Garden Bridge and crossed over the parkway to the Philadelphia Museum of Art. She ran the steps to the top, pausing, not because she needed the air, but because she loved the way the city unfolded beneath her, perfectly aligned, the wide parkway rimmed with multicolored flags of every nation. The city from this angle was open, accepting, cultured, alive. She liked the way she felt from the top of those steps, and she wanted an extra dose today after all the time she'd spent in Kingsessing and in the Alternative Detention Center yesterday. Those places had nothing to do with the Philly she grew up in. This fact unsettled her more than she'd realized.

She ran up and down four more times before taking off down the parkway. She connected with Arch Street by Love Park's towering fountain, then headed past the Convention Center, through the electric bustle of Chinatown, past the detention center and finally in through the wide glass doors of the Federal Building. She chatted with the security guard, mourning the Eagles' loss with him despite her complete indifference, and then headed down to take a quick shower in the basement locker room. She changed into the extra white blouse and navy trousers she kept hanging in her locker. She wound her hair into a knot, secured it with an elastic, and walked meditatively up the eight flights of stairs. Two overly hair-gelled junior attorneys from the AUSA's office brushed past her, trying to find a secluded area to smoke. She knew that Saturday's corpse would already have made its way to one of Monty Watt's drawers and she cringed, remembering, and wondered for a moment if she shouldn't have followed her teammate Michaela into a nice, safe career as a personal trainer.

The din of ringing phones, both office lines and cellular, hit her like a wave as she pushed open the door to the eighth floor. Wansbrough was alone in their cubicle, and looked up as she walked in. "You look fresh from a run."

She looked him over. "And you look worried. Did something happen with Fulton?"

"I heard from the AUSA he's pleading not guilty to the rape and murder."

Nora sank into her chair, processing this. "How can that be?"

John shook his head. "Stranger things have happened. But because we still can't find the murder weapon, it doesn't surprise me."

"But the DNA . . . "

"I don't know what he's up to. But that's not the worst part . . . " John continued.

She raised her eyebrows, questioning him.

"It's my twenty-fifth anniversary."

She laughed, despite herself. "Is that all? Okay, how are you celebrating?" Nora asked.

"By not putting a gun to my head."

"Did you get Olivia something?"

"I'm working on it."

"You're still working on it?" Nora demanded.

"I'm *working* on it," he repeated tersely.

"You got reservations somewhere?"

"*I'm working on it!*" he snapped.

"Oh my God," she said. She powered on her laptop. "You're lucky it's a Monday, you might still be able to get reservations somewhere." She began browsing the Internet. "Modern Asian fusion? Spanish tapas? Old-world steak house?"

"I could take her to your dad's place . . . "

"Cheapskate! Answer the original question."

"Steak?" he shrugged.

She made her way through to Butcher & Singer's reservations page. "What time do you want to go?"

"Dinner time. Seven. Seven thirty," he said, as though it was obvious.

Nora gazed at the screen and then smiled at him. "They have openings at five thirty or nine forty-five."

"*Jesus . . . *"

" . . . likely won't be there. Now . . . which one?"

He shook his head. "Can't you see about some other place?" he asked plaintively.

"How can you skimp on the twenty-fifth anniversary dinner? Nothing less than a Stephen Starr restaurant will do."

"I don't even know who that is!" he protested.

"*Olivia* does, trust me." Nora entered the rest of his information after he reluctantly passed her his credit card to hold their place. "And she'll be *very* grateful."

"You mean I might get lucky?"

"Eww. I meant she *might* decide to stay married to you."

She could see, though, that he was contemplating the confluence of his twin ideals of steak and sex.

"You're alright, Nora Khalil," he said finally.

Nora shrugged, ignoring the fact that he was still mispronouncing her name after six months. "You'd better call her. She'll need time to primp."

As Wansbrough carried his cell phone into the bustling hall, Nora looked at her own fingernails—which she'd trimmed the night before with a toenail clipper while taking a break from her computer screen. She indulged in a thirty-second fantasy about a dim, romantic restaurant, a clingy black dress, and Ben Calder pulling out her chair. A second later, she spied Calder and Burton as they stepped out of the elevator together and started walking toward their cubicle. Nora tugged her brain into focus.

Burton didn't say good morning. "Did you hear about the plea?"

Nora nodded. "Good morning, gentlemen," she said, pointedly.

Ben Calder smiled at her. "Good morning, Officer Khalil."

"So. What's next?"

"Less sleep," Ben said. "More *investigatin'.*"

"You should have that on a throw pillow," Nora observed.

Wansbrough stepped back in, pocketing his cell phone. "Did you get in to see Jane Doe, Nora?"

She nodded. "Jane Doe needs to be in a psych ward. Like, immediately. She's completely traumatized. And guys, I think she's really young. I spent a lot of time trying to link her with someone—anyone—in the missing persons databases. I found nothing."

John nodded, writing himself a note. "I'll get her transferred today. What about you, Eric? I heard you were working up a report for us. You ready to go with that?"

Eric said, "Actually, I believe the project is proving successful. The PPD is helping a lot, to be honest—Officer Cook aided in the arrest of two lower-level members of the Junior Black Mafia late last night, a boy and a girl, both minors. Both demanded lawyers, so we're forced to wait to talk to them."

"Where did you find them, Eric?" Nora asked.

"Basement of grandma's house," he answered smugly.

"Bad Granny!" Ben exclaimed, shaking his head.

"So, surnames are helping; we can thank Mrs. Baker for that one. In the meantime, I've made a layout of Junior Black Mafia territory."

Eric finished hooking up his laptop to the plasma screen on their wall, and a bright map of Southwest Philly popped up. "Okay, so as we know, the Junior Black Mafia and the A&As are both transitioning from territorial into corporate gangs. If we can chart the perimeter of JBM territory, we're looking at basically this area of Kingsessing—from 54th down to 59th and from Springfield to Whitby. Dewayne Fulton's house is here," he paused to point at the bottom southwest corner of the screen, "and our newest crime scene is here." He extended his finger to point nearer to the northwestern edge of the screen. "The most drug business is on *this* strip, as we know," he said, pointing at the line representing 55th Street.

With the press of a button, a half-dozen pulsing circles began to glow. "These are the locations of drive-by shootings. This is the most recent A&A drive-by that felled—" he checked his notes, as Calder piped up, "Shane Dillard, age seventeen, a.k.a. Benzo."

Burton nodded. "Dillard. So, as you can see, most JBM activity is within these few blocks—both the drug dealing and the drive-by shootings. Investigating the local businesses and the community centers in this exact area has netted several leads that we will be pursuing while you guys are gathering intelligence on your stabbing victim."

Wansbrough was nodding, impressed. "All right, Eric, nice work. Make sure you have enough backup, keep PPD in the loop like you have been, and keep your vests on. These kids are running scared. And they're probably a lot more scared of the cartels supplying them than they are of you."

Burton nodded. "That's a fact, John. We have plenty of backup."

"Okay," Wansbrough said. "Nora?"

She pulled a stack of papers out of her drawstring backpack, and handed each of them a map of the neighborhood. She motioned at the houses generally. "We're still holding to the theory that this graphic a crime is meant as a message to someone, so we're concerned with who lives close to the corpse. I think we would be well-served by going house to house within eyeshot of the crime. I haven't found any direct link to the gang so far, although there are gang symbols everywhere down there. I attached a house-by-house report to the map explaining ethnic origin insofar as it could be determined, household income, and any relevant federal or state infractions."

Her colleagues looked through the pages she handed them as she spoke. "There are two felons in the neighborhood—Elise Garcia at 5601 Chester for tax fraud and Byron Mack, at 401 55th Street, for drug possession; both did minimal time. Mr. Evans, Mrs. Chambers's white neighbor, has been charged with domestic violence twice. Charges were dropped by his wife both times. The others noted there are almost exclusively people who've had misdemeanor drug possession arrests."

She made sure they were caught up with her, then continued, "We have four abandoned homes, one slotted to be taken over by the city."

"Was that the one next door to Mrs. Chambers?" John Wansbrough asked.

Nora shook her head. "No, amazingly, that one *is* inhabited. Or it is, according to this. The nearest abandoned home to her place is three doors down. In a couple of cases it seems clear that the owner is not living on site; I found one, if not two, other properties coming up in their possession."

"So, renting them out?"

"Probably without an official rental contract. To sum up, I couldn't find any gang links between any of the names that came up as owners of these houses. Meeting the residents face-to-face may tell a different story. For your reference I attached the pictures of the neighborhood homes that the techs sent me yesterday after they finished up out there."

"Okay, good Nora. What about the neighborhood mosques?" Wansbrough asked.

"There are four in the general area. One is basically a storefront," she offered. "The other three are converted townhomes, one a double."

Wansbrough nodded. "Okay—Burton, can you do some research into the neighborhood imams, find out who they are and what they're up to, how best to approach them? As soon as we can get an ID from Watt or, worst-case scenario, a facial reconstruction, we can go talk to the imams. See if they're missing any of their flock?"

All the agents nodded.

"Okay, kids, we're not ruling out anything—our primary objective is to meet with the neighbors now, and Nora and I will also go chat with Mrs. Chambers's hairdresser."

Ben said, "Seriously? The hairdresser?"

John stared at him. "What, are you new? Hairdressers have the pulse of a community, especially an impoverished area like this one."

Ben nodded, chastened. "Okay, duly noted."

John continued, "I'll look for Burton's report by tomorrow, and then we can ask questions in the mosques. Ben—why don't you go ahead and call Watt now and ask him to get an artist to re-create that face for us. You two call us if you need anything out there."

As they rose to part, Nora could tell that John wished Schacht hadn't prioritized their newest case, and that they were joining their teammates instead. She met Ben's eyes, and said, "Call me if you have trouble running 'em down."

Ben shrugged, giving her a half smile. "I might call anyway."

Tress It Up's small, grubby storefront belied the bright, warm atmosphere within. Plastered to the wide glass windows were large, faded posters of black women with masses of tiny braids; the posters served to effectively hide the store within, and as the agents entered, they understood why. The seven customers inside were in various states of undress, and all had either fat rollers or huge aluminum foils jutting out of their heads. Three stylists commanded bright pink barber's chairs, and the row of four hair dryers was at full occupancy.

Dead silence followed the bell-tinkling that announced their entrance.

A large-chested woman came forward, still holding a spray bottle. "Can I help you?" Three huge hairclips sprouted from the edges of her black apron, and her makeup struck Nora as alarming for eleven in the morning. Her short, spiky hair had lavender tips.

"We're looking for Cheryl," John said.

"You being who?" the woman demanded.

Wordlessly, they pulled out their identification and showed it to her. She scrutinized their badges, then asked, "Is there a problem?"

"Are you Cheryl?"

She nodded.

"Can we talk privately?"

Cheryl pursed her lips, then said, "Gimme a second." She walked back to the wide-eyed woman in her barber's chair and rapidly rolled two more fat pink rollers into her thin hair. After securing them with clips, she sprayed a foul-smelling substance liberally over the woman's entire head and ordered her to wait. She lifted the dryer from the head of another woman, instructed her to go to the rinsing station, and seated her other customer in the newly vacated seat.

At last she looked at the agents, not bothering to disguise her annoyance. "Follow me."

She led them into a back office, where they asked her full name, and she gave it as Cheryl Thomas.

"What is this all about, now?" she demanded.

Nora said, "We're simply looking for some information about a recent murder in the neighborhood. When we questioned one of your clients, Mrs. Chambers, she suggested that we find out what you know about the gang activity in this area."

Cheryl thought for a moment. "Elfreda Chambers? That's a good woman, right there." She paused, studying them. "If it's Miz Chambers who sent you . . . " her voice trailed off, wavering.

"She did, and she spoke very highly of you," John said. Nora suppressed a smile.

Cheryl Thomas seemed to sit slightly higher in her chair. "Well, this last murder was right in her backyard now, wasn't it?"

"Have you heard anything about gang activity?" John asked.

"Oh, now you're coming around to ask us about 'gang activity'? These bangers are killing us up in here. What, was the lady white, is that why there's this sudden concern?" She gave Nora a once-over, but didn't seem able to classify her. "Where you from, honey, Mexico?"

"Philly," Nora said acidly.

John said, a little self-righteously, "The lady was not white. We've had a lot of trouble with both the A&As and the Junior Black Mafia these days. This is the third killing in a short amount of time— she might not be connected to either gang, but the location of the body suggests it was a message for the Junior Black Mafia."

"Killings I don't know about. But I did hear that the A&As are trying hard to get some of the JBM business, which is why they've been messin' around in JBM territory, shootin' things up. Since the A&As started distributing Mexican drugs, they got serious masters now. After serious money."

"How do you know about links to the cartels?" John asked.

Cheryl shrugged. "It's what people say. The A&As started working with the Mexicans, so the Junior Black Mafia started pimpin'. Tryin' to keep up."

"Wait, what?" Nora demanded. "What are you saying?"

Cheryl leaned back in her chair. "Boy, you all don't know nothin', do you? The A&As are getting more drugs, cheaper, from Mexico. That's why they got the cars now, why they got bank. The Junior Black Mafia don't have the same connections. And Reality ended up in prison last time he tried to hook up that way—"

"Reality? Dewayne Fulton?"

"Yeah. So he's gang-pimpin' now. One girl who come in here, her daughter just . . . " Cheryl shook her head. "She just gone. Little girl, too. Just fifteen. And see, now they got the Facebook, got the Internet, they can set everything up online. No street-walkin'. Orderin' the girls online so they just show up at the door. One girl can go to seven, eight guys a night, sometimes more. And they never see none of that money. Reality—Dewayne—he takes it all. Girls get some meth, some heroin, maybe. Maybe they get some nice clothes to wear, a nice bag, that's it."

"Where do all the girls come from?" Nora asked.

Cheryl spread her arms wide. "Right here in paradise, girl."

John nodded. "It's not the first time I heard of gang-pimping. Just the first time I heard of it here in Philly."

Cheryl worked her jaw. "And now you heard about it, you gonna be stoppin' it. Right?"

"That's my job, Ms. Thomas."

Cheryl looked nonplussed.

"And—I'm a father. So what do you think?"

Her features relaxed slightly. "Alright, father. That's good enough for me." She tilted her head, letting a smile creep across her features. "You a *married* father, too?"

Wansbrough tried to suppress a laugh. "Twenty-five years."

"Alright, just askin', now," she said, laughing, as she patted her spiky hair.

"Tell your client whose daughter is missing to come to us," Nora said, handing her a card.

Cheryl rose and crossed to a bulletin board near her desk. She pulled pushpins out of the cork and handed Nora a missing persons flyer. It showed a picture of a young African American girl with a shy smile. Tameka Cooper, aged fifteen. The information had been written by hand and run off on yellow copy paper. "Her mama already gone to the police three times . . . "

Nora took the flyer, then tapped the card she'd given her. "My direct line," she said, meeting Cheryl's eyes. "Have the mother call me."

Cheryl blinked her outrageously long lashes, then asked. "Y'all gonna answer if I call you and say the JBM figured out I talked to you. Right? Because, for the record, this salon ain't one of those set up by girls in the crew, a drug money salon. I built this business from the ground up. It's all I got."

John nodded somberly. "Ms. Thomas, your safety is a priority for us."

"But not, like, the *top* priority . . . "

"The top priority. You just call if you need anything." He handed her his card as well. She tucked both cards into her apron as she headed back to check on her client under the dryer. John and Nora thanked her and headed out onto the street.

Nora plunged her hands deep in her jacket pockets. "Well, that's a twist. I've seen a lot of female gang members in the last six months, and it was clear that some were exchanging sex for drugs, but getting pimped on the Net? Who would put up with that?"

John looked at her. "I don't want to keep telling you you don't understand anything about being poor, but it's pretty clear to me that you still don't really get it."

Nora winced, regretting her words. She was silent for a moment as they walked, then said, "If Lisa Halston was a madam and not just a hooker, it's possible she was helping with the gang-pimping operation."

"Making the contents of that computer all the more critical." John looked around at the grim span of ramshackle homes and weedy, littered lots, then took a jagged breath.

Nora tilted her head. "You okay? John?"

"What's that statistic I'm always quoting at you?" he asked distractedly.

"The one about eighty percent of the murders in Philly being gang-related? And how if little white kids were scared to walk to school the way little black kids are scared to walk to school, there wouldn't be a gang problem?"

"I came up out of a neighborhood just like this one, Nora. My mother . . . " his voice trailed off. "If it weren't for my grandma, I would have been gangbangin' myself."

"Crazy grandma?"

He smiled. "*I* made her crazy. She wasn't always crazy. Growing up, she saved us from the streets by taking us out of my mama's house. Making sure we had food every day, making sure we went to school and came back home again."

Nora nodded, watching a boy of no more than six straggling along on the opposite sidewalk, unattended. He seemed to feel her gaze, and he looked up. Their eyes locked, and then he continued his silent walk. She said at last, "And so the latest victim . . . "

"Could have been one of Dewayne's girls," John finished.

Nora twisted this around in her mind. "I guess anything's possible."

"Maybe those calluses are from praying for forgiveness," John said.

Nora looked at him askance. "Maybe. Do you think Cheryl's right about the A&As being more successful with the cartels?"

John shook his head. "Dewayne wasn't hurting. He's gotten from Colombia via New York City. He's not unconnected. And we know he's been distributing as far away as Camden and the Main Line. The prostitution thing is probably just an additional source of income." They kept walking for a few more paces, before he said, "The smart ones now are going to be figuring out how to produce their own product. Keep supply-side costs down—and eliminate some of the danger of dealing with the cartels. The cartels make our gang-bangers look like choirboys."

Nora asked, "What if the cartels had a part in these killings?"

John was nodding. "It's exactly what I was just thinking. It would explain the really graphic side. It's not just your ordinary revenge for a drive-by—not the typical MO."

The rest of the neighborhood was not receptive to their questions about the Junior Black Mafia, the A&As, or the recent murder. They knocked on door after door, receiving a standard answer. *Didn't hear anything. Didn't see anything. Gangs? I don't know anything about the gangs.* Those who answered their doors were almost exclusively African American, though a few looked and sounded to be West African.

They stood for a long time near the crime scene, studying the houses and walking the small path where the truck or van must surely have stopped to discharge the body. Nora stared at the dark, listing structures. Almost all the windows had heavy bars installed across the glass. A few were missing their windows altogether, while not a few had boards across them.

"I feel like I've memorized this scene, John. The layout, the houses, which is closest, which would have had the best view. But it's not helping. I wish people would talk to us." She turned slowly around, looking up at the homes, scrutinizing every brick and each bit of trim.

John shrugged. "These kids are from here. Talking gets punished. People are terrorized. What I wouldn't give for a bigger budget. Stop kids from going into gangs—just bar the door and not even move outta the way—the same way we shut down whole airports to keep guys from flying off to Yemen to join up."

It was after three when they finally gave up and headed back to the field office, which seemed even more frantic with activity than when they had left that morning.

As they entered their cubicle, John's desk phone began trilling, adding to the cacophony of sound on the eighth floor. John picked it up, spoke briefly, and replaced the receiver. "Jane Doe has been moved to the psych ward at Thomas Jefferson. Still not speaking, but the doctors there have placed her age at sixteen."

Nora considered this. "I'll try to get in to see her later." She checked the time on her phone. "Speaking of seeing people, don't you have somewhere you have to be, John?"

Wansbrough looked at his watch. "*Shit*." It was going to be a struggle to get home, get changed, and make his dinner reservations on time.

He stood to go, patting his pockets for cell phone and keys, as Burton and Calder walked in. They had arrested two more marginal members, this time of the A&As. Burton was sporting a black eye and a cut across his jawline.

"You guys okay?" Wansbrough asked.

"Yeah," said Ben Calder. "Cake."

"What happened?" asked Nora.

Burton answered, "Running tackle out the back of the Kingsessing Community Center. We hit the concrete stairs, and I got an elbow in the face."

"But you got the bad guys . . . "

"Just kids, Nora," Ben said, sounding tired. "X-Box and Rico. A lot of tattoos, very little info. X-Box thinks Kevin Baker has left town, though. That's the one thing we got so far."

"Going where?"

Both agents shook their heads. "The kid couldn't say," Burton answered. "Seems he's genuinely too far down the totem pole to know. But we'll see how he feels after a night in lockup."

"Alright," Wansbrough said. He quickly briefed them on the information from the hairdresser, then made to leave. "Burton, I'm gonna need that report on the local imams and Bureau policy for approaching them for questioning. We need to do everything right and get our information fast and efficiently. Calder, you and Nora need to go downstairs and see what Monty Watt has come up with."

Calder tried to keep from grinning.

Wansbrough caught his look. "Are you grinning, Agent Calder? You like morgues, young man?"

"I do," he answered, as Nora shook her head in exasperation. "Very much, sir."

"Excellent. You get to type up the report, then."

"See?" she said, after both Wansbrough and Burton had stepped out. She waited for Ben to tuck his phone into his pocket. "See what you get yourself into?"

"Nora, I don't mind typing up a report if it means I get to spend time with you."

"That would make more of an impression on me if we weren't talking about going to the morgue."

"Do you spook?" he asked.

"Mmmm. Let's just say my thick skin is a little slow in growing."

"Alright. I'll tell you what helped me."

"What's that?"

He gave a half bow, gesturing that she should leave the office first. As she reluctantly passed by him into the hall, he said, "I stopped looking at the bodies for, like, their wounds and stuff. I just think of them as people who have problems and need my help. They're just stuck in the morgue until I can fix what's wrong."

Ben started for the elevator, but Nora motioned toward the stairs. "Come on, it's healthier. So you don't have to shoot the people who are in better shape than you."

He sighed. "Only for you, Nora."

She returned the conversation to its track. "Is that why you joined up?" she asked, falling into step next to him on the stairs. "You're someone who fixes things?"

Calder thought for a moment. "I don't know, it just seemed right for me. I was really good at science in school."

"A nerd!"

"I *knew* the jock in you would say something about that...."

She laughed out loud.

"I knew a lot about drugs ... "

"As a user?" she interrupted, only half-joking.

"Noooo. Well, not much ... " Then he grinned lopsidedly. "Not enough to disqualify me from working here, anyway. No, I went to the Bronx High School of Science. So, public school, right, so I just found out all I needed to know about drugs. And then I studied chemical engineering at City College," he said, "but I figured out pretty quick I didn't want to hang out in the lab all my life."

"And the FBI ... "

"Looked like a good place to be a badass and get to shoot guns."

"Nice," she said, tsking a bit.

"No, look, Nora. Seriously, I saw some scary things. Back then, the drug trade had New York City as the distribution center for Colombian drug traffickers. I saw what street distributors did to the neighborhoods, and I saw what users did to themselves. I ... "

Nora looked at him, aware that he was having difficulty saying something. "What is it?" she asked gently.

He riveted his eyes on the stairs as he descended, then continued. "I had a girlfriend. She had a coke problem that became a crack problem. It ended our relationship. She's . . . still in rehab, and this is four years later."

"Ben, I'm so sorry—"

He cut her off, "So if you want to know, yeah, I wanted to fix that. Still do."

Nora didn't know what to say. Suddenly she was jealous, she realized, as she imagined Ben with this unknown woman, as she imagined him aching over her and wanting her whole again. The pain of it made her furious with herself.

Watt seemed overly glad to see them. "Hey, guys!" he almost called out lightly, giving Nora the sense he got too few living visitors a day.

"How's our victim?" asked Ben.

"Which one?" retorted Watt.

"Latest," Ben clarified.

"Still unidentifiable," Watt answered, leading them past two of his team members who were bent over the corpse of an elderly white male. Nora noticed for the first time the red-haired young woman in her twenties who seemed to be collecting bullets from the body. She had clear, porcelain features, and her ponytail bobbed as she worked. Nora wondered how much say Monty had in the hiring of his crew.

On the other side of a dividing curtain they stopped at an autopsy table.

Nora steeled herself to look again at that mutilated body. The pallor of the skin had taken on a grayish color, except where her wounds gaped open. Nora's gaze lingered on the victim's long, thin fingers, noting what looked like ink stains in addition to a lot of dirt. "You ran her prints?"

He nodded. "Turned up nothing. No records, no nothing."

"Immigrant?" Nora asked.

"If she is, she's not one who entered the country legally."

"First generation, maybe," Calder was saying. "Rape?"

Watt shook his head. "She wasn't raped. In fact, she's a virgin."

Nora looked up. "That rules out being one of Dewayne's gang prostitutes."

Ben nodded. "What do we know about her wounds?"

Watt flipped open his laptop and walked them through the scenario he was proposing using a computer schema illustrating an assailant sitting on the victim's back and then slitting her throat from behind. "You can't inflict a wound like that unless it's from behind. The chipping angles on the trachea suggest that she'd been flipped onto her stomach with someone maybe straddling her from behind, lifting her head—possibly by the hair."

Nora and Ben peered in to stare at the screen.

Watt continued. "But, backtrack a little—the other wounds, body and eye, were probably made first. Then the throat was cut to finish her off."

Nora shivered.

He flipped to the next screen. "For those other wounds, she would have been lying down at the time on a carpet—there are tons of fibers under her nails. I'm doing trace analysis of her wounds to see if I can find any rust traces from the knife blades. I didn't find any rope marks, but I did find bruising. So I assume someone else was holding her down—" he gestured again at the screen for illustration. "There are hairline fractures in each radius bone, as though she were struggling and had her arms smashed down to hold them still."

"So, you're saying she was stabbed multiple times while lying down, and then flipped over to have her throat slit?" Ben asked.

"That's what I'm saying," Watt answered. "It's a theory, but I think it's consistent with the information we have so far."

"Are you thinking she was maybe wrapped in the same carpet she was killed on?"

Watt was nodding. "Yes, that's exactly what I think. There were bits of lime and lye under her nails as well, fingers and toes. Typical of area basements. And one more thing—we found a tire print in the muck yesterday: BFGoodrich Rugged Terrain T/As."

"SUV?"

"Yep. Something big. And heavy."

Nora and Ben both nodded. Then Ben said, "Look, Monty . . . "

"Yeah, I know. I heard that Dewayne Fulton is pleading not guilty to the murder-rape. I made a jpeg for you of what the weapon has to be, man. You have to take it from there." Watt walked over to his printer and retrieved a photo of the knife. "Hunting knife, eight and a half inches, weighing about six, six and a half ounces. You can buy it at any Cabela's or Sports Mania in the country. Or online."

"Shit," Ben murmured.

"I did check the Baker girl's wounds for rust, or trace particles that might have been on the blade. They're all clean—like, laboratory clean."

"Meaning?" Nora asked.

"I'm willing to bet it's a new blade. Maybe even purchased just for this kill."

Nora and Ben looked at each other. "Less sleep, more investigatin'," Nora said.

Ben nodded somberly. "Good work, Monty. We'd better go." They thanked him, then headed out of the swinging metal doors just as two other agents walked in. It seemed to Nora that the other two looked just as irritable and anxious as she and Ben felt.

Ben pulled out his keys. "Let me take you home, Nora. It's been a long day. And it's cold."

She shook her head. "No, it's okay. I'll run home, I need the exercise."

He narrowed his eyes at her, a half smile on his lips. "You ran to work this morning."

"What? How did you—?"

"Your hair was still wet when I came in the office. I could smell the shampoo."

"Okay, you sound like a stalker. I'm not getting in any car with you," she said, unable to suppress a smile.

"Oh, come on, we'll talk about our caseload the whole way."

Nora peeked into her backpack to make sure she had everything she needed, then followed Ben to the parking garage, where he made his way to his slightly dented Ford.

"So when do *you* get the big black Suburban?" she asked.

"You know," he said indignantly, "I've been asking everyone that, and no one will give me a straight answer."

She settled into the passenger seat and strapped on her seat belt, then asked, "How did that poor woman wind up brutally murdered like that?"

"Muslim woman," Calder corrected. "Maybe she's not so random? How about terror? She knows something? *Saw* something, hence the eyes being cut out."

"That's dramatic, but possible," Nora admitted, as they passed by the garage attendant's booth. Then suddenly, she said. "Hey, you didn't just connect her to terror because of my Muslim theory, did you?"

He pointed innocently at his chest. "Who, me?"

She shook her head, unsmiling. "You are *such* a racist!"

He held out his hand, stopping her. "Nora. It's a possibility. We'd be stupid to overlook it, and I know we're not stupid. We need to ID this body."

She knew he was right, but she didn't like the turn the conversation had taken.

As they turned on to Market Street, he said in a conciliatory tone, "Look, let's get something to eat on the way."

Nora gaped at him. "That's completely outrageous. Were you just in the same room with me and the dead body? How can food even cross your mind?"

"Come on, Nora. You have to eat. It's part of the thick skin thing."

She shook her head in silence.

Ben continued, "There's a cart that sells cheesesteaks almost as good as Geno's."

"I don't—"

"You don't eat cheesesteaks? No *way*."

"Way. I only eat halal meat. Like, Muslim kosher."

He took this in. "So . . . no cheesesteaks?"

She nodded slowly. "I've never had a cheesesteak."

"And you're actually *from here*?"

She nodded again.

"You do know that people come here—from foreign countries, even!—to eat the cheesesteaks?"

"Yes, and I've lived in Philly my whole life. What can I tell you, I'm a hopeless case. Better give up while you still can."

His phone flashed to life; it was Burton. Ben hit speaker. "I just got a call—we've found two JBM up in Strawberry Mansion."

"Off their turf. They must be running scared. Address?"

"Thirty-third and Diamond. Crack house."

"My favorite!" said Ben. He glanced at Nora. "You in, Officer Khalil?"

She grinned. "I saw what the toddlers did to you guys in Kingsessing. I will never knowingly let you run after anyone without me again."

"My hero," Ben said. "Got a vest?"

She shook her head. "In my locker," she said, waving a hand eastward to indicate the field office.

"Extra Kevlar for the resident speed demon, please," he said, loud enough for Eric to hear.

"Okay," came Burton's reply. "Fifteen minutes. Meet up at the playground."

They assembled at Mander playground. She saw Jacobs and Lin, as well as the two sheriff's officers—who were apparently only good at showing up for raids—and two junior agents whom Nora had

only met briefly. Nora slipped on the vest and the Safe Streets Task
Force windbreaker.

Burton drove up in his Jeep, locked it with the remote, and with
only a perfunctory greeting presented them with a printout from
Google Maps of the row house they would be attempting to enter and two full-page mug shots. The male had shaved his head,
the better to display the upside-down crown with intersecting
pitchforks tattooed onto the flesh of his scalp. The female had leaden
eyes haloed by a mass of short dreadlocks. "The kids we're looking
for are Tyreek Perkins—known as 'Grapevine'—and Rita Ross,
also called 'Rox' or 'Roxie.' Tyreek did time with Dewayne when
he went in for his last meth bust. Rita is one of the JBM first girl
members—in it almost as long as Dewayne himself. In and out of
rehab three times. Did time at the juvenile detention center back
when it was still on the parkway."

"Which means she's definitely not a juvenile anymore," Ben said.

"She's Nora's age," Eric said, in a tone that seemed a bit snide to
Nora, but she felt like her heart was thumping too quickly to allow her to call him on it.

Ben added, "And she knows a lot about the JBM's drug supply
lines. It would be great if we don't shoot her."

Agent Lin said, "Listen, it'll be dark soon, and this building is
kind of a death trap. Everyone will need to take extra precau-
tions."

Nora peered at the picture, poring over the façade of the row
house. It was of peeling, beige-painted brick. The two ground-floor
windows were boarded over. The second-floor bay window hovered
so precariously above the front door that it looked suicidal to stand
at the doorstep.

"There's no street access to the backyard, so a few of us should
come up Natrona Street, here, in order to seal off the back," Lin
was saying.

Ben said, "Nora, maybe you should go with Eric and Agent Lin.

Based on our last encounter, I think the first instinct is to run out of the back. And we don't know how many more are in there."

Nora nodded.

"John will be sorry he missed all the fun," Ben said, checking the ammo clip in his Glock.

"Brokenhearted, I'm sure," Nora replied, doing the same, then tucking the gun back into its holster at her back.

The leaves of Fairmount Park cradled the last remnants of daylight as the nine agents reentered their vehicles and headed back toward 33rd Street. As they waited at the stoplight, Nora looked out of her window and found a little boy staring at her, his hand clutching that of his older sister who was shepherding him home from the playground. Nora gave him a smile, but he only stared at her, his round eyes wide.

"I guess we're not a very subtle-looking crew . . . " she murmured to Ben.

He smiled his lopsided smile. "I love twinning with you. I'm thinking argyle sweaters for Christmas."

"Eid," she corrected him.

"Eid," he conceded, as he guided the car across the intersection.

"Try not to shoot anyone, Ben," she said.

"Come on, Nora. I hardly ever shoot anyone on Mondays," he answered.

She exited the car and found Burton and Lin, both of whom broke into a run up Natrona Street to the thin corridor leading to the backside of the grim strip of row houses. The last easily decipherable sound she heard was Ben pounding on the door, announcing them, "Federal officers!"

The backyard of the ramshackle row house was mined with pieces of mangled metal and broken glass. It exploded into activity as bodies came charging out of the row house. Lin and Burton waved her on; those fleeing were not Grapevine and Rox. She and Burton reached the back door simultaneously.

"I'll cover you," she said, pausing at the door frame and drawing her weapon.

Burton nodded and darted in, as Nora fought to make out figures and faces in the dimness of the building's interior. The back door was just off a grimy kitchen, and Nora's eyes fell immediately on a bearded white man with long, greasy hair. He sat on one of the sections of the floor that still retained its flowered linoleum tile, gazing up at them in a drugged haze, immobile, seeing them and not seeing them. The stench of the house tore into Nora's mouth and nose—human waste and rotting garbage and what could only have been vomit.

Above them, she heard the thumping of feet and shrieks; there were at least three others in the building aside from the band of agents. Chest heaving, weapon sweeping across the shadowy rooms, she trailed Burton as he darted from room to room on the ground floor. In the squalid living room he shouted, "Clear!" almost immediately. But as he entered what was once a dining room, he stopped short; a figure had darted through a door that led either to a closet or a basement. He turned back, met Nora's eyes, and motioned for her to follow.

Lin pounded up the stairs to join Ben and Jacobs in trying to subdue the crashes of breaking furniture and the unabating eruptions of profanity. Burton had opened the door off the dining room to find the basement, and, after confirming there was no electricity by flicking the light switch on and off several times, he was signaling to Nora to follow him down. She remained on the top step and trained her gun on the stairwell, covering him as he began to descend. Burton was almost to the bottom when they both heard the shattering of a windowpane. The sound came from inside and outside simultaneously, and Nora realized that it was the sound of someone kicking through a basement window to escape into the backyard.

"I'm in pursuit!" she shouted down to Burton.

"Go, go, go!" he cried, turning to run back up the stairs.

Nora raced out into the cool twilight, and saw Rita Ross's crown of dreadlocks retreating down the alley and out onto Natrona Street. Nora navigated the perilous stretch of yard and then darted out onto the street, just in time to see Rita vanish between two houses heading toward Douglass and 33rd beyond. Nora pounded across the pavement, her eyes riveted on Rita Ross, who was fast—very, very fast. It had been a while since Nora had had any serious running competition, and she found that all of her senses had sprung to life. Suddenly the air she was sucking into her lungs was sharp and bright, and it made her eyes water slightly; she narrowed them to keep Rita in her sights. She could imagine for a moment that the gun in her hand was a relay baton; she found a burst of speed and was flying. She vaguely registered the shouts of bystanders from their porches. She was close now, but Rita had darted into the traffic on 33rd Street and then into the park.

Let it be deserted, let it be deserted . . . Nora prayed, terrified of traumatizing a little kid. But she raced past empty swing sets with relief. And then they were passing the basketball courts, and Rita Ross was starting to turn, and Nora could see the blade in her hand, and the fury in her eyes at being outrun; Nora shoved her piece into the holster at the small of her back, and barreled into Rita at full speed. Both women went sprawling onto the cool, wet grass of the field. Laying beneath her, Rita tried to slash at Nora with the blade, but Nora slammed her wrist against the ground, then flipped her over, pinning her arms before she could even gasp for breath.

In a seamless motion, Nora pulled the cuffs off her belt. "Where'd you run track?" she demanded, once they had clicked into place.

"Bitch!" Rita shrieked, struggling, trying to kick Nora off of her.

Nora shook her head and rolled away, then rose, pulling out her weapon again. She called Ben who didn't pick up, and wouldn't have heard her anyway under the stream of expletives tumbling out of Rita.

Nora took a few steps back and waited for Rita to tire herself out. She asked her again. "Where did you run track? You're really fast."

"Are you fucking stupid?" Rita shouted. "You think I'm your little girlfriend or somethin'? I don't have to say shit to you, Bitch!"

Chest still heaving, Nora walked it off, waiting for Ben and Eric. "We could talk about Dewayne Fulton then."

Although she was panting, Rita's gaze was molten lava as she struggled up off the dewy grass and stood facing Nora.

"Okay," Nora pressed. "Then how about Kylie Baker?"

Rita made to spit at her, and Nora pointed the Glock at her in alarm, putting on her fiercest face. Rita's eyes darted between Nora's face and the tip of her gun. Finally she sputtered, "I'm not sayin' *shit* without my lawyer."

"Oh, fine, whatever." Nora's phone lit up soon enough, and Ben let her know they had taken Tyreek into custody. It was less than a minute before Eric Burton drove his Jeep over the soft expanse of field next to the basketball courts, and the two of them guided a still cursing Rita Ross into the backseat, installing her next to Tyreek. Agent Lin rode with Eric to escort them back to Center City, with Agent Jacobs following in his own car.

Nora and Ben remained standing on the now-dusky field, Nora still panting.

"You okay?" he asked, regarding her closely.

Several long coils of hair had escaped her chignon, and she pushed them away from her face as she asked him, "Is it bad that I thought that was kinda fun?"

"Completely twisted," he said, as they started for his car.

"Really?" she frowned.

"Of course not. It *has* to be fun. Why else would you stay?"

"Health insurance?" she ventured.

He laughed. "Well, okay. That too." They walked in silence for a bit. "You did great though," he added after a while.

She grinned. "Well, thanks, Ben. You too. I have no idea what you did, but I'm sure it was fabulous."

He held open the door of the Ford for her. "Yes, I'm planning on billing double for tonight's services." She started to sit, but Ben caught her arm.

She looked up, startled at his touch, and found his eyes bright.

"Nora," he said, his voice warm.

Her breath caught.

"Give me a chance, Nora."

"I—"

He leaned toward her, his lips almost brushing hers, but she pushed her hand firmly against his chest and stepped back, pressing herself against the icy frame of the car.

"I can't," she said, her eyebrows furrowing in a sad frown, as she shook her head, her breath coming in quick, hazy puffs in the crisp air. "I can't, Ben." Without looking at him again, she settled into the passenger seat and drew the seat belt across her.

His shoulders sagged as he pushed her door closed and circled to the driver's side. They drove in silence. It was only moments after departing the grim, hollow-eyed houses of Strawberry Mansion that they found themselves at Boathouse Row, the exclusive rowing clubs housed in wide, stately houses along the Schuylkill riverbank. Ben turned the car onto Kelly Drive and they passed the museum as they pulled onto the parkway.

"Look, Nora." He glanced at her, then focused on the street. His face was suddenly serious. "I'm trying to understand. I know you like me. Even if you don't want to admit it."

She looked up at him and inhaled, her stomach writhing. She

hated the words that came out of her mouth. "Ben, I . . . I think we're done. Okay? We work together. We're friends. But I can't have you keep on pressuring me."

"Is it something I said? The terrorist thing?"

"What? No, Ben, it's not that. Look, my family is everything to me, and I just don't want any stress, don't want any more drama than we've had, which is enough for a lifetime—"

"What? What does that mean, Nora? Talk to me."

"I'll tell you about it someday, I swear. But the interracial dating thing, I've seen what happens . . . If I start up with you, it'll be like exploding a bomb right in the middle of my life."

He stopped at a traffic light and turned to look at her in silence, his gaze somber. "You do know that we are officially the same race. The census says so. The census does not lie, Nora."

She let her eyes dwell a little too long in his, then she looked away. "Ben, please. If you like me even a little, just . . . back off. Please." The final word was no more than a whisper.

Ben Calder studied her, then turned away as the traffic began flowing again next to them. He was silent until they had neared the Cairo Café. Finally, he nodded. "Okay, Nora. I get it." He forced a thin smile. "I did my best, right?" he said.

"I'm sorry, Ben—"

"Don't worry. All business from here on out; I'll e-mail you a copy of my report on our meeting with Watt."

She sighed, feeling hollow, then said, "Thanks for the ride."

He didn't look at her. "See you tomorrow."

She opened the passenger door and emerged into the cool air. She stood for a while, watching him drive away.

Her father wore a serious look. The restaurant held only a few customers, and Ragab had been delivering a plate of food to a single diner sitting by the window when Nora had exited Ben's car. He stood, now, waiting for her as she passed the perpetually empty hostess's stand.

Ragab didn't even greet her, only walked with her, speaking in rapid Arabic. "Who was that?"

Nora stared at him blankly. "What?"

"You just got out of a young man's car. I know your partner, John Wansbrough. This man was not John Wansbrough. John Wansbrough is a father like me."

Nora sighed in exasperation, then cast a glance at the few tables. She spoke to him in Arabic, "Are you serious?"

"*Ya Noora*, who is this man you were riding with?"

"A colleague of mine on the task force who was nice enough to bring me home after a long day of work. Is there a problem?"

"*Ya Noora*, you know how I feel about that."

"Well, you might consider how I feel!" she retorted, surprised at her own tone of voice.

Ragab stared at her. "Are you raising your voice to me?" He looked both hurt and angry, but Nora couldn't tell which one prevailed.

"Baba, I'm tired—I've been working all day . . . "

"Nora, you're still my daughter. I expect you to respect my rules. You have a car. If you don't want to drive it, and you need a ride home, call me, call Ahmad. Men? You don't ride in the cars of strange men. You *know* this, Nora. You have known this all your life. It doesn't look right."

"To whom?" she demanded irritably.

"To *me*," he said, giving her his back and heading toward the kitchen. He turned at the swinging door, speaking in a carefully controlled voice for the sake of the customers. "Until you're married, you need to worry about what *I* think. After you're married, let your husband worry about whose car you're riding in."

Nora's jaw dropped. Furious, she stalked past him through the kitchen and climbed the stairs, slamming the door behind her.

She was being drugged.

It was not the first time.

She lay on the bed, her arms spread wide across it, feeling such a heaviness pressing down,

down,

down upon her.

She could not move, could only listen, detached, trying to categorize the sounds that drifted in through the partially boarded-up window. *This one can only be the shouts of children scuffling. This is a honking car horn, and this other a faulty car alarm awaiting deactivation by its absent owner. This is the slam of a door. And this louder one, what is this . . .*

. . . oh, yes, this is the sound of her lungs gathering up the air of this dank room and using it to prolong her life. She tried to will the lungs to stillness. Or the air to cease entering.

When she had first come, when everything was finally explained to her, and she finally understood, the tall one had given her a choice. She could take the pill before meeting with the first man . . . or not.

But if she met him and resisted him, they would beat her.

He had listened to her wailing protests, even patted her coldly on the back. She had wanted to work in America, he told her. This was the work for someone like her.

She owed him for the hellacious journey in the stinking cargo box with fifteen other weeping, seasick girls; owed him for the food she ate; and still she hoped to make enough money for her family back home,

home,

home . . .

She refused to take the pill: the thought of vacating herself was too terrifying. And when the man entered the room and began to shed his clothes, she had been determined to endure him. But when *he touched her, and she smelled his sweating skin and the stench of his breath, something snapped within her and her fist sank into his eye with a fleshy, sickening thud and he howled and shrieked in pain, cursing in his own language, clutching his face.*

They poured into the room, her cousin among them, and gave her such a beating that even now she limps from it.

It was easier, after that, to take the pill. It was a mercy, she decided, and the pain and the shame and the disgust eased and her mind could go away,

go home,

and she could walk barefoot along white-hot sand, one hand clutching a long, wobbly fishing pole, and the other a woven basket, as her eyes scanned the sparkling blue-green water for just the right spot, the spot that would offer up enough fish for her and her mother and sisters.

Enough.

She had only ever wanted to have . . . enough.

And now the heaviness held her still, inhaling, exhaling until his return.

She had not understood that the mercy could come in powdered form as well, that it could be snuffed up the nose

like the water for ablutions.

CHAPTER 5

It was just past nine in the morning when Wansbrough texted her. "Recd miss pers rept."

Nora ran up the back stairwell and arrived sweaty and panting. He shook his head. "We do have an elevator."

She flopped onto her chair, which skittered slightly on its wheels. "That elevator is why you're so slow, old man."

"Speaking of speed, I read all the reports from last night. Nice going there."

Nora grinned. "Dewayne has a power track star on staff. I underestimated him."

"You guys talk to them yet?"

She shook her head. "Both asked for lawyers. And so we wait. But what's this about a missing persons report?"

"Looks like your cappuccino strategy worked. Officer Mike Cook sent this over himself this morning. Usually takes two or three days before they connect the dots that way for us willingly." He handed over the report. The black-and-white copy of the picture was slightly grainy, but it showed a woman in a paisley headscarf, a quiet smile adorning strong features. Nora peered at it thoughtfully, then scanned the paper. This woman's mother had made the report late last night in what was, according to the report-taker, barely passable English. It was not normal that Hafsa al-Tanukhi, aged twenty-two, slept outside her home. She had not called to check in for over twenty-four hours.

"What do you think?"

Nora lifted her gaze slowly from the thin sheet of paper. "Our corpse's outstanding feature at this point is her hair, and obviously I see no hair here."

"But the age matches. Background matches. Timing matches," Wansbrough said.

"To a T."

"Let's go?"

Nora glanced at the address. "Northeast. You drive."

He smiled at her, gathering his keys from atop his desk. "I let you drive us once, and you have some kind of fantasy that I might do it again? No, my sister. You just let that pretty Ford keep rotting in the garage downstairs."

She fell into step next to him, lingered a moment at the door to the stairwell, then followed him to the elevator bank when he ignored her. "What's wrong with my driving?"

"You drive like my crazy grandma," he said immediately.

"And how is that?"

"You turn all the way around in your seat to check for cars before getting in the next lane. You never turn left when you can make it, only when there are no oncoming cars within a mile radius. And you can't listen to music because it distracts you. These are the characteristics of ninety-year-old women drivers with humps and cataracts."

Nora punched the "L" button and glared at him, particularly peeved because everything he had said was accurate.

The ride into Northeast Philadelphia was long and tedious. They had gotten off the jammed I-95, only to find that the inside streets were a chaos of repair crews and detours. When they arrived at the al-Tanukhi home, though, they took an extra few moments to talk.

"I don't want anyone to see that body who doesn't have to," she said. "We have to be absolutely certain. Can we ask them for a hair or something for a DNA test?"

John thought for a moment. "It's a good idea, not bad. If they'll agree."

"If it is her, though, they're gonna want to take possession of the body immediately. Muslims bury their dead right away. No chemicals."

John sighed. "We can't do that, and she's already been pumped full of preservatives if I know Watt. So far her body is the only evidence we have."

"I know," Nora answered miserably. She stared for a while at the small, squat home. The door was decorated with a wreath of plastic autumn leaves. "We'll have to stall, then."

It was almost ten thirty when they walked up the path and Wansbrough pushed the doorbell.

It was not long before a man with a full salt-and-pepper beard pulled the door open. John and Nora showed him their badges. The man was of medium build, dressed in a button-down shirt that was starched and pressed but untucked; khaki pants; and Adidas flip-flops. He regarded the badges with a fierce frown, then ushered them in, muttering a perfunctory *welcome*.

"Why did the FBI come and not the police?" he asked suspiciously.

"We can explain that to you, sir," John answered, his voice implying that they would need to sit down for such an explanation.

They stood in expectant silence for a moment in the ceramic-tiled foyer, next to a crowded shoe rack. Then Nora looked pointedly at John.

"Shall we remove our shoes?" he asked, and she could tell from the way he said it that he had no desire to do so.

Their host clearly appreciated the question, though, and his frown eased slightly. "Yes, please," he said. His English was heavily accented, and Nora knew with certainty he was Arab. She guessed Iraqi. She slipped out of her laceless Puma Osu Nms, and watched bemusedly as John unlaced and removed his shoes, then adjusted the tip of his right sock to hide the hole over his big toe.

They entered an immaculate, if airless, sitting room. Nora was very still, taking everything in. Imitation Louis XV furniture, heavy glass coffee table, and handmade doilies . . . There were no pictures on the walls, only gold-embroidered Qur'anic verses in elaborate frames. A vase full of fake flowers sat on the mantel of a fireplace that was eerily clean.

"I am Omar al-Tanukhi. Hafsa is my daughter." He sat stiffly on the dainty couch as John and Nora took their places in the regal chairs on either side.

Wansbrough checked his notebook, then said, "The person who made the police report was Hafsa's mother, a Sanaa Faraj. Is she present?"

She was. She had been waiting and listening, apparently, and she walked in as soon as her name was spoken. "I am Sanaa Faraj," she said, carefully, as though she had plotted out the sounds before shaping the words. She wore a long abaya and a pale peach satin headscarf. She was plump, though not obese. Around her neck was a long gold chain, dangling with charms that bore the phrases, "What God Wills," and "Thank God," and the shape of a hand encrusted with slivers of cubic zirconium. Nora had at least fifty of these charms in her jewelry box, gifts from her grandmothers.

Omar al-Tanukhi looked irritated at his wife's sudden entrance, but also looked as though he had surrendered to her tsunamic emotional state. Sanaa Faraj's eyelids were red and swollen, and she looked dangerously close to breaking down as she offered them something to drink.

Both Nora and John declined. As the woman took her seat next to her husband on the gold-edged Louis Seize, Omar al-Tanukhi repeated his question. "My wife called the *police*. Why is the FBI here? Is it because we are Muslims?"

Nora proffered her badge. "I am a police officer, Mr. al-Tanukhi," she clarified. "We are part of a joint task force between the police, FBI, and local sheriff's offices designed to keep Philadelphia's streets safe."

Nora heard the father mutter in Arabic, *"Look what they've sent us, a woman and a nigger."*

Nora leaned forward, eyes narrowed, and said in very precise Arabic, "My partner is the best investigator in the FBI. I expect you will treat him with the respect he deserves, as he is the best chance you have for finding your daughter."

Omar al-Tanukhi stared at her for a charged moment, then lowered his gaze.

But Nora's Arabic had the effect of unleashing a dam in Hafsa al-Tanukhi's mother, who had clearly been trying to figure out how she was going to communicate important information with her very official guests, all in English. She slid to the end of the couch nearest Nora's chair, seized Nora's hand, and began speaking in rapid, nearly hysterical Arabic. "Something's happened to my daughter, I just know it! Never in all her life has she gone out and not returned. How can she not call me when I am sick with worry!? I have asked everyone she knows, and no one has heard from her. Please, please help me find her! Please assure me she's alright!" As she spoke, tears streamed down her pale cheeks.

Nora grasped her hand and spoke softly. "We will do everything we can, Mrs. Faraj. But what we can do depends on you. Try to calm down a little and help us sort out some things that will clarify everything, God willing."

She glanced over at John, then, who was patiently waiting for the drama to die down. Nora chose her words carefully. "First, I need to see a picture of Hafsa without her hijab, so I have a better idea of what she looks like."

Mr. al-Tanukhi tensed. "There's nowhere she would go without her hijab," he said. "You don't need that."

"If, God forbid, Hafsa is hurt, she won't be in a hospital wearing a headscarf. Please, Mr. al-Tanukhi."

But Sanaa Faraj had already bustled out of the room. We heard her opening and shutting drawers in an adjacent room, and she returned with a snapshot. The picture was of a high school–aged girl with a wide smile and a tumble of curly black hair. The corpse on B-level had no eyes, and Nora found her gaze lingering on a pair of dancing, cocoa-colored eyes. She looked at the photo perhaps too long, then seemed to awaken, knowing that if she showed it to John at this point, Mr. al-Tanukhi would balk.

"May I keep this?" Nora asked.

Mrs. Faraj hesitated, then nodded.

Nora said, "This picture is of a teenager. Your report to the police stated that Hafsa was twenty-two. Don't you have a more recent picture?"

Mrs.. Faraj shook her head, retaking her seat on the couch. "She has worn hijab since she was fourteen. She no longer has her picture taken without it." The mother was silent a moment, then new tears began sliding down her cheeks. "She is such a good girl . . . "

Nora shifted in her seat, going over her options. She had a thought, and she patted Sanaa Faraj gently on the knee. "Do you have any mint tea? It would calm everyone down, don't you think?" It was an appalling breach of etiquette, asking for the tea instead of waiting to be asked again, but Nora took a chance. She wanted to get the woman alone and let John get Mr. al-Tanukhi's story.

Mrs. Faraj was slowly nodding and swiping at her wet cheeks with the edge of her scarf. "Of course, where are my manners?" she said slowly, starting to rise.

"Let me help you," Nora said.

"No, dear, don't trouble yourself," the woman answered, squeezing Nora's hand.

"I insist," Nora said, and they walked together toward the kitchen. "We're going to make some tea," she said to John as they passed. She ignored Omar al-Tanukhi's suspicious look.

She heard him ask, "Is she Egyptian? She speak with Egyptian accent." John, who knew perfectly well, said, "I'm not sure . . . "

Sanaa Faraj was filling a stainless steel kettle with tap water. If she had questions about Nora's origins, they were obscured by her worry for her daughter. "I just can't imagine where she would be. We sent her brother out looking all last night and the night before, and he did not find her anywhere . . . "

Nora sat at the small, round kitchen table. "How old is Hafsa's brother?"

"Twenty, may God protect him," she replied, pulling glass teacups out of a neatly arranged cupboard. She set them before Nora. "He's going to be an engineer, *in sha Allah*." God willing.

"Where did you send him to look, Mrs. Faraj?"

Mrs. Faraj sighed, thinking. "The mosque where we pray the Friday prayer. The homes of her friends. And the mosque where she volunteers sometimes."

Nora didn't want to scare her off by writing anything official-looking on a notepad, so she took very specific mental notes, a trick she'd learned in training; she imagined what these things would look like written down on a notepad, whether she wrote in cursive or block letters, and what words she would have underlined. She even picked blue ink.

"Can you tell me a little about her friends, and share with me some of their names so I can visit with them?" She asked this as she held out her hand for the canister of tea bags, smiling at her hostess who reluctantly gave them to her as she considered her request.

"I suppose . . . " Sanaa looked worried, and Nora sensed she didn't want to scare Hafsa's friends by having a police officer, even a female one, show up at their houses.

"When we've finished our tea," Nora said, trying to put her at ease.

Sanaa nodded. "Of course."

Nora placed a bag in each waiting glass mug, as she asked, "Where was she volunteering?"

Mrs. Faraj made a tsk-tsk sound with her tongue. "At a mosque all the way across town. In the black section."

"And what does she do there?"

Sanaa shrugged as she placed a few mint leaves in each glass. "Whatever she can. She went because she wants to teach immigrant women to read and write English. She has a friend there, they are close, so she is often there, but it takes up far too much of her time, if you ask me."

"What kind of immigrants is she teaching??" Nora pressed.

Mrs. Faraj shrugged again. "Africans, I think. There are a few Arab women there, although how they can stand to live in that part of town, I don't know." She caught herself then, as though just remembering the very black man in the other room. "I don't mean . . . "

Nora kept her features still, trying to encourage Hafsa's mother to talk. The woman looked slightly flustered. "It's just, you know . . . all the crime . . . "

Nora tried a different tack. "Can you show me Hafsa's room, Mrs. Faraj?"

She had been about to pour the boiling water. "Her room? Why do you need that?"

"Any clues I can get about Hafsa's habits and personality can help me figure out where she is now."

Mrs. Faraj glanced at the kitchen wall, as though her gaze could reach through into the other room where her husband sat. She poured the water over the tea bags, then slowly nodded. "Of course. While the tea steeps."

Nora followed her down a short, dim hallway to a small, colorful room. Hafsa al-Tanukhi had stenciled flowers on the white walls of her room. A twin bed was pushed against one wall; the bedspread was a kaleidoscope of color, and it was decorated with bright throw pillows. A desk sat next to the bed, with a notebook and a few ballpoint pens in a mug bearing the familiar T for Temple University.

"Does Hafsa attend Temple University?" she asked, reminding herself urgently to keep to the present tense.

Mrs. Faraj shook her head. "No, no. Her brother."

"Where does Hafsa go? Or has she already graduated from somewhere?" asked Nora.

The mother frowned slightly, then said softly, "We only had enough money to send one of the children."

Nora processed this. "So Hafsa has not attended college at all?"

"No, not yet," repeated Mrs. Faraj. She could not seem to meet Nora's eyes as she said, "Her brother's prospects were brighter, so it seemed right to let him go first, even though he is the younger. When there is more money in the future, when God makes it easier, perhaps Hafsa—"

It was at this moment that Mr. al-Tanukhi appeared at the door, with John on his heels. "What you doing?" he demanded in English, his face pinched and flushed.

Nora frowned. "You called in a missing persons report—how are we supposed to help you without gathering information—"

But he began shouting at her in Arabic. "Yes, the information I give you—me! Not information you steal from behind my back! I knew this was some kind of investigation. FBI comes here, instead of police, what, you think we're stupid? This is just some trick to get the Muslims—well I won't have it! You get out of my house. I know my rights, you need a warrant to go snooping through my house. I asked you to find my daughter, not go snooping through my house. Get out, get out of here!"

Wansbrough looked furious; he could figure out the content of that diatribe without understanding a word. "Nora, that's our cue."

She looked at Mrs. Faraj, who had begun crying again. "I can't help you if I can't learn more about Hafsa." She pressed several business cards into the hand of Sanaa Faraj, then brushed by Mr. al-Tanukhi and followed John to the door.

The shoe issue made for an exit with little flourish. John jammed

his feet into his shoes, leaving them untied, and stomped toward
the car, all to Omar al-Tanukhi's invectives.

Traffic was even more intense on the way back to Center City. Sade
filled the silence and Nora was grateful for the music to calm her
furiously thumping pulse. She glanced over at John, then out the
window, before finally saying, "That went well." When John responded only with silence, she continued, "Seriously, we do not get
to rough people up enough in this line of work. I hated that guy."

"Man, so did I," he admitted. John was silent for a moment, and
then looked over at her. "Do you think it's the right family?"

"It would be very hard for the hair in this snapshot to be anyone else's." She pulled it from her blazer pocket and handed it to
John.

He glanced between the photo and the road for some time before saying, "And do you think al-Tanukhi had something to do
with his daughter's disappearance?"

Nora hesitated. "Maybe."

"Honor killing?"

She hated that term. "What does that even mean?" she demanded.

"Hey, easy," said John, holding up a hand. "It isn't just Arab cultures who engage in that kind of thing, I'm not implying anything.
Objectively, what do you see? Does that guy look like the kind of
guy who would kill his daughter if she was sleeping around? To save
face in front of his community?"

Nora inhaled deeply, considering. The father had anger issues.
Nora found herself nodding slowly. "It's not impossible. There was
just so much wrong with the story I got." Nora related to him all
that Sanaa al-Faraj had told her, down to the scene in Hafsa's room
in which her mother had explained how Hafsa had been denied her
university education.

"Dust?"

Nora smiled. "It looks like Sanaa has nothing better to do on the planet than to clean that house. Like, rabidly."

"So you think Hafsa might have been using the teaching as a cover to be meeting someone? Dad got wind of it?"

"Maybe. Her mom said she had a close friend, and she spent too much time over there."

"It is, after all, the bad part of town," John said.

Nora felt a twinge of remorse for having related that part to him.

"Are you gonna ask me what I got outta the dad?"

Nora snapped out of it. "What did you get out of the dad, Special Agent Wansbrough?"

He arranged his thoughts. "They came as refugees during the first war with Kuwait. He works as a school maintenance man, a job someone thought he was qualified for because he'd studied engineering in Iraq. His English was never good enough to work in his own field. He's a little bitter because he could never get anything better. Apparently he's *seen* stuff, though, which is why he insisted on sending his kids to Islamic school."

"*Seen* stuff?"

"High school kids fucking in the bathroom. Drugs. Alcohol. Bullying."

"Oh, you mean he works at my old high school?"

"No, mine, apparently." The two exchanged wry glances. "Actually it's up here in Northeast, Goodman High."

"So what did he say about Hafsa?"

"That she's a good girl who wears the hijab. He said that at least twice. That she does what she's told. Her one flaw is that she is not yet married, but he has been working on it."

"I'm sure he has," Nora said. "He had a potential suitor? Did you get a name?"

"No, that was about when he realized that the tea was a long time coming, and he went looking for you and the mama. And then you insulted him by intruding where he didn't want you. So I'm thinkin' we won't be getting much more info out of the al-Tanukhi family until we get Schacht to get us a warrant and a summons."

"Yeah, I wanna talk to her brother really bad. See what's up there."

"Well, phone it in, then." He glanced at her, smiling. "What's that thing your dad always says? 'Yellow'? Doesn't it mean, 'get a move on'?"

Nora laughed. "*Yalla*," she corrected as she pulled out her phone, and was about to tap Special Agent-in-Charge Schacht, when it rang.

It was her father.

Her brow furrowed as she recalled their altercation of the night before. She dismissed the call and went ahead and called Schacht. As succinctly as she could, she gave him the details of their conversation with Mr. al-Tanukhi. Schacht said he'd work on a warrant to search the home as well as summonses for the father, mother, and brother.

She was preparing to hang up when Schacht stopped her. "Nora. Put me on speaker. The latest is that Dewayne Fulton's claiming that he and Kylie Baker had consensual sex. He dropped her off after that near her home. What happened after that, he says, had nothing to do with him."

"That's crazy!" she found herself shouting. "She was just a little girl!"

"Well," Schacht said slowly, choosing his words carefully. "This version of the story has Kylie lashing out against her brother and trying to put herself in Dewayne's path every chance she could. He finally gave in and had sex with her—on more than one occasion, he says."

"At the very least that's statutory sexual assault—"

"Which means a fine and less than ten years."

"Oh my God." Nora felt sick.

"Just thought you should know. The AUSA is very pissed off at all of us right now."

"Okay. Should we go back to Mrs. Baker's?"

"Yes. Burton and Calder have spent the day looking for the murder weapon *again* and working their contacts. You need to see if you can find any truth to this version of the story. And if the mother doesn't say much, see if you can track down some of Kylie's friends."

After they hung up, Nora looked at John.

"What do you think of all this?"

He shook his head. "We have to admit the possibility. But it would mean we have a lot more work to do."

"Who else would have motive to kill a fourteen-year-old girl?"

John answered her with silence. He guided the car onto the 676 to head once more toward West Philadelphia.

Nora's stomach felt tight. "Mrs. Baker's gonna slap us for hitting her with a story like that."

"It's not our story, it's Dewayne's."

"She's not gonna like it." Nora stared out the window. "I'm gonna need some tea on the way. And to think, I was *this close*. The mint leaves were *really* fresh."

"All I can offer you is the Starbucks at Thirty-fourth and Walnut."

"Reeks of coffee in there," Nora complained. "You come out and it's, like, all in your clothes . . . "

Wansbrough shrugged. "Life is hard, what can I tell you?"

She looked over at him. "John, if this case isn't open and shut, then maybe the killing that started all this isn't either?"

"It was a drive-by in broad daylight. Kevin Baker's car. Open and shut, Nora."

She nodded. "Open and shut."

Mrs. Baker was not happy to see them.

"Did they find Kevin?" she asked, as she pulled open the door.

The agents shook their heads. "I'm afraid there's a new wrinkle in our investigation," John said.

Mrs. Baker invited them in, silencing a late-morning talk show with the remote in her apron pocket. "What?"

John didn't try to sugarcoat things. "The DNA tests came back, and they match with the samples provided by Dewayne Fulton. The problem is, Dewayne is going to claim in court that he had a consensual sexual relationship with Kylie."

Mrs. Baker sagged in her chair. "My God. That monster."

Both agents were silent, neither wanting to press on. Finally John began, "Mrs. Baker, if we could interview just a few of Kylie's friends . . . "

But she was shaking her head, giving herself over to a fit of coughing, then said, "What kind of monster would say such a thing? How could he defile my baby girl's memory that way, suggestin' *she* went to *him*. . . ."

Nora looked at the floor. "Did Kylie have a boyfriend?" she asked softly.

"Of course not," Mrs. Baker sputtered. "It was strictly forbidden for Kylie to date, she's just a baby herself. She has a strict curfew of sunset, and she's asleep by nine every night. *Every night without exception*." Mrs. Baker was shaking with anger, and didn't seem to realize that her speech had shifted into the present tense.

John Wansbrough waited for Mrs. Baker to stop talking, then he said, "Could we take a look at her room?"

Mrs. Baker stared at them in disdain. "Top of the stairs," she muttered, waving them off. "I can't do stairs anymore. Just, just go on . . . "

The agents walked in silence up the stairs. They could hear Mrs. Baker talking under her breath and stifling a few coughs as they ascended. And then they heard the television spring back to life, and the living room filled with the sound of a couple in the midst of a talk-show paternity dispute.

Kylie's room was adorned with several posters—mostly rappers, and one country scene with a jet-black stallion grazing in a sun-dappled meadow. She and John exchanged glances, then Nora pulled plastic gloves from her backpack and handed a pair to John. "All this feels backward to me. We should have started here a long time ago."

John nodded. He crossed to the window and carefully raised it, then looked out. The window opened onto the roof of the back porch. He climbed out and walked to the edge, then looked down. Slowly, he ducked back in.

Nora read his mind. "She could have snuck out?"

He shrugged. "Screen's out of this window, not the other. It's an easy drop off the porch."

"Could someone sneak in?"

"Someone like Dewayne? Not his style."

"Unless he was really out to mess with Kevin Baker's mind," Nora pointed out. She pulled out her spray powder and dusted a soft line onto the window frame from the inside and out. She carefully pressed fingerprinting tape against the painted frames, and then applied the tape to the white paper in the kit.

John picked up a backpack that had been left on the bed. He unzipped it carefully and started pulling out notebooks and textbooks, rifling through them gingerly.

Nora was just sitting down at Kylie's desk when she heard her partner grunt. "What do you think of this?"

He passed her an open biology text. The chapter was on amphibians, and the margin was decorated with "I love Dewayne," written in wobbly cursive.

Nora shook her head. "Wow."

"*Wow* is an understatement."

"How'd you know to do that?"

"Hey, I raised two girls."

"Doesn't mean he didn't rape and murder her," Nora said, then suddenly coughed, her throat uncomfortably tight.

"It just means she might have helped him out." John replaced the books in the backpack and shouldered it, coughing slightly himself. "Let's ask Mrs. Baker if she'd mind us taking this to the office. I think she hasn't dusted in here for ages."

They walked down the stairs. Mrs. Baker saw them carrying her daughter's backpack. She didn't move from her chair, but said, almost listlessly, "Where you going with her school pack?"

John said, "Mrs. Baker, could we take this with us to the lab for analysis?"

"It's her school pack. What are you gonna analyze in her school pack?"

"We can run her things for prints, see if we get any leads on who she was hanging out with . . . "

But Mrs. Baker wasn't really listening. She had refocused her attention on the television, and she waved them off again. "Take it," she muttered.

John and Nora thanked her and headed for the door. John checked his watch as they headed toward the Suburban. "It's just past noon. Let's get this to Watt and see if there's anything else we can find. Then, I think we should have another talk with Dewayne."

Nora was about to agree when a shiny black Escalade skidded around the corner at high speed. Before she could react, John tackled her, and the two crashed onto the Bakers' lawn as the air erupted with bullets.

Stunned, Nora looked wildly about her. John's chest was heaving on top of hers, and she struggled for breath. As soon as the SUV had careened out of sight, he rolled off of her. "Are you okay? We have to get to the car—are you okay?!"

She nodded, wordless, and followed him in a running crouch to the Suburban. He yanked open the back door and they both tumbled inside, even as he was shouting into his cell phone.

"Agents under fire at Sixty-fifth and Montenegro. I repeat, agents under fire—Black Cadillac Escalade, one or more shooters. I need *immediate* backup!"

Nora shouted, "And EMTs!"

"And EMTs!" he added, punching off his phone. "Are you hurt?"

She shook her head, "No, John, you are!"

He looked himself over to see his left arm oozing blood from above the elbow. "Goddam it!" he shouted.

He started looking around for something, and Nora immediately pulled off her jacket. Instead of pressing it against his arm, he started wiping at the upholstery.

"You're insane," she snapped, yanking her jacket back. "This is to stop the bleeding. Take your shirt off, quick—can you?"

The two fumbled for a moment, and finally pulled off John's jacket and shirt. He was breathing fast in his sleeveless undershirt as Nora swabbed at his wound. "Hold that against it. Is there a first aid kit?"

He nodded. "All the way back."

She scrambled over the backseat and into the trunk area, noting the massive cracks in the back and side windows where the bulletproof glass had weathered the storm. She dug the first aid kit out from the sidewall compartment. "Gauze, gauze, gauze . . ." she muttered as she rifled through the contents, finally pulling out a large roll of gauze. She climbed back into the backseat and started wrapping his arm.

"Is there an exit wound?" he asked.

She craned her head to look at the back of his arm. "Yes, I think so. It's a lot of blood, man, just hold on." She started wrapping, fighting the wooziness that surged over her.

"You okay?" he asked, noting her face.

"Just worry about yourself, got it?" she retorted, relieved to hear the wail of sirens bearing down on them. She looked over her shoulder at the Baker house as she worked, but saw no movement.

John followed her gaze. "Any broken glass?"

She shook her head. "It looks okay to me."

"It was Kevin Baker's car."

Nora's eyes widened. "No way. Shooting at his own home?"

"Or shooting at us. Or both. Nothing surprises me."

Nora tied off the gauze and looked at him. "Thanks, partner. I was slow out there."

"You'll catch up, Nora. You just gotta stop assuming the best about people," he said with a wink.

She laughed softly, as a flood of police cars skidded to a halt around them. "I'm gonna go check on Mrs. B."

"Yeah, I'll talk to these guys."

Faces had started tentatively appearing at windows and on front porches, peering nervously at the crowd of law enforcement officers and at John Wansbrough who was talking rapidly as the EMTs began attending to his wounds. Nora walked up to Mrs. Baker's door, belatedly realizing her hands were covered in blood. Under the wide-eyed gazes of Mrs. Baker's next-door neighbors, she wiped her hands on her trousers before knocking rapidly on the door. "Mrs. Baker! Mrs. Baker, are you all right?"

After a lengthy wait, Nora heard the familiar sound of dead bolts being pulled to one side. She sighed in relief as she saw Mrs. Baker standing in her foyer. The woman's voice was choked, "What just happened—another drive-by?"

Nora nodded. "Yes. Are you okay?"

"I'm fine," the woman answered, looking around. "I don't think anything came in. You all okay?"

"My partner was hit in the arm, but he's going to be fine—Mrs. Baker, my partner identified Kevin's car."

She narrowed her eyes at Nora. "That's not possible. Kevin wouldn't shoot at his own home."

"Still, I have to ask you again, has Kevin contacted you at all in this period?"

Mrs. Baker shook her head, simmering with anger. "What you're saying is impossible. It was a car that looked like Kevin's."

"Please, Mrs. Baker, you have to know how concerned we are for your safety . . . "

"And you have to know that I am a mother who has nothing, *nothing* to say to you all anymore. Now go on about your business!"

Nora blinked, staring for a long moment at the door that was shut emphatically in her face. She glanced at the neighbors, then started back down the front walk, just as Ben Calder and Eric Burton drove up, adding their car to the growing group around the Suburban.

Ben jogged over to her, intercepting her on the front walk. His face was etched with worry. "You okay?"

"Yeah, just a little bruised from the linebacker tackle. John's hit, Ben."

"I know, we heard already. What happened?"

She recounted for him the screech of tires and hail of bullets from the Escalade. "Everything happened so fast . . . .."

Her voice trailed off, and the two stood for a while surveying the scene. Eric Burton was standing next to Wansbrough, listening intently as he continued giving orders to Philly PD and Bureau personnel about strategies for finding Kevin Baker's vehicle. Already, a few squad cars had headed out, sirens shrieking.

Ben continued, "You're very lucky, Nora. Come on, I can't believe you're still walking around every day without a vest—especially after having a gun aimed at your head the other day!"

"A vest wouldn't have helped me with Lisa Halston. But I get it, I won't go out without it anymore."

Ben looked at her, his eyes bright with concern. "Promise."

She looked at the ground, unsteady under that gaze, and recalling how hurt he had been the last time they had spoken. She met his eyes. "I promise, Ben. If you will, too."

He held her gaze, then nodded.

The EMTs were forcing John Wansbrough into the back of the ambulance. He looked furious.

"Nora!" he practically shouted.

"John?"

"This is ridiculous—it's just a flesh wound, but they're taking me in. I told them we don't have time for this . . . ."

Ben piped up, "You have time, John, just take it easy."

Wansbrough ignored him, saying, "Nora, the keys are in my blazer pocket . . . "

"Don't worry," she said. "I'll get the car to the evidence techs at the garage and meet you at the hospital."

He said, "I was gonna say give them to Calder."

Ben laughed out loud.

"Ha-ha," she answered testily. "Guess what, Special Agent Wansbrough, your Suburban has already been shot at and bled on today. I can't do much worse to it than that."

Wansbrough tilted his head, considering this. "Then again . . . "

"Alrighty then—see you at the hospital," she said, smiling brightly as she helped the EMT shut the ambulance's back doors.

After determining that John would be released that evening, Nora said good-bye to him and Olivia, who had met them at Hahnemann Hospital. After promising to check in often, Nora took the elevator to the gift shop, bought a bottle of Aleve and the cuddliest bear she could find, then took the elevator up to the psych floor. She would have taken the stairs, but she was still in pain from John's tackle. She was starting to think she had sustained a bruised rib, and she paused at the drinking fountain to swallow two pills.

The frames of Nurse Bedford's reading glasses were dotted with tiny purple rhinestones. They dangled from a chain around her neck. Slowly, deliberately, the nurse unfolded them, perched them on her craggy nose, and then peered through them with distaste at Nora's badge.

Nora tried to be helpful. "You have all of her information on file. The Bureau transferred her to you from the holding tank. My name is on the paperwork as well."

"Visiting hours begin at six and last 'til eight," Nurse Bedford insisted.

Nora smiled as sweet a smile as she could muster. "This little girl is my case. She's all alone. I have twenty minutes. It's five o'clock. Please. Help me out."

The nurse was silent, nostrils flared, lips pressed. "Well, if she's your case, then you'd better know. The doctor ran a full gamut of tests on her when she heard she'd been prostituted so young. She has gonorrhea."

Nora blinked, feeling queasy. "Please let me see her," she said simply. She brandished the teddy bear for good measure.

"She doesn't know yet. We'll tell a guardian whenever you produce one." Nurse Bedford rose as if in pain and guided Nora through a secure door. They passed a man in his midtwenties who was clutching himself in a hard embrace as he sat on a vinyl-cushioned bench. An obese woman shuffled aimlessly along the hallway, her ankles bulging over fluffy blue slippers.

Jane Doe's room was the furthest from the nurse's station, and her window had a full-brick view of the parking garage wall. She lay listlessly in the bed, staring at the mute black screen of the TV.

"Hey, there," Nora said, approaching the bedside. "I'm glad to see you."

The girl turned her head ever so slightly to glance at Nora, then turned away.

"I was hoping maybe you'd talk to me today," said Nora. "Help me figure out who you are, where you came from."

Silence.

"I brought you a friend," Nora said. She tucked the bear between Jane Doe's thin arm and the dense, retractable side rail.

Jane didn't move or acknowledge the gift.

Nora sighed softly, then pulled up a chair. "How about I just sit here for a minute?"

This time, Nora was determined to respect the silence that Jane had built. She listened to the stillness of the room, to Jane's breath, to her own. She only hoped she could be there when the girl found her voice again.

After asking Nurse Bedford to call her if there were any changes, Nora left the hospital and stood for a few moments on Broad Street, deciding what to do. It was almost six, and the streets were still so congested that walking back to the office was more efficient than sitting in a cab. Reluctantly, Nora huddled into her Windbreaker and made her way gingerly along the crowded sidewalks. Realizing she was famished, she bought herself some vegetable dumplings from her favorite storefront in Chinatown, then continued on her way. She ate as she walked, remembering how her mother had always insisted that it was incredibly rude to consume food openly without sharing it. And yet given the day she'd had, Nora decided Mama wouldn't have faulted her.

She greeted the evening security guard and submitted her badge for scrutiny. Then she made her way down the stairs and through the dank basement to the shooting range where she plowed bullets into targets for an hour, trying hard not to think of what might have happened had the drive-by shooter found his mark. She was exhausted and aching by the time she returned to her cubicle. There she was stunned to find John Wansbrough wearing a hospital-issue T-shirt, his arm wrapped in a huge bandage.

"What are you doing here?" she demanded immediately.

"Olivia's in the car. I just came in for my laptop. Apparently I've been ordered to stay home tomorrow, so I'll need it. Nora, why are *you* here?"

She shrugged. "I stopped by to see Jane Doe. In addition to the meth dependency, they are treating her for gonorrhea. I didn't know what to do, or how to undo what's been done to her, so I came and shot my gun."

John nodded grimly. "With runaway kids, sometimes it only takes forty-eight hours to be approached by a pimp."

Nora shut her eyes. "Even if she starts talking, I don't think we'll ever understand the circumstances that put her in that loft that day."

John sighed. "Life is short, Nora." He gestured with his head toward his bandaged arm. "Just ask me—"

"Thank God you're okay, John. It was really close—"

"—You should go out more," he concluded.

"Yeah, that's gonna happen," she answered.

"What about Calder?" he pressed. "He likes you. Hell, looks to me like he *loves* you."

Nora felt a violent blush skate across her skin, and she looked down. "You know the rule about workplace romances."

"Yeah, I know that no one pays any attention to it. What's your real reason?"

Nora was silent for a moment, and then sat back down in her chair, saying slowly, "Can't bring a non-Muslim white boy home to Daddy."

Wansbrough shook his head. "Girl, what's the matter with you? You are a grown woman. You gonna tell me you can't date who you want to date?"

She raised her chin, almost defiantly. "I can't and won't date at all. My family is really close, really conservative, and my dad's been through a lot. It would kill him."

John stared at her, his strong jaw working back and forth. Then he sat down and powered on his laptop.

"What's up?" she asked. "Is something wrong? Isn't Olivia waiting in the car, John?"

"Look, I feel like I need to tell you something that could change your perspective on all this. I think . . . I think I'm going to upset you, but eventually you're going to thank me."

Nora stared at him. "Upset me how?" she demanded. "What's this all about, John?" Cold fear was beginning to clutch at her insides.

His eyes were gentle. "Nora, many of us know your dad's story. In fact, it was kind of famous around here. Our epic post-9/11 mistake."

She was nodding, frowning, trying to follow where her partner was going.

He turned to his laptop. "Not everyone knew all the details, though. But this was a special case, because so much was in the media about it, and there were so many rumors circulating that tried to explain what happened. How could we have messed up so bad? Arresting an innocent man . . . "

Nora sat forward in her chair, looking over John's shoulder intently. "What *details*?" she demanded, her heart beating furiously.

John called up Google Images, then looked at Nora. "It being a terror investigation, we weren't obliged to relate all of the details to the press. Normally, I wouldn't know any of this. But this part of the case became common knowledge because the woman involved was very vocal—she'd show up in the lobby even after your dad was released, asking for Schacht, asking for her idea of justice."

"John, you're really scaring me. *What details?!*"

"Nora, the anonymous tip that resulted in your dad's detainment after 9/11 wasn't anonymous. It was from a woman who. . . . Well, a woman he knew very well."

Nora's insides crumbled as John told her about the dental hygienist who had worked on Market Street and had been coming regularly to the restaurant for lunch. He told her about her small apartment in South Philly, where her dad would disappear on his way to or returning from the Italian Market for eggplant or tomatoes or lettuce.

John told her that she had been beside herself when Ragab had refused to leave his wife and children for her. In an act of scorned fury, she had called the FBI and told them that the Egyptian owner of the Cairo Café was plotting to bomb several Market Street skyscrapers, including the one in which she worked.

Nora listened in complete silence. When her partner was done speaking, she said, working hard to keep an even tone, "Did you go to Google Images to show me a picture of this woman?"

Wansbrough nodded, then turned back to the monitor and called up the photograph. She was lean, bottle-blond and hairsprayed, exactly what Nora would have expected from Wansbrough's story. Nora gazed for a long, long time at the woman's features. Limpid blue eyes, mascara-lengthened lashes, small pink lips, no discernible cheekbones, a tiny pug nose.

"The Bureau had every intention of prosecuting her for the false tip. But she was clearly mentally unstable, so we knew we didn't have a case . . . "

Nora nodded, feeling as though she might vomit at any minute. She understood everything now. She sank her fingers deeply into the arm of her chair, fighting hard for control. When she spoke, the words came out hoarsely. "My mother would have begged them not to anyway. So we wouldn't find out. To protect us."

"Yes, actually. I was told that your mom was relieved to hear about the psych issues because Schacht had had every intention of prosecuting. And she just wanted it all to be forgotten."

Nora suddenly pushed back the rolling chair and stood up. Wansbrough followed suit, wincing as he moved. "Look, Nora," he was saying. "Let's talk about it! I'm sorry if I overstepped. You're like a daughter to me, you know that."

"John, you did the right thing. I just need . . . You know, a little time. To . . . sort it out."

She brushed by him as she made her way down to the women's locker room to change.

She was glad for her old Temple sweatshirt, a soft red buffer against the icy night air. She should have put her Windbreaker back on, but she hadn't been thinking clearly, hadn't been thinking at all, had only known she needed to be out of that building and outside, running. She sprinted as quickly as she could through Chinatown, dodging pedestrians and bicyclists and taxis that could now dart swiftly through the streets in the post-rush hour lull. She crossed Broad Street and the sweeping expanse of the parkway, oblivious to the fast-filling pubs and restaurants that lined the streets of Center City. Soon she found herself by the river, where long eddies of white light from the street lamps splayed across its mute surface. She knew as soon as she started running that she should have stopped immediately and gotten someone to look at her rib. But she couldn't think about that now. She just . . . she just needed to run.

Your father is a good man, but he is not wise.

Nora almost laughed out loud, finally understanding what her mother had meant by this.

Oh, Baba you are so, so stupid.

Theirs had been a marriage of opposites. Nora had always felt this. Her mother was shy and introverted, seeking refuge from the noisy city in the records of Abd al-Haleem and Umm Kulthoum and the poems of Nizar Qabbani. Her father was always talking, laughing loudly and deeply, clapping people on the back and plying them with food. He would pause now and then from tickling his kids to tell them that their mother had eyes like the ocean or a face like the moon. Ragab had a near-infinite ability to love intensely, but no tolerance for sitting still long enough to listen to his loved ones.

Even when—or, perhaps, *especially* when—it came to religion they were very different. Their mother's Islam was a warm, still pond, filled with books and knowledge and light. She prayed meditatively and emerged calm. One of Nora's favorite memories from childhood was the sound of her mother's voice, lush and low, reciting Qur'an during the most silent hours of the night.

The Islam of their father was more of a vague ideal he didn't quite understand. He prayed only sporadically but fasted the month of Ramadan with titanium precision, breaking his fast on a cigarette. His main fatherly concern was to get his daughter to wear longer skirts, baggier jeans, and blousier T-shirts. *Because Muslims don't dress that way!* was the only justification he could ever come up with for badgering her to dress more conservatively than she already did. Her father tried to force, cajole, and ultimately to bribe her to pray. No overnights, no dances, no prom. And she could never, under any circumstances, marry a non-Muslim man. *I would disown you. You would no longer be my daughter . . .*

Nora had been sure that her parents loved each other, but equally sure that, had it not been for their children, they would have gone their separate ways. Even when Fatin had been loneliest or most frustrated in her marriage, Fatin could not have separated her husband from his children. Ragab adored his kids, and would do almost anything for a kiss or to elicit their laughter. And they adored him, for he was tall and strong and handsome and funny, capable of fixing everything broken, and known for giving them gifts they didn't need when they least deserved them. Above all, they loved watching the effect he had on people, whether customers or guests in their home, and the light that he brought to a room.

He must have been lonely as well, she said to herself.

Oh, God, but some South Philly skank? Really?

Nora's breathing was hard and fast, overcome by the memories of the pain and fear following her father's disappearance. That horrible picture in the papers of him being led away in shackles, that picture for which she was bullied and mocked for so long afterward, even after he was let go, even after he was proven innocent . . . It was cold and getting colder, but Nora's mind was churning, and she barely noticed anything beyond the boundaries of her mental minefields.

She saw a few different courses of action open to her.

One, she could confront him, demand to know how he could have cheated on Mama, attack him for his twisted double standards, and generally make a big scene.

In this scenario, Ahmad would find out, and his image of his father would be trashed, just as hers had been.

It felt bad. It felt so, so bad, and Nora couldn't imagine doing that to Hammudi. Especially not now, with the SATs looming.

Shit.

Two, she could pretend she didn't know anything about it, and they could all go on about their lives.

But that was what her mother had done for her. Protected her.

Would things have been different if she had known?

Shit, shit, shit . . . Her feet pounded harder as she ran even faster, refusing to submit to the pain in her rib.

Her father needed to know she knew.

Because things just couldn't stay the same after this. Because everything was different now.

She found herself at the top of the museum steps. She sat down painfully on the top step, looking at the light-adorned city stretched out before her. She listened to the din of traffic—distant sirens, the screech of brakes and gunning of motorcycle engines unleashed on the beckoning parkway. She listened as her own jagged breathing came slowly but surely under control.

All she knew *was that her blood was on fire.*

She couldn't think, couldn't link together two actions, or align in her head the steps necessary to walk out the door or bathe herself or make it to the bathroom or call for help or even just to slash her thin, brown wrists.

But she could see her mother's face, knowing she would surely have preferred that she be dead of starvation at home instead of here. Anything but this. And now she was oceans away . . . Rahma pictured the ocean, pictured herself floating in it as she tried to cool the fire in her blood. If all the sea were ink . . . *Rahma's mind trailed off, searching, searching for the rest of the verse, but it hid, elusive in the gray depths of her mind.*

Her mother knew the verse. Her mother knew. When he entered the room not long after sunset, he found her curled into one corner, rocking, rocking, rocking. Mama knows, *she said, tears pouring down her cheeks.*

Not you, not you . . .

He stood over her for a moment.

All that Rahma could register was the revulsion on his face.

He hoisted her up to a standing position and steered her into the bathroom; cockroaches skittered as he flipped the light switch.

Mama . . . *she sobbed.* Mama . . .

He twisted back one of her arms, then shoved her into the tub and turned the shower on over her. He gruffly rinsed the worst of the filth from her before dragging her back to the sagging mattress.

CHAPTER 6

The pain in Nora's rib cage was searing when she awakened the next morning. She gathered herself slowly and painfully, determined to come up with some kind of breakfast for Ahmad before school. When he walked into the kitchen, he found her pouring hot milk into matching mugs that held Lipton tea bags.

He stopped to stare at her before sitting down. "What's the matter with you?"

She shrugged, laying out slices of soft white cheese and Kalamata olives on a plate. She flicked on the stovetop burner and warmed a pita over the open flame with the tongs, then handed it to him, doing the same for herself.

He looked at her suspiciously. "Did you get hurt?"

"No, I didn't get hurt, I'm completely fine, thank you." She sat down next to him, trying not to groan, and, as if for proof, took a long sip of the warm, milky, tea.

"Trouble with Special Agent Colleague?"

"Ahmad!"

"Then what?" he asked, as he chewed a huge mouthful of bread and cheese.

She knew if she told him about the drive-by he'd be totally unable to concentrate. She reached over and tousled her brother's hair. "Just up late worrying about a case."

"The gangbanger?" he asked, smoothing his hair.

"Yeah." She studied her brother's face thoughtfully. "You got gangsters at school?" she asked, sipping at her tea.

"*I'm* pretty gangsta." He set down his mug, then flashed a hand

sign at her, his thumb and first two fingers widespread, and his final two fingers curled over tightly.

Nora laughed. "Yes, you are, I can tell. Do you even know whose
sign that is?"

Ahmad shook his head. "No idea."

"Well, don't go flashing it anymore, it'll get you killed in some
parts."

"Why, whose is it?"

"Latin Kings. Where'd you learn it?"

"Kid in class. Does it all the time, mostly when he's angry at the
teacher."

"Yeah, you just stick to SAT signs, okay?"

He regarded her thoughtfully. "Is it worse to be thought of as a
gangbanger or a terrorist?"

She sipped her *shay bi-laban* slowly. "Gangbangers do more dam-
age in the long run. But since the victims are usually people who
can't speak up, or when they do no one pays attention, we don't really get it. A bombing holds people's attention a lot better than a
shooting in a 'bad' part of town."

Ahmad looked away. "Doesn't help to have the wrong kinda
name."

She leaned forward, laying her hand on his arm. "Someone mess-
ing with you at school?"

Ahmad sighed, glancing at the clock. "Nothing I can't handle."

"Ahmad, look at me—"

His warm, brown eyes met hers.

She spoke quickly. "There is *nothing* you can't handle. Don't you
let some punk get inside your head. You stay focused on what you're
doing and you do it with dignity, you got it? The stuff people say,
that's on them, that's all about whatever crazy situation they're coming from. It has nothing to do with you."

Her brother nodded, then looked suddenly ten again. "When I
think about this test I want to puke."

"Come on, you're gonna do great, *in sha Allah*. It's a day of your time—and *in sha Allah* it will mean a four-year scholarship, right? Now, you want more *shay bi-laban*?"

He looked at his near-empty mug. "Yeah, as long as you're spoiling me, might as well take advantage of it."

She stood and walked to the refrigerator. As she took out the milk, she said, "You want me to drive you? I can run get the car from the garage."

He stared at her. "Ummm, I had plans to arrive alive, actually."

"Boy!"

"Yes, yes, I know. You have a gun . . . "

She left just after Ahmad, going in the opposite direction. She decided to ride the bus, and she wedged herself in among the dour-faced commuters, descending painfully just outside the William J. Green, Jr. Federal Building.

In the crowded security line, she was keenly aware of every small brush of a shoulder or jostling by a swinging briefcase. Her entire body felt electric with pain. She eyed the doorway to the stairwell, then immediately discarded the idea and stood with the throngs in front of the wide bank of elevators. Of all the people Nora didn't want to see at that moment, Ben Calder topped the list.

He squinted at her. "What is this? Nora taking the elevator? Without being bullied by Wansbrough?"

"Good morning," she said evenly.

"Good morning," he replied. His voice took on a serious note. "Are you okay?"

She tucked her earbuds into her bag. "I'm perfectly fine, thank you."

"Whatcha listening to?" he asked.

She hesitated. She had picked the music because she woke up thinking of her mom, imagining her pain, and understanding why she had spent so many years as a hopeless romantic. After a moment, though, Nora admitted, "Umm Kulthoum, Star of the East."

"Hook me up," he said, pulling out his own earbuds.

"Oh, no, no way. She's an acquired taste." Nora hesitated, then gave Ben a half smile. "I won't have you making little white-boy grimaces. The woman was—is—an *institution*."

He took the bait, still clutching the earbuds. "Racist. Racist. Racist." She moved to protest, but he interrupted her, saying, "I will Google this woman. I will buy her albums. I will sing her songs all day long. And you will see. What's good enough for Nora Khalil is good enough for her white-boy buddy Ben." The elevator opened and they stepped on, along with a small crowd. "How's John?" Ben asked.

"He wasn't too hurt to come back for his laptop last night. But I hear Schacht actually forbade him from coming in today. So it's good you're here. We're expecting the brother of Hafsa al-Tanukhi any time."

"Sure, no problem." Ben studied her. "What were *you* doing here last night?"

Nora shrugged. The elevator paused at the fifth floor, discharging a few of its passengers. "Shootin' stuff." She lowered her voice and leaned in, inadvertently catching the scent of his aftershave. "Our little Jane Doe has gonorrhea, by the way."

Ben frowned. "Shit," he murmured, as Nora pulled away. Their eyes held for a moment, and Nora was grateful that the doors swooshed open.

They emerged from the elevator with three other agents and two hairsprayed administrative assistants. When they entered their cubicle, Nora sank into her chair with relief she hoped was not visible.

But Ben was regarding her, noting her drawn features. "You don't look right to me. Was it the shooting yesterday? Or are you upset about Jane Doe?"

She sighed. *Yes. All that. And bruising a rib, losing a father. Where to start?* "I'm good, Ben. Let's just get through today."

"Okay. Any word from Libby and Jonas about the computer?" he asked.

Libby called back, "Whatever was on it was wiped or saved to disk. End of story."

Nora and Ben shared a look. "You are no longer the best computer geek ever!" he called.

"Thank you, Benjamin!" she returned tartly. "And you are no longer the best agent because you can't find where they put the *data!*"

He shook his head and said, softly, "Maybe when we are grown-ups we will get an office with real walls."

The morning passed quickly, the eighth floor dense with activity and the sound of ringing phones and laser printers spewing out reams of paper. Within their cubicle, Nora and Ben worked side by side through a blur of phone calls, e-mailed reports, and files, as they rushed to finish their own paperwork while filling in the gaps left by John Wansbrough's absence. Eric Burton would appear, then exit silently, then reappear at random moments throughout the morning; Nora did not ask him what he was working on, and, as usual, he never volunteered information or spoke out of anything but necessity.

Just after eleven, Nora's direct line rang. It was the mother of Tameka Cooper.

"Cheryl from Tress It Up gave me your number," came the voice. The woman sounded so exhausted and listless that Nora shuddered.

"Yes, Mrs. Cooper. I'm glad you called me." Gently, Nora began asking questions. Tameka's mother was in a fog and seemed to know almost nothing about her daughter's habits. The only thing she knew for certain was that her daughter knew Dewayne Fulton, who she always referred to as "Reality." How they had met was completely obscure. The extent of their relationship was unknown. But shortly after coming to know him, she began coming home with Louis Vuitton bags and Coach sneakers.

And then she didn't come home at all.

After Nora hung up, Ben turned to her, his eyes a question.

Nora gestured to the phone with her head. "Mother of a young girl who may be caught up in this gang-pimping thing—Dewayne's day job when the meth trade is slow."

Ben nodded. "Renaissance man, that guy." Stretching, he looked over Nora's desk. It was covered with photos of the crime scene and the neighboring houses. She had set up all the pictures the techs had taken of the neighborhood homes, and reconstructed a mini version of the Kingsessing block there on the desk. Photos of the corpse were laid in the center.

Pulling up the empty chair from Wansbrough's desk, Ben leaned in to study the layout.

"We're missing something important, Ben, I can feel it."

He contemplated the scene from various perspectives.

Nora said, "I'm totally confused about any connection between Dewayne and our newest victim. But I'm honestly still trying to figure out the connection between Kylie and Dewayne. The whole sex with Kylie thing is still freaking me out."

Ben looked up. "What if he was pimping her like this other girl?"

Nora's eyes widened slightly, surprised she hadn't thought of it.

He sat back in John's chair, thinking. "Well, why not? I mean, especially given what you guys found out from the hairdresser."

"Monty would have found traces of other semen, then," Nora said.

"Would he?" Ben jumped up.

Nora frowned. "What?"

"Well, I'm just a lowly drug guy, but if I were checking a rape victim, I'd probably stop as soon as I found semen. But if she had had sex with someone the previous day, she probably would have washed herself from the outside." Nora shifted in her seat, keeping her face very still. Ben continued, "But there's nothing she can do about her insides. And former science guys like me happen to know that sperm can live up to five days in the right conditions . . . "

An aide poked her head in the door. "There's an Akram al-Tan . . . al-Tan . . . " She looked down at the sheet of paper in front of her, wrinkled her forehead, then looked blankly back at them. Finally she said, "You have a visitor in interview room six."

Nora gathered her things. "Will you call Monty and suggest that he look more thoroughly? Maybe see if Kylie had gonorrhea, too? If Dewayne's what they had in common . . . " her voice trailed off. Then she shook her head as though to expel any thought of Dewayne Fulton, a.k.a. Reality. "I'll get started in room six."

Akram al-Tanukhi fumbled with his visitor's ID, clipping and re-clipping it to his sweater.

It had not been difficult to get him to come in. The agent who took the summons found him at home. Akram had asked to bring his own car because he had an afternoon class; he looked hollow-eyed with worry and seemed eager to help.

Nora exhaled slowly before beginning with Akram. The scene with the father had not ended the way she hoped, and she was determined not to cause more problems than she solved this time. She started by asking him for the one thing she most regretted not getting from his mother: the names and addresses of some of Hafsa's friends. He began writing down some names of family friends on the pad of paper she pushed toward him.

"No doubt your parents described to you our visit to your home," she said.

Akram shifted in his chair. "My dad was pretty upset," he volunteered cautiously. "My mom . . . well, she's been upset for a few days now, so that was nothing new."

Ben walked in, and Nora introduced them, then asked cautiously, "Why was your father so upset?"

"I'm not sure," Akram answered. "I think he felt like you guys overstepped; he took offense that you were poking through the house. As though you might think we had something to hide."

"Do you?" Nora asked.

Akram's eyes widened slightly. "Of course not. My sister's disappeared. We just want to find her."

"Then why was your dad so angry when I was in your sister's room?"

Akram shrugged. "He's pretty protective of Hafsa."

"And yet, he sent you to college instead of her. Sacrificed her future for yours."

"Well—it sounds bad when you say it like that," Akram protested. "Hafsa understood. She was sad and all, but I made her a promise."

"What kind of promise?" asked Ben.

"I told her that as soon as I have a job, I'll pay for her college education. If she wants to go to Harvard, I'll pay for it. If she wants to go get a Ph.D., I'll pay for it. And that's her plan."

"*You* are her big plan?" Nora didn't mask her irritation.

Akram frowned. "No, but, you know, to hang on. Not give in to Baba."

"To give in to what?"

Akram seemed to think he'd said too much. He looked flustered. "I—"

Nora and Ben regarded him in expectant silence.

Finally, he said, "Well, Baba feels like she should focus more on marriage and children."

Nora bit back ten different acerbic remarks. "And how do you feel about these options for your sister?"

"Oh, you know. . . ." Akram made a long, heavy exhalation. "You have to understand who Baba is. He left Iraq against his will, a refugee, but did it because the situation had become so bad."

Ben and Nora waited for him to continue.

"He just . . . Well, making sure that Hafsa gets married is all he knows how to do to protect her and make sure she has a happy future."

"And Hafsa, does she still want to go to college instead?" Ben pressed.

Akram nodded. "More than anything. So I guess . . . her idea of a happy future and his are different."

I've heard that one before, Nora thought.

Ben said, "Can you describe a little more how your father and sister interact?"

Akram looked nervous. "What do you mean?"

Nora offered, "How do they talk to each other? Do they joke a lot or fight a lot?"

"Well, Baba's not much of a joker," Akram began. "But I guess that in the last few years their relationship has been . . . well, more tense than it was when Hafsa was younger."

"Because of his pressure on her to marry?"

"Yeah, I guess so," Akram said.

"Do suitors come over to the house?"

"Oh, yeah, all the time. It makes things really crazy. Mama's always cleaning and baking to host some new guy for Hafsa to meet."

"And Hafsa's reaction?"

Akram smiled ruefully. "She rejects every one. Usually because they are so strict—like really super *salafi* guys, really big beards and stuff. No smile. Hafsa is—well, she has a strong sense of humor, and the guys Baba has been inviting home . . . Three or four of them were already married."

Nora sighed, pursed her lips, then asked, "Has he ever hit her or threatened her when she rejects a suitor?"

"No. He . . . " Akram looked at the floor and his voice became soft. "Well, he has threatened her sometimes. He has pulled her hair sometimes, and Baba shouts a lot. One time he pulled off his belt like he was going to use it on her. But he never has."

Ben asked, "Is it possible that he hits her when you aren't there?"

Akram considered this. "I think she would have told me. And Mama wouldn't have been silent about something like that. Mama's scared of Baba's shouting, but she can shout when it comes to Hafsa."

"Tell us about her volunteer work."

Akram said, "She goes to a few different mosques. She tries to help women learning to read and write. She can help American women with Arabic and she also helps foreign women with English."

"So where does she teach?"

"Well, she's been out to al-Aqsa mosque and to a mosque in Germantown. The last few months she's been in Kingsessing. Sketchy neighborhood. More than sketchy, really rough. But she's really committed to going."

"Do you remember the name of the mosque?" Ben asked.

Akram shook his head. "No. I've driven her there a few times, but I honestly don't remember—"

Nora interrupted him. "If we read you a few names could you tell us if one of them sounds familiar?"

"Sure, I'll try."

"Masjid Bilal? Rahman Mosque? Unity Masjid—"

Akram looked up. "Yeah, that's it. I remember now. I did see the name on the door one time. They have, like, a neon sign, too. Broken."

Nora and Ben exchanged glances.

"What has she said about her experiences there?" asked John.

Akram shrugged. "Not much. She has a friend she's always talking about. Basheera . . . "

"Basheera what?" Nora pounced.

He shook his head. "No idea. Black girl. Not a family friend," he said, tapping the pad of paper in front of him as if to emphasize she was not on the list.

"No record of her phone number, address, contacts—does she go to university?"

Akram hesitated. "Her number would be in Hafsa's phone . . . but that's with Hafsa for sure. And she's not . . . well, she doesn't answer . . . "

His shoulders sagged slightly, and Akram looked tired.

Ben gave Nora a heavy look, then asked Akram for Hafsa's cell number so that they could obtain its call history. It would take two days, though. It was time Nora didn't feel like they had. She pressed on.

"Did it ever occur to you that she might be meeting someone, or using her mosque sessions as a cover for some secret relationship?"

Akram looked genuinely shocked. "That's nuts. If you know Hafsa, you know that's impossible."

"Why?" Nora asked.

"Because she's so . . . She's just so good. Like her and this Basheera, all Hafsa said they talk about is helping out, looking out for girls in the neighborhood, helping sisters with their reading and stuff."

Ben said, "We believe you, Akram. But let me ask you this: how would you feel if you found out your sister was in a relationship, or meeting someone?"

"Maybe . . . maybe I should get a lawyer now?"

"How would your dad feel?" Nora asked gently.

Akram looked away, chewing his lip.

Ben tried a different tack. "Have you ever heard Hafsa mention gang violence in the area?"

"Nah, her biggest complaint is the imam. She hates him."

Nora leaned in. "Why is that?"

Akram shook his head. "Honestly, I wasn't really listening when she was talking about all that. I think he's really conservative, maybe. The lessons he gives are really backward, bad for women. That's the kind of stuff that bugs Hafsa."

Ben sighed. "But the neighborhood itself?"

"Well, we fight sometimes 'cuz I think it's too bad a part of town—like if Baba saw it, no way would he let her go there alone, you know? And she keeps saying she needs to go back. She says it's a violent neighborhood, but also that she never feels threatened."

"Have you ever heard of the Junior Black Mafia? Or the A&As?"

He shook his head again.

Nora asked, "Akram, did you drop Hafsa off at the mosque the afternoon she disappeared?"

Akram flinched. "I did. Does that make me a suspect or something? I think I should really get a lawyer now . . . "

"Is it her habit to take a backpack with her? Notes, something like that?"

Hafsa's brother looked lost in thought for a moment. "She keeps all her stuff in her backpack . . . " He suddenly met Nora's eyes. "But she left her backpack in my car that day, said her and Basheera'd just be talking to the imam about something after his lesson. She just took her bus pass and her phone."

Nora and Ben sat up straight in their chairs.

"Do you still have it?" Ben demanded, his voice slightly louder than he had intended.

Akram looked unnerved. "I—Well, it's Philly. I put it in my trunk when I went to school so it wouldn't get stolen, then I just . . . I guess I forgot about it."

"Is it still there?" Ben pressed.

"I—yeah, unless Baba or Mama took it in. But I don't think—"

Without another word, Ben grabbed Akram's arm and nearly dragged him downstairs to the parking garage, with Nora close behind.

Hafsa al-Tanukhi's ragged blue backpack proved to be a treasure chest.

After they dismissed her brother, Ben and Nora stood over the backpack, their hands encased in white latex gloves, each one silent. Then they began searching every inch of it. They found two English as a Second Language textbooks, and a book of how to write the Arabic letters in all of their various forms. Lodged in the front zipper pocket—along with two pens, a pack of Trident gum, and a couple of crumpled receipts—was a hair elastic, yellow, with four strands of long, wavy hair clinging to it. Nora galloped down all eight flights of stairs to place it triumphantly on Monty Watt's slick, stainless steel table.

She stood over him, panting slightly and clutching her aching rib. She watched as he aligned the sample from the corpse with a hair from the elastic under the imposing lens of his digital microscope. It wasn't long before he pulled away to smile at her.

"It's a match. A perfect match. Look," he moved aside, allowing her to see the screen better. "The medullary patterns are identical, both fragmented. The cortical fusi are identical in pattern as well. I could run a DNA test to be sure, but it can only confirm what I'm telling you now."

Nora thought she would feel triumphant at having attained the identification, but now that the corpse had a face and a name, the fact of the murder could truly sink in. A woman, looking not too different from Nora herself, had suffered terribly before dying. Suddenly, Nora found herself sinking onto the bottom step of the stairwell, completely unable to climb up to her office. She tried hard to figure out how she was going to keep from seeing the image of Hafsa's body every minute of every day of the rest of her life. *Oh my God*, she whispered. She pressed her forehead to her knees and fought for breath.

There were many times when she wondered what she was doing in this building, badge on her belt, gun under her armpit.

Oh my God, I should have listened to Baba . . .

That idea made her so angry with herself that every other thought
in her head ceased. "Shit," she said aloud, lifting her head, yanking her hair out of the elastic and then winding it all up again into
its chignon.

She sighed. *I have to go upstairs.* This thought was followed by
another one:

I have to figure out who did this to her.

Still, the ascent was not quite long enough.

Even though she'd texted him right away with the news, Calder
had lingered in the interview room until she returned from the
basement. "Well, what have we come away with?"

Nora sank into a chair, thinking. "We know for sure that the last
place she was seen alive was that mosque."

"Yes, so someone needs to go there first thing tomorrow—John
will be back, or, you know . . . I could go with you if you want."

She held his gaze briefly, then said, "I'll ask him. See what he
wants to do. In the meantime, I'll touch base with Burton before I
leave today and find out what intel he's got on the imam."

Ben watched her. "Breathe. Don't stress, Nora. It's going to take
some time."

She shook her head slowly. "You're forgetting something. Now
that we know it's Hafsa, we've got to tell her family."

Ben inhaled sharply. "Yeah, not me. Anyway, you'll need a victim specialist with you. Or Chaplain Rogers."

Nora tilted her head. "The one time I really want you with me
you don't want to come?"

"*This* is the one time?" he countered.

She opened her mouth, then closed it again. "They don't like me
very much there," she said, pensively.

Ben gave a half smile. "With good reason. You're maddeningly insensitive." He extended a hand.

"Me?" she protested, accepting his hand and rising from her chair.

He released her hand swiftly and picked up his BlackBerry from the table, sliding it into his pocket, then gathered his notebook and pen. When he realized she was waiting for an explanation, he shrugged and pointed to his chest, then at her.

"Me?" she protested again, softly, watching his eyes.

"Yeah, you, Officer Khalil. Those Philly PD guys may take stuff like you laid on me yesterday in stride. But we federal officers are a breed apart, see? *Sensitive.*"

She nodded, feeling his sadness despite the lightness of his tone. "I see."

"No, Nora, I don't think you do, actually," he replied, as he headed out the door. He paused, then motioned for her to follow. "Come on, then," he said brusquely. "Let's track down the chaplain. He's more sensitive than both of us put together."

Chaplain Rogers was a sixty-seven-year-old black man with sharp eyes and graying temples. He was, without doubt, a sensitive fellow. However, he was entirely unprepared for the scene that Sanaa Faraj put on when Nora told her that her only daughter was dead.

It had been with great trepidation that Hafsa's father stood aside and ushered Nora and the chaplain into his home. He knew, Nora realized. He knew as soon as he saw her.

When the chaplain invited Omar al-Tanukhi to sit—an absurd thing to say in the man's own home, Nora realized, and a dead giveaway—he refused.

"No. No, I will not," he insisted.

It was loud enough to bring his wife to the living room, breathless, her headscarf not quite pinned into place. She looked from Nora to the chaplain, struggling to piece together the reason for this new visit.

"*As-salaam alaykum*," Nora murmured in greeting.

Mrs. Faraj responded, then softly asked to know what had happened. She turned to her husband and found tears streaming down his cheeks and disappearing into his vast beard.

"*La'a*," she whispered. *No.*

The chaplain began to speak, saying as gently as he could that the body of their daughter had been found in gang territory, and that they had only just positively identified it as Hafsa. He spoke the name carefully, having practiced its pronunciation with Nora on the drive over; he clutched the usual sheaf of papers that included numbers to call for counseling and case manager contacts. Chaplain Rogers understood that the family would ask for the body to be buried right away, and he was ready to explain that the Bureau needed to keep the body for a few more days as evidence that would help them find the killer.

But he couldn't get beyond the first sentence. Sanaa collapsed in devastated, unremitting screaming. "My daughter," she howled, falling to the floor.

Nora had expected the worst from Hafsa's father, but he simply stood, rooted to the beige carpeting, weeping silently, looking lost, and ignoring his wife completely.

Meanwhile, Sanaa slapped her palms against her face, shrieking. The torrent of words that poured from her startled Nora. "Hafsaaaaaa—" she cried. "My daughter!"

Nora had explained to the chaplain that he should not touch Mrs. Faraj, but that he could offer advice and comfort, and his usual hugs would be perceived as a breach of etiquette. Still, he inadvertently took a step toward her, wanting to lift her off the floor.

Nora stepped in and tried to coax Mrs. Faraj to a standing position, but she would have none of it. She shrieked Hafsa's name over and over, pulling at her clothing, tears sluicing over her thick, black lashes.

The scene set off in Nora a clear memory of appearing unannounced on the dim threshold of her grandmother's Cairo apartment. It was a sweltering July day. Her grandmother opened the door to find Nora and Ahmad standing there, sweating hands clutched hard together, and Ragab panting up the steep, dark stairs to the fifth floor . . . Nora had seen the quick joy of the surprise dissolve in the realization that their coming, tear-stained and somber, could only mean that an airport van was navigating the crush of afternoon traffic with a casket in its hold. Nora remembered the scream, the collapse, her aunt running in alarm from the kitchen.

What did her aunt say? Nora had the presence of mind to ask herself. She squatted next to Sanaa, gathering the time-worn words—

But the woman surprised her and suddenly sprang up, hurling herself at her husband, beating him with her fists. "This is your fault! We should never have come here. I told you it would be better to die in our country than be strangers in America! I told you, I told you! I begged you, you stubborn bastard! I begged you! You bastard! America! We will be safe in America, you said! Well, there's your America, they've gone and killed her!"

When Sanaa clawed her husband's cheeks with her unpainted fingernails, drawing blood, Nora pulled her arms away and began dragging her from the living room to the bedroom. Sanaa did not stop shrieking her daughter's name or cursing her husband, but Nora began murmuring the words she'd found in her memory. *We are God's and to Him we return*, she repeated over and over, convinced she was not heard, but equally convinced that she had nothing else to say.

When Sanaa found herself deposited on the bed, she looked up at Nora, her eyes bewildered and bereft. She reached up and grasped

Nora's hand, desperately. "I never wanted to come here," she said, her tone pleading.

Nora hesitated, weighing her words. "But you're here," she answered finally. Then she added, "Your son will be home from class soon. He'll need your help to get through it. Help him. You don't have the luxury of falling apart, do you understand?" Nora's father had said these things to her when Mama died. Pretending to be strong for her little brother had kept Nora from crumbling.

Sanaa's wet eyes held Nora's for a moment, and she clutched her hand harder before releasing it. Then she curled in on herself, her weeping softer. Nora pulled the throw blanket over her and slipped out of the room, exhausted.

Hafsa's father had remained in his fog, oblivious to the chaplain's practiced soothing. Even after the chaplain and Nora had gently explained that they must keep the body for a few more days, but would return it to them soon for burial, Omar al-Tanukhi did not speak. It seemed to Nora that he was reviewing every moment of his life that had led to this one, every sacrifice he had made and indignity he had stomached with the hope that life would somehow be better for his children.

They left their cards, along with numbers for grief counselors and case managers on his coffee table, and walked quietly out the door. Nora was relieved that the parents were so horrified by the death of their daughter they had not demanded details. She did not know how she would have gone about explaining that Hafsa's eyes had been cut out and her naked body dumped in an alley.

When they left him, Omar al-Tanukhi was still standing stock still in his living room. Silent tears skated over the thin, red scratches on his face, wetting his graying beard.

Eric Burton was sitting at his desk, his long fingers flying over the keys of his laptop.

After being with Hafsa's parents, Nora had wanted only to rush home to bed, but she had returned to the office to get her own laptop. She was relieved Ben wasn't there, because she knew something would break inside her if he invited her to talk about what had just happened. "Hey, Eric," she greeted him. "We ID'd the body."

He looked up, interested.

"Hafsa al-Tanukhi, Iraqi-American." Nora pushed away the emotion that swirled up now as she said the name. She swallowed, making her voice as even as possible. "Apparently she taught literacy at one of the mosques we were talking about. I called Wansbrough; he asked me to see what you've found out about the imam at Unity Masjid—her brother says the imam is possibly very conservative. We need to talk to him tomorrow."

Burton nodded, then called up a document on his screen, sending it to print. He tugged it off the printer and handed it to Nora. It was a single page, but dense with print on the front and back.

Nora scanned Burton's report. Shaykh Anwar was a Syrian who had answered the call of the rather squalid Unity Masjid when his options with the Syrian government had run out. The deal they gave him, while still well below the poverty line in the United States, was infinitely preferable to a stint in a Damascus prison; he had just been drawn into the revolution, and he had realized quickly that the stakes weren't for him. He was a *salafi*, an ultra-conservative, and the congregation had shown no signs of protesting his views. The African Americans in the mosque looked to him as an authority because he was coming with a diploma from a respected religious institution in Syria, and the few Arab Muslims in Kingsessing were relieved to have one of their own after the previous imam who often mispronounced the Qur'anic verses.

"You're going to be interviewing him with Wansbrough?" Burton asked.

"Yes," Nora said, coming to the end of the page and meeting his gaze.

"Maybe you aren't the right person to do that," he said.

"Why not?" Nora, surprised, demanded hotly.

Burton regarded her with narrowed eyes. "Because you don't belong here, Nora. I believe you were accepted to the task force because someone somewhere decided it would look good to have a Muslim girl from the 'hood' on board. Striking some kind of *visible ethno-religious counterpoint.*"

Nora felt a chill on her neck, and her breathing quickened. She glanced into the hallway, wondering if anyone had overheard him, wondering what he knew and how he knew it. She was so busy straining for the sound of Jonas and Libby bickering at their desks that she almost forgot to be angry that he was suggesting she didn't merit her position.

"Come on, Officer Khalil—" he accentuated the heavy first consonant of her last name in a way that left her no doubt that he was mocking her. "What do you bring to the table? Athleticism? That may be enough for Philly PD, but it doesn't count for much here. Mental acumen? Hardly."

She could barely register his words, she was so surprised at the attack. She scrambled to focus.

But Burton wasn't done. "I know what you've been hiding about your father—"

Now Nora was on her feet, furious. "That's not a secret, Burton, and I have nothing to hide! Any idiot could do a Google search. He was wrongly accused, and his name was cleared completely! End of story."

"It could be the end of story," Burton countered, "unless you have a bone to pick with the FBI— "

She gaped at him. "What, do you think I would sabotage you?"

"Why wouldn't you? Either way, you can't possibly be impartial."

"Impartial how?" she said, her voice going icy cold.

"You will always have a propensity to be sympathetic toward Muslims and Arabs."

"What are you even talking about?"

Burton rose, bringing his face close to Nora's. His blue eyes were narrowed and cold, but his breath was hot against her skin as he spoke. "It was a massive error in judgment on Schacht's part to let you on the task force—let you get your foot in the door of this organization. You're just another terrorist waiting to happen. So you better know I'll be watching you very, very closely, and reporting everything you do and everything you say." As he walked out into the near-empty hallway, he looked back at her with disdain. *"Everything."*

It was well past seven when Nora left the office. She wanted to run home, but the pain in her rib was unrelenting now. She sat numbly on the thirty-three bus, a rich combination of Sanaa's screams and Burton's accusations thumping in her head.

Everything within her had wanted to kick Burton in the sternum. It was Fordham High all over again; this time, instead of sucker punches she had been verbally slashed. But the wounds were the same: being doubted, having her loyalties questioned. The surprise came at having to deal with it in the workplace, just when she'd thought things had been going so well.

It was almost seven thirty when she walked into the Cairo Café. It was a good crowd for a Thursday night. Nora nodded at the two servers who were weaving between the tables, palming massive dishes of kabob and kofta. The smell of curried lamb hit her hard, and she realized she was intensely hungry.

Ragab's face broke into a smile as she pushed through the swinging doors. It was clear he wanted to forget their altercation over Ben's car. The flame from the grill rendered his face flushed and hot; she kissed his cheek lightly. She knew she had to talk to him eventually about the other woman, but now was not the time. She had to figure out how to handle it.

"What can I make you?" he asked in Arabic.

She considered this, and then, thinking of Ben, said wistfully, "Cheesesteak."

Her father looked aghast. "You have to be kidding! With the mushy bread and the canned cheese?"

"Come on, this is a Philadelphia restaurant. You should have some version of a cheesesteak. *Halal* cheesesteak. Think about it."

Ragab eyed her. "I'll think about it. For now, how about lamb curry?"

Nora admitted to herself that that was exactly what she wanted. She nodded.

"Okay." And then, cautiously, he said, "How was your day, *habibti*?"

"Productive," she answered blithely. She watched her father sideline the order he'd been cooking in order to prepare her food, and she smiled. "Ahmad back from SAT study session yet?"

"Upstairs," he answered.

"Good. Is he okay? He's really worried about the test. Did he tell you anything?"

Ragab shrugged. "With Ahmad, it's always hard to tell. He doesn't talk much, like his sister."

"Yes, well, an important trait we learned from our mother." Her tone was bitter, she realized. But Ragab seemed not to notice.

"Three antisocial people in one family, and I am the only normal one." He gestured heavenward with his long aluminum spoon. "Why?"

"Aren't you enough of an extrovert for all three of us?" she asked. "*'So that you don't lose the balance,'*" she added.

"Your mother always used to quote that verse, may God have mercy on her." Ragab poured her curry into a to-go carton. "I made double—feed your brother. You want baklava?"

"Already got it," Nora said, showing him that she had pulled two slices out of the dessert fridge.

"*Yalla*, go on."

"Thank you, ya Baba."

"Your aunt Madiha says she sent you a message on the *Fays*." This was Ragab's designation for Facebook. "Send her back a message, be polite."

"*In sha Allah*," Nora responded, having no intention whatsoever of doing so. She pecked him on the cheek as she made for the stairs.

Ahmad was praying when she walked in. She removed her shoes, carefully set the food on the kitchen table, and waited for him to finish. He looked tired.

"*Habibi*, how was your day?"

He shrugged and sank down next to her at the kitchen table. He groaned softly and placed his forehead on the table.

Nora reached out a hand and rubbed his back. "Come on. Did you have a bad practice test or something?"

He groaned again. "Yes. Of course. I mean, not the math. But I have so much to do, just homework. And still I have to study for this stupid test." He turned his head to look at her, letting his cheek rest fully on the table. "I hate the English language."

"I know you'll do fine, Hammudi. I know it, you'll see. You are studying so hard." She took her hand and ruffled his hair.

"It doesn't make any sense. And the words are too long!"

Nora chuckled; she felt the same way. Which was why the idea of more school had made her queasy, and she had jumped at the police academy chance when it came her way. Eric Burton's words came back to her.

What did she bring to the table, after all?

John Wansbrough was waiting for her outside the Cairo Café at 6:30 A.M.; they had decided to try to catch up with the imam after the dawn prayer. John had refused to take any more time off. Nora had delivered the Suburban into the custody of the forensic team, and it was now parked at the FBI's garage in South Philly. They had issued him another black Suburban, this one slightly older and worn, and he looked as though in mourning for his bullet-riddled ride.

"How's the arm today?" she asked, strapping on her seat belt.

He shrugged, guiding the car into the scant traffic. "Hurts like hell, thanks for asking."

"Still getting sympathy at home?"

"That well ran dry yesterday. Would *you* ever ask a man with a gunshot wound to take out the trash?"

"That depends on the trash, I guess," Nora said. "Did you hear back from ballistics about what went through your arm?"

"Semi-automatic, .22 caliber. They pulled four of them out of the side of my fine vehicle, too. When I find the bastard . . . "

"Completely unconcerned about the arm, outraged over the car. Men are so ridiculous." Her voice had a slight edge to it.

He glanced over and noticed the dark shadows beneath her eyes. "What is it? Is something wrong?"

She did not reply for a while, and he was about to ask his question again, when she finally said, "Do you think I'm here as part of some sort of affirmative action thing for Muslims?"

He turned to face her fully as they paused at a light. "Why would I think something like that?" he asked carefully.

She fidgeted with a crease in her trousers, then said, "Burton said that."

John was silent, watching her intently. "Do you believe him?"

"I don't know," she answered. Nora worked her jaw, looking away. She had wanted immediate confirmation that she was essential and valuable and valued.

John read her reaction. "Nora, you are bright and strong and smart and the fastest young agent, man or woman, I have ever had the privilege of seeing rocket across the back alleys of Philadelphia. You get me your reports before I even ask for them. You stay up half the night working and preparing when the rest of us are asleep. Do you really need me to tell you this?"

She met his eyes. "I—I don't know," she answered. "I was so surprised by what he said to me."

John tilted his head. "What'd he say?"

"He thinks I won't be able to be impartial when the subject matter is related to Arabs or Muslims. And that I'm a terrorist waiting to happen."

John rolled his dark brown eyes. "Oh, boy . . . hey, listen, it's part of the thick skin thing, Nora. I can go after Burton if he harms you in any way, or if he obstructs your work in any way. But I can't do anything to him for thinking you're part of a sleeper cell. Sticks and stones, girl."

"Oh, John. This is more than sticks and stones. This is my colleague."

"And half the country. Maybe more. So prove him wrong." Wansbrough glanced at her, eyes flashing. "*And them.*"

She listened, looking steadily out the window at the city as it began to stir.

"I'm *tired* of having to prove myself," she said irritably.

John threw back his head and laughed. "How old are you?"

She knew he knew, so she remained silent.

"You're just getting started, girl. You have a long, long road ahead of you, and you will have to prove yourself every day in every way. And your victories are gonna come at a higher price than everyone else's, and your mistakes are gonna be scrutinized harder than everyone else's, and that's just what it is. Believe me, I know this inside and out."

She held his gaze, feeling small.

He continued, his tone softer. "Look, Nora, Eric Burton is very smart. His input is usually very valuable, and he's *very* good at his job. He wants to watch you, let him watch. Show him what you've got. Don't you back down from anyone, and don't let anyone scare you. Just keep doing what you're good at, with good intentions, and the rest will work itself out."

Nora shook her head, realizing she'd just said the same thing to Ahmad yesterday.

"And hey," John continued, turning onto Walnut Street. "Chaplain Rogers told me about how things went with the victim's family yesterday. You calmed that woman down, and that was invaluable. You had the Arabic skills, the cultural skills—Who else was gonna be able to do that? Let's say for argument's sake that you were included because of your ethnicity. I don't see how that's a bad thing these days."

She listened silently, watching the buildings slide by. She considered his words, wincing again despite herself at the memory of the scene with the al-Tanukhis. Finally she said, "We have to fast-track that body."

John nodded. "Monty is digitizing every inch of every knife angle, trying to get it home to them today, don't worry. But don't forget that however impressive his grief, her father is still a person of interest in this case. Now, come on. We'll stop at that smelly Starbucks at Thirty-fourth. I'll buy you some mint tea. I owe you one for setting up my anniversary dinner."

She had forgotten to ask him about it. "It was a good night?"

"I'll be paying it off through next year. But yes, it was a *very* good night . . . "

As he drove up onto the edge of the curb, he looked like he was about to add something by way of elaboration, but Nora held up a hand. "Leave it right there, Old Man."

He laughed out loud, then shoved the gearshift into park and jogged into the Starbucks. There was no line at that hour, and he soon returned holding two steaming cups. He handed Nora hers, asking, "So are we ready for all this? You got all the information you need to ask the right questions?"

Nora considered this as she popped off the top to cool her tea. "I'm not sure, John."

"Okay, go over it with me."

"Okay. Hafsa is found, throat slashed and eyes cut out. We can assume that the eye thing means that she's witnessed something that could get someone else in trouble All this is in the heart of gang territory when we're in the middle of basically a war started by a drive-by and culminating in a rape and stabbing. Is she connected to all that in some way? We need to find out. Meanwhile, her dad's sort of a classic, potential honor-killing suspect, her brother doesn't really fit the part, but all we really know is that the mosque was the last place she was seen alive."

Wansbrough continued, "So, for this reason, we're on our way to dawn prayer, ridiculously early, to see if we can find out something about her murder. And the imam?"

"Hafsa apparently disliked him—'hated him,' according to her brother, although it's unclear why. She had wanted to talk to him about something on the day she disappeared. Burton gave him a pretty negative report. Says he's *salafi*."

"*Salafi?*"

"Yeah, like people who are keen on getting back to what they think is the pure religion. Catch term for ultra-conservative."

John took a long sip of his coffee, studying her. Then he said, "So what are we going in with here? What's our goal?"

"We need to know what happened the last day Hafsa came here. We need to know who Hafsa's friend Basheera is and where we can find her. We're going to ask the imam how his lesson went that day, and we're going to ask him for his help."

Imam Anwar of the Unity Masjid was frowning at them.

They had caught him in the hallway outside his shabby office, where he had headed after completion of the dawn prayer. He was shocked to see two visitors to the mosque that early, and his first reaction was to ask Nora to cover her hair. When they showed him their badges, and mentioned that they needed to ask him questions with regard to a crime, he was visibly disconcerted.

"I'm afraid your partner needs to cover her hair," the imam insisted, "It is very disrespectful . . . "

"We're not in the actual prayer area of the mosque, Shaykh Anwar," an irritated Nora reminded him. "And I don't think you're grasping what's going on here. We are investigating the murder of a young woman."

The imam swallowed audibly.

John said, "Hafsa al-Tanukhi was a young woman who taught literacy here—right here in this very mosque. On a regular basis."

Shaykh Anwar's face remained impassive as he entered his office and took his place behind his desk, gesturing at them to sit.

John continued, "She was recently murdered, Shaykh Anwar. Are you saying you don't know her?"

The imam frowned deeply, thinking. "This is a terrible thing, but I do not think I have heard this name before. I cannot say for sure."

Nora felt anger bubbling in her stomach. She reached for the file and plunked the pictures of Hafsa's corpse down on the desk in front of him. The picture she had taken from Hafsa's home was clipped to the inside of the file folder.

The imam's gaze fell on the pictures, and his face wrinkled in disgust. "This is *haram*, you should not allow a Muslim woman to be exposed in this way."

"We didn't expose her," Nora retorted. "Her killer did."

The imam sighed. "This is a terrible crime, very sad. What did you say her name was again?"

John Wansbrough leaned forward, tapping the desk with his index finger for emphasis. "We know for a fact that this young woman visited this mosque regularly. We also know that this mosque was the last place she was seen alive. I find it hard to believe that there are that many women teachers willing to volunteer their time here."

The imam shook his head. "None of this is anything more than nonsense to me. How can I know the intimate details of all the Muslims who come to this mosque? I do my best to counsel with and get to know the young men, but women too? It simply isn't possible."

"Well, perhaps it's something you'll need to work on," responded Nora. "You were scheduled to teach the afternoon that Hafsa disappeared. She came with the intention of talking to you that day. And you still say you don't know her?"

"I'm not sure you understand the way a mosque functions," the imam said, struggling to make his English keep up with his displeasure. "Anyone can walk in and pray here, any time. We don't keep records of the people who worship here or attend classes. And I certainly don't ask the women in my class who they are or what they're doing there. I come, I teach, I leave."

"So you do not know Hafsa al-Tanukhi?" John pressed, botching the name's pronunciation.

"No, I do not."

"There is a woman named Basheera, a friend of Hafsa's. How can we get in touch with her?" Nora asked.

"I do not know the women in my mosque," he answered defensively. "I have no way of knowing this."

Nora spoke. "And, with the understanding that making false statements to federal investigators can get you convicted and sentenced to prison, you assert that you do not know that an Iraqi-American woman was teaching literacy in your own mosque?"

The imam glared for a charged moment at Nora before looking away. "You might be speaking of the sister who came here volunteering to teach reading and writing to some of the more ignorant women."

"Yes, exactly," Nora confirmed, even though the imam was continuing to address Wansbrough.

"I did not know her."

"You didn't want to see if she was qualified to teach?"

The imam answered quickly, "I sent my wife to sit in on one of her sessions."

Nora smiled pleasantly. "Then we'll start with her."

"No!" the imam practically shouted. "That's impossible."

John Wansbrough leaned forward, his patience exhausted. "Why?"

"She—she doesn't speak to strange men," Shaykh Anwar said thinly.

"My partner can interview her privately, if she prefers."

"But—but she doesn't speak any English!" replied the imam, his voice taking on a desperate edge.

John turned to Nora, who said in dulcet-toned Arabic, "Is there any other reason?"

The imam's eyes darted between their faces, and his shoulders slumped.

The two agents stood. Wansbrough said, "We'll come to your home this afternoon to interview you both. At that time, you can decide if you'd like to be more forthcoming with information, or if you'd prefer to come downtown."

The imam was silent. He did not escort them to the door.

"That guy is really scared about something," John said, as soon as they'd entered the car.

"I agree," Nora said.

"Involvement in the murder?"

Nora shrugged.

They were interrupted by an incoming call. Wansbrough hit speaker.

"Hey guys, it's Ben. The semen thing was right, Nora. Monty stayed late last night and I just found his e-mail."

"How right?"

"At least three other males besides Dewayne had intercourse with Kylie in the days before her death."

John Wansbrough almost swerved into a car. "Jesus, I'm absent one day—"

Nora frowned at him. "We think Dewayne was pimping her."

John shook his head. "God, that poor kid. It's a miracle she wasn't dead from some sexual disease already."

"Well, she did have gonorrhea. Monty found out with a cervical swab, but it's hard to die from that. How do you want to proceed?" Ben was asking.

John thought. "You guys have a JBM girl in custody, right?"

"Rita Ross," Ben answered. "Eric and I keep hoping to talk to her about supply lines."

"Let's talk to her about pimping first." John glanced at Nora. "Maybe *you* could talk to her."

Nora took a deep breath, remembering how Rita had cursed her. "I can try. She gave me the impression she wasn't talking without a lawyer."

Ben volunteered, "She's dismissed two lawyers already."

"Dismissed?" John asked.

"Won't work with them. Apparently she's a handful."

John grinned. "Then Nora is just the right person to speak to her."

Nora walked into the room, trying to exude confidence. Rita Ross's file was under her elbow, and two mugs were in her hand.

The woman looked up at her with disgust. "You?"

Nora smiled; she knew John and Ben were standing in the dimness beyond the mirror. "No one's ever happy to see me anymore."

"What do you want?" the woman growled at her.

Nora placed the mugs on the table; the smell of the mint filled the small room, and Rita Ross frowned, staring. "I want to drink a cup of tea with you," Nora explained.

The other woman pushed back her chair. "*Fuck you.*"

Nora had asked that she be uncuffed, and they'd debated this lengthily, but finally came to an agreement—provided that Ben and John could be close enough to intervene.

"Look, you can drink it or not. It's tea with mint and sugar in it . . . "

"I can throw it in your face," Rita said.

"You could. But then I would almost certainly shoot you for wasting the perfect cup of tea."

Rita stood and walked over to the mirror. "What the fuck is this? Can you get me a real cop up in here?"

Nora picked up her mug and held her ground, choosing to lean casually against the wall, even though it took real effort not to walk right out of the room. "So I told you what *I* want. What do *you* want, Ms. Ross? Looks like you've been firing a lot of lawyers lately."

"I want some respect. They seem to think I'm some kinda gang ho."

Nora nodded, finding her first opening. "I know, Ms. Ross. You are a full member of the crew. Without you, Dewayne Fulton's operation would fail."

"What do you know about it?" the woman asked scornfully, leaving the mirror to walk back to the table and reoccupy the chair, folding her arms.

Way too much, Nora wanted to respond. "You helped Dewayne build something. You were just getting to the place you wanted to be. You guys had made all the right connections, you were ready to take it all to the next level. Then Dewayne starts taking the organization in a different direction altogether . . . "

Rita Ross regarded her with narrowed eyes.

Nora continued. "He starts pimping. Sets it up on the Internet, sends out some runners to watch over the merchandise. Keeps the girls high so they keep coming back . . . "

The woman looked away, drumming false, blue fingernails against the tabletop.

"Starts working with a white hooker named Lisa Halston. Wants to take it up a notch . . . "

Nora watched as Rita's face darkened.

"But that's not your style, is it, Ms. Ross?"

She rounded on Nora. "Oh, I see where this is going. I say again, Bitch. *You do not know me.* I ain't your friend."

Nora sat down across from her and looked her square in the eye. "Well, that's too bad. Because it's been a long time since anyone made me work to run them down. And I respect that."

Rita glanced up, then looked away again. "Why, you think you pretty good?"

Nora said, "I do alright."

"If I'd had my piece I wouldn't have had to run," she said.

"Where was your gun that night?" Nora asked.

Rita was silent. Nora gently pushed the warm mug toward her. She took it, sighed, and sniffed at it before taking a small sip. "I had to trade my piece," she said finally. "For shelter."

"You'd left in a hurry," Nora surmised. "So it was all you had with you."

"This crew up in Strawberry Mansion, said they had a safe house where we could ride it out under the radar, but they wanted somethin' in return. Didn't know they'd put us in a fuckin' crack house."

Nora regarded her for a while, recalling the stench of the house and the chaos within. "Why . . . why didn't you just get out of town?"

Rita gave her a scathing look. "You ever traded your blanket for food?"

At Nora's silence, Rita continued. "You ever steal some cough syrup for your baby sister so she can sleep through one night?"

Nora faltered, "I . . . "

"Situation like that, the gang steps up. The crew is your family. Got your back, you got their back. You don't run from that. You don't just get outta town. You in it. For life."

Nora tilted her head. "And Dewayne? You think Dewayne still has your back?"

Rita was silent.

"He's been busy these days, right? With the girls. With Kylie Baker . . . "

Rita Ross tsk'd softly, then lifted the mug of tea to her lips again.

"Kylie was in love with him," Nora ventured.

Rita harrumphed. "She mighta thought she was."

Nora looked a question at her.

"You think I don't understand Kylie? Kylie saw Dewayne, with his Beemer and his bank. And it couldn't've mattered less what he did or how he did it or what he asked her to do. She just wanted to hold on to the idea that there was a way out."

"But Kevin had that. He was taking care of his family, wasn't he?"

Rita's face darkened. "Kevin Baker is a *piece of shit*. He don't take care of nobody but Kevin Baker. Soon as he got himself some Gs, he was buyin' the flashy ride and then movin' out of his house, wearin' the gold. His mama was sick, she *still* need an operation so she can walk better, fix her knees, he don't even give her the time of day . . . Kevin Baker is worried about one thing: Los Zetas. He's gotta sell and sell some more. If he can't hold on to the turf here and keep the supplies flowing, they will find someone who can. And that will be that."

Nora couldn't keep from glancing up at the mirror as she digested this.

Rita Ross stared into her mug. "Girl like Kylie wants to be taken care of. Sometimes you wanna get so spoiled you forget what it was like to be hungry. And you want someone to lie to you and say you can have it all. Dewayne was like that with me in the beginning."

"And then . . . ?"

"And then he got tired of me." She took a swallow of the tea. "He coulda gotten rid of me. But he kept me. Trained me to make the connections he needed."

"You mean, made you use your body to build his network."

Rita didn't answer.

"And then made you watch him start pimping girls. Some of them little girls."

She inhaled, staring down at the spot where one of her electric blue fingernails had popped off, exposing a stunted, broken nail, bare of paint.

Nora pulled out Jane Doe's picture and slid it across the table. "We found her. We have no information on her. She won't talk. She's scared and alone."

Rita looked at the picture, then looked away.

"Do you know her? Rita?"

She shook her head. "Nah, I don't know her. But if she's one of the girls, she'd be on the disk."

Nora straightened in her chair. "What disk?"

"Flash drive. Lisa Halston and Dewayne had been putting together information on all the girls. For marketing purposes," she said icily. "Dewayne called it his moneypot, but Lisa was behind it. Ms. In-Control. Had the girls' real names and their street names and how much they brought in. And their . . . special talents."

"Where was this disk?" Nora asked, leaning in.

Rita shook her head. "The bitch always kept it with her. So she could stay in the game, she said. So Dewayne wouldn't cut her out. She was the expert at bringing them in, see? Showed the girls her fancy loft, her shoes, her shit. Once in, Dewayne knew how to keep them. Anyone change her mind, he pull her by the hair into the street, slam her head against the pavement. Tell the whole neighborhood, 'This bitch is mine!' Used his belt on them, used his ring. Used his cigarettes. One girl, he tied her up three days in his bathroom. Every time he needed to go, he went and pissed on her, then kicked her a few times, then left. Three days, until she swore never to turn down a customer again for the rest of her life."

Nora watched Rita's face. "We can help you," she said softly.

Rita met her gaze and held it, then whispered, "There's no help for me. That's the thing about hell, see? You don't get to leave."

The two looked at each other for a long moment, and Nora nodded slowly. Reluctantly, she rose to leave, and was almost at the door when she heard Rita murmur, "West Philly High."

"Excuse me?"

"I ran the 100, 200, and four-by-100 meter relay. West Philly High."

Nora nodded again. "Thanks," she said, gently closing the door in place behind her.

He was moving her.

Slowly she realized he was covering her hair with a black scarf, and then pinning a long black niqab over her face.

You have to walk now, you understand me? You have to walk. No sound. No sound at all.

She understood.

She had been moved often.

No one ever told her where.

No one had to tell her why.

She did not know the name of the city where she now was, only that she and the six other girls had been brought here at night in the back of a van with blackened windows.

She knew the others had already been taken away, the first night that the police came and took the body in the alley.

They had been left there long enough to see the message, long enough to learn their fear anew.

And the people of this new town had gotten the message, and had surely begun to fear as well.

Whatever hope had invaded her at the sound of the sirens was driven off now by the sound of the door closing behind them. He seized her by the elbow and steered her down the crumbling cement stairs, as the cold midnight swallowed them whole.

CHAPTER 7

The home of Anwar al-Islahi was slightly less ramshackle than the neighboring row homes. An optimistic hand had once painted the intricate trim teal; now, it struck a tinny dissonance alongside the other weary facades.

John and Nora stood on the porch.

Nora paused before rapping on the outer door. "He's not going to be happy to see us."

"Get used to it, Rookie."

"I completely hate it when you call me that," she said, knocking.

"Yes, I know. But that was a very rookie thing to say. Toughen up. We're not baking cupcakes here, we're fighting crime."

Nora gave him a half smile. "I'll make a note of it."

Imam Anwar wore a gelabiyya that grazed his bare ankles. He was not happy to see them at all. Before opening the outer door, he looked uncomfortably at John. "I thought that the sister would be coming in alone."

John asked, not masking his irritation, "Is it a one-room home, sir, or is it possible to speak with you in a dining room while Officer Khalil interviews your wife in the family room?"

The imam blinked rapidly. "I need to be present while my wife is interviewed."

Nora answered firmly, "That's completely impossible. May we come in please?"

The imam stepped to one side, bristling. The house was spare, the home of a new immigrant, free of inherited furniture and the accumulated clutter of years spent in one place. An IKEA shoe rack designed for a closet was placed prominently in the foyer, and Nora promptly slid out of her shoes, with John reluctantly following suit.

The imam ushered John into a dining room that held a bruised and rather wobbly-looking second-hand table surrounded by six mismatched chairs. Nora watched him scan the room for every exit, noting every feature before seating himself at the head of the table.

She then followed the imam into the living room. Two small sofas faced each other, each covered in bedsheets that apparently masked the flaws or stains of the original upholstery. A straight-backed chair was piled high with neatly folded prayer rugs. On one wall was a large poster of the Ka'ba back-lit by neon-laced minarets; the surrounding open mosque was packed with thousands of devoted pilgrims. The walls were completely bare except for this. The north end of the room ended in what Nora guessed was the basement door, not far from steep stairs ascending to the second level. Shaykh Anwar called upstairs to his wife, and she descended, cloaked in full niqab.

Nora watched her apprehensively. Her form was slight, and her steps were measured. When the woman greeted her with an accented *Hello*, Nora replied by saying *As-salaam alaykum*. Shaykh Anwar narrowed his eyes at Nora, then explained to his wife in Arabic that he would not be allowed to sit in on the interview, and he would be in the dining room with the other agent.

She followed his retreating form with her eyes, and Nora saw through the slit in her face veil that they were light, almost amber-colored. When Shaykh Anwar entered the dining room, John rose and closed the door, giving Nora a pointed look.

Nora held out her hand to shake that of the imam's wife. She was met by a tiny gloved hand that felt birdlike in her grasp. "My name is Nora. May I ask yours?"

The woman nodded slightly. "Khulood."

"It's nice to meet you," Nora said, but the woman did not reply. "Madame Khulood, I need to ask you to remove your face veil for our interview," Nora continued, as gently as possible.

The woman sat stock still, considering this. "I don't—" she began

Nora cut her off. "You know that the face veil must be removed for praying and for performing the pilgrimage . . . " she said, gesturing at the poster on the wall. With a start, Nora realized that she had been paying attention to her mother's occasional discussions about Islamic law after all. "You must also remove it for official appearances like marrying and giving witness. This is an instance of giving witness."

Khulood's light eyes met Nora's. Slowly, reluctantly, she pulled the veil up over her head. Her face was thin and her cheekbones high. She had a pointed chin and a small mouth. The lashes that surrounded the light eyes were pale and feathery.

"Did you know Hafsa al-Tanukhi?"

The woman nodded slowly. "Yes, yes I did."

"Did you study English with her?"

Khulood narrowed her eyes. "A few times . . . yes."

"I need to know the names of the women who studied with her. In particular I am trying to find a woman named Basheera. Do you know a woman named Basheera?"

Khulood looked worried, and cast her eyes at the closed door to the dining room. "I don't think so . . . "

Nora tried hard not to show her irritation. "What did you think was the purpose of my visit today, Khulood?"

She received no response.

"Were you there for the lesson your husband gave on Saturday?"

Khulood looked flustered. "I'm not sure . . . "

"You're not sure if you were there or not?" Nora pressed.

Khulood quickly shook her head. "No, no, I was there, of course, I just . . . I can't remember everything . . . "

"Well, try to remember one thing."

Khulood shrugged. "He gave the lesson. We listened. We all left. Nothing happened unusual."

"What were the names of the women who attended your husband's lesson?"

The woman began to tremble and her eyes started welling with tears.

Nora didn't back down. "Did Hafsa speak to your husband that day?"

The small woman widened her wet eyes. "No!" Then she looked again at the dining room door, giving off the aura of being adrift.

"Khulood, I came all the way over here to save you the inconvenience of having to come to my office. I would be very happy to call you into the office if it will make it easier for you to share information."

Khulood shook her head slightly, then murmured, "May God forgive you. Basheera Johnson. I do not know her telephone or address. There were others, another black woman named Karima . . . something. Some Arabs like Fatma al-Bakry, Marwa Abd al-Hamid, they had taken some of the English lessons because they had no language skills at all. And very little Arabic literacy, frankly."

Nora was scribbling in her notebook. "Why would Hafsa have wanted to talk to your husband, Khulood?"

"She had no reason to talk to him at all. She taught language. He taught religion. That was all," the woman replied simply. "I'm sure whatever happened to her was God's plan for her."

Nora's pen paused in midair over the notebook page. "Her eyes were cut out, Khulood. Her throat was slit."

Khulood dropped her eyes. "God is the most merciful," she said softly.

———

Both agents were quiet as they headed back to the Philadelphia field office.

John finally spoke. "How did it go?"

Nora shook her head. "She lied. A lot."

John Wansbrough nodded. "The same with her husband. He was very scared, very on edge. I think his life is being threatened."

"Did you let him know you thought so?"

"Yes. He said that was preposterous. I wasn't very convinced."

"I think he coached his wife. She had a script she was supposed to stick to. She really didn't want to give me the names I got."

"We're gonna need to track down those names," John said, guiding the car over the South Street Bridge.

Nora asked, "Could one of the gangs be threatening him? Is that why he's so scared?"

John shook his head. "That could be the link. But why him—what he has that would concern either gang, I don't know."

It was the middle of the night when she got the call.

The shaykh's house had burned to the ground.

Nora was up and dressed in less than a minute.

"Where are you going?" her father asked as she came out into the kitchen. He was wearing plaid pajama bottoms and a sleeveless undershirt, and he was watching the Food Network. "It's one A.M.!"

She finished twisting her hair into its tight bun. "Work," she said.

Her father pursed his lips, muting a rerun of *Chopped*. "I say again, it's *one in the morning!*"

"Well, you should let the criminals know, Baba, okay?" she snapped.

He watched as she stuck one arm into her jacket. Finally, reluctantly, he said, "Okay, you hungry?"

She shook her head. "John's on his way to pick me up—*salaam*."

She heard his response as she made her way out onto the street to wait. She couldn't wait inside; she wasn't in the mood to talk, and her heart was pounding against her chest; she felt sick. John had said the couple was in intensive care; the imam's wife was in critical condition, while the imam himself had suffered serious burns all across his body. Nora fought against the feeling that she was responsible.

When John Wansbrough drove up, she entered the mercifully warm car, then looked up and saw her father watching her from his bedroom window. She slammed the door, making John look at her as though she'd slapped him.

"Hey, now, we're just breaking in this beauty. Be gentle."

She ignored him. "What do we know?"

He shook his head. "The fire department thinks it was a Molotov cocktail thrown through the front window. The first floor was nothing but old wood, and it went up fast. They pulled the Islahis out from a second floor window."

"No witnesses?"

"Of course not. Are you new here?" he said.

She sighed. "I feel . . . "

John looked at her with a deep frown across his features. "This one isn't about feelings, Nora. This isn't our fault. The imam was scared, scared of maybe just this. If he had told us from the beginning who he was scared of, then maybe he wouldn't be in this position. You yourself told me that you thought his wife was lying to you. Honesty might have prevented this whole thing. Are we clear?"

Nora nodded. "So what's next?"

"We're going to the hospital. Watt's going to the scene to be our eyes and to see if he can assist."

They passed swiftly through the empty streets and soon arrived at the Hospital of the University of Pennsylvania. Wansbrough left the SUV on a curb outside the emergency room, and they walked in. After flashing their badges at the desk, they were guided by an indifferent nurse to Anwar al-Islahi's room in intensive care.

"Can he talk to us?" John asked the nurse.

She nodded. "He's conscious. Might be a little loopy from the morphine, but conscious."

The imam was, yet again, not happy to see them. His black eyes managed to produce a look of fury. They greeted him, and he turned his face away.

John circled to the other side of the bed. "Mr. al-Islahi, what's happened here is very alarming. Do you think you're ready to tell us the truth now about what's going on at your mosque?"

The imam's voice was a harsh whisper. "This is your fault. I told you to leave us alone . . . "

"With all due respect, sir, if you knew there was a threat, it was your obligation to inform us. Now, who is responsible for burning your home and putting you and your wife in the hospital?"

At mention of his wife, the imam's eyes filled with tears. "Khulood," he murmured. "My wife is pregnant, you bastards. How could you do this to us?"

Nora felt sick, and she looked desperately at John before saying, "Shaykh Anwar, you must tell us who's responsible so we can prevent another attack on another family. *Please.*"

He turned on her, his eyes flashing. He spoke rapidly in Arabic. "You fools, do you think if they can do this just to scare us, they won't kill us if I tell you anything? I didn't come here to die. I didn't come to this country to die!" He broke down in tears then, and Nora watched in shock as the imam sobbed. "I will not speak to you. You cannot make me, you cannot!"

The nurse who had ushered them in returned, her shoes squeaking against the highly polished floor. "I said you could speak to him, not that you could give him a nervous breakdown," she said angrily. She patted his hand and injected an extra shot into the dangling bag of saline.

As they watched Shaykh Anwar slide into unconsciousness, Nora asked about Khulood. The nurse shook her head. "She's in critical condition."

"Outlook?"

"I couldn't say," the nurse replied. But her eyes said enough.

The four of them sat grimly at their desks, at an impasse, as Schacht stood looking from face to face.

Finally, Nora said, "Look, a price has been paid already for these names. Time is ticking. And I'm not seeing how these women should be considered armed and dangerous." She did not bother to mask the frustration in her tone.

Burton said, "Let's think about that for one moment. Not armed and dangerous. Except, maybe they are the perfect killers."

Nora listened intently, trying not to hate everything that came out of his mouth.

He leaned in, seeming to address her colleagues, in much the way the imam would only talk to Wansbrough. "A woman in full veil binds up her hair, covering it. So she's leaving nothing behind. And she's wearing gloves. No fingerprints. Plenty of immigrant women still know how to slaughter an animal using a simple kitchen knife."

"Motive?" Nora demanded.

"You tell us," Wansbrough countered.

She thought for a moment, trying to settle her brain into this theory. "He said 'they.' *If they can do this just to scare us . . . . . . they can kill us for giving you information.* Or something like that."

Ben offered, "So if it's not one of the gangs we already know and love, then it's a new gang or group."

Nora said, "I don't think it's anything we can understand unless we talk to the women whose names Khulood gave me."

Wansbrough said to the group, "I don't want to keep sending

Nora into a situation alone simply based on her gender. I think we should request that these women report to the Bureau and answer questions."

She could tell that Ben Calder had wanted to say exactly that; his features expressed vigorous assent. "Any interviews have to be done in pairs, and it would be way better to do them here," he said.

Nora shook her head vehemently, directing her protest to Schacht. "Like the imam's wife, these women will never talk freely unless they're in their comfort zones."

"But if the result of talking with the FBI is that their homes are burned, how can you put them in danger by entering their homes?" Burton countered. "Obviously the neighborhood is under close surveillance."

SAC Schacht looked again from face to face, thinking. "How about if you hold the interviews in the mosque?"

Nora considered this, nodding slowly.

He continued. "Is it one of those mosques with a separate women's prayer section?"

Nora recalled the physical layout of the mosque from when they had visited after dawn prayer. Slowly, she nodded.

"Good," he said. "You can interview them in the women's section. And there's no reason why you can't take another female agent with you."

"From outside of the task force?" she demanded. "Seriously?"

But Schacht was nodding. "We can make a temporary appointment. There's strength in numbers. You have no idea what you might encounter. You need a partner for backup, and maybe to record the conversations."

Nora sighed, hating the idea of working with someone new.

Ben said, "Ooh, you could take Libby. That would be fun!"

"I heard that," Libby's voice pierced the divider.

Ben whispered to Schacht, "We need walls . . . "

Schacht ignored him. "And I think it's safe to say from your last experience that you have learned the value of wearing a vest."

"We'll pick the right person together," John said, as though to console Nora.

She sighed, nodding, unable to imagine who that might be.

The Philadelphia field office had fifty-eight women agents. After sifting through their files, Nora and John selected and received Schacht's approval for the inclusion of Special Agent Laurie Cruz on their team. With her dark hair and chestnut-colored skin, Cruz looked slightly more Arab than Nora herself. She was about thirty-five, fighting her weight, and had distinguished herself tracking drug routes from the streets of South Philly deep into Mexico. She had initially trained Calder, helping him become the resident expert on domestic interstate drug trafficking issues. It had been with great reluctance that she had passed him off to Safe Streets.

Nora liked Laurie Cruz, and she knew the feeling was mutual. They had greeted each other amicably enough in the halls before, but now they spoke comfortably on the way to the mosque. Laurie, too, was the only woman on her team. She drove her Buick aggressively, bullying the other cars. Still, even as she was cutting people off and running red lights, Laurie chatted away. As unobtrusively as possible, Nora slipped her hand into what Wansbrough called the "*Oh Jesus!* handle" anchored above the window; she gripped it tightly.

Agent Cruz told Nora about the day that a rookie Ben Calder had been chasing a carrier who held a bag full of heroin; when Ben tackled him, the bag exploded and they both got noses full, making for a very affable Ben. Nora laughed out loud. "No wonder he just shoots the perps now."

"John Wansbrough brags about you, you know. Says you're the fastest feet in the building."

Nora flushed, pleased but flustered. "I—"

"And very modest," Laurie added. "Listen, I don't know as much about the local gang scene as I do about their international suppliers, especially Los Zetas. Mixing in this whole religious and immigrant subculture introduces so many new variables to this puzzle. I'm curious what you expect to find today?"

"I don't know," Nora responded honestly. "We had to work hard to get these names. We didn't send summonses, because we're sure the neighborhood is being watched. I'm hoping to catch some of them after the noon prayer, but it may be hard to get anyone to talk to me. That's if they're even attending prayers—probably recent events have them spooked."

Laurie listened intently. "Sounds explosive. Look, I know it's awkward bringing in someone new. But I think they're right. You need someone to have your back."

"Don't get me wrong, I'm glad you're here, Laurie. I just don't think these women pose a threat, you know?"

"No, but it's not that. It's just that we have partners for a reason. One can sense something the other doesn't, can't . . . Can be aware of responses that the questioning partner can't perceive. It's not a perfect system, but it helps to have someone on your side. And to back you up in court, of course. But you know all that."

Nora sighed. "Well, I guess the other thing is just that . . . I think that at least one or two of these women will be Arab immigrants with a deep, inbred fear of authorities."

Laurie nodded. "I've seen that in Latino populations. The secret police are so brutal and so random down there that they expect the worst up here. And the African American population deals with similar issues in this country with our own police." She glanced at Nora. "No offense."

Nora shrugged. "My cohort at PPD has been made up of some really good people. I know not all cops are. I guess more than anything I'd like to gain trust today and see if it gets us anywhere."

Laurie looked over at her and smiled. "Good luck with that." She paid for her inattention to the road by having to swerve to miss side-swiping a poorly parked car. As they approached the mosque, Nora wrapped a cream-colored scarf around her hair, and handed a light blue one to Laurie. Nora had taken both scarves from a shoe box in her mother's closet, and she refused to dwell on the fact that her mother's scent was still infused in the silky fabric.

Unity Masjid was a revamped twin, with a tiny gravel parking lot behind it that seemed merely symbolic. Undaunted, Laurie Cruz wedged her Buick between two battered compact cars. "Did I do it right?" she asked Nora, pointing at the scarf. Nora tucked in the edge and added a straight pin, careful not to poke Laurie.

"Fabulous," she said, and they got out.

The building was gasping for a new coat of paint, and parts of the roof looked to be worn through. Nora pushed open the door marked SISTERS' ENTRANCE. Her eyes adjusted to the light, and the first thing she saw was a child. The little girl had a crown of excited curls tamed by a Dora the Explorer headband.

Nora and Laurie removed their shoes and added them to the tall shoe rack by the door. Then Nora and Laurie took places on a long bench at the back of the prayer area.

Nora regarded the scene, trying to remember the last time she had prayed in a mosque. She had stopped praying altogether when her mother died.

It was not Friday, and so the noon prayer was sparsely attended. Less than a dozen women stood aligned with precision along the patterns traced in the carpet. Nora inhaled deeply; the bowing and prostrations of the praying women crashed and receded like waves on the shore of her own limbs. But she remained completely still as she watched them.

As the prayer ended, each woman uttered words of peace over her right and left shoulders. It was then that Nora walked over and knelt on the carpet next to the last woman in the row. "*As-salaam alaykum*," she murmured, extending her hand. The woman looked Arab, and Nora hoped that she would return the greeting.

The woman's eyes narrowed slightly, but she gave the appropriate response, reluctantly shaking Nora's hand.

Nora placed her badge in front of the woman on the carpet, and spoke in Arabic. "My name is Nora Khalil and I am investigating a murder. Please, sister, I'm in need of some help. Are you, or do you know, Marwa Abd al-Hamid? Do you know Basheera Johnson or Fatma al-Bakry? A woman called Karima?"

The woman paled and withdrew her hand. Her voice riddled with fear, she hissed in rapid Arabic to the woman next to her, who had begun praying a supererogatory prayer, "It looks like they've sent the intelligence agency—"

The praying woman heard her and, to Nora's surprise, broke off her prayer. She pulled her niqab over her face and started walking swiftly toward the door.

Nora felt panicked; it was her only chance to talk to these women. "Please, sisters—One of your own sisters has been killed. I am working hard to find who did this, and to understand who is terrorizing your neighborhoods. Please help me. Help me help you. I have just a short list of names of women who might have the right information. We're here in the mosque, where no one can see you speaking with me. If I have to get a warrant to speak with you, it will be very public, very open."

The woman who had been making for the door turned to regard her. Her dark eyes glistened with tension.

"Who are you looking for?" she asked, her voice emerging from behind her veil strongly but on edge. Her dialect was as Egyptian as Nora's.

Nora recited the names again, realizing that a few of the African American women were watching the exchange anxiously.

The Egyptian woman said, "I'm Fatma al-Bakry. I won't speak for any of the others."

"Thank you. Thank you so much. I just need a few minutes of your time." Then, Nora looked at the small cluster of black women. She said in English, "Does any of you know Basheera Johnson? Or a woman named Karima? Marwa Abd al-Hamid?"

Two of them exchanged glances. Against a general murmur of discontent, an older woman stepped forward, a gray widow's peak protruding from beneath a satiny black scarf. She looked closely at Nora, "Who are you, sister? Are you even a Muslim?"

Nora noticed that Laurie had risen from her place on the bench just behind the group. Nora displayed her badge. "I'm Officer Nora Khalil of the Safe Streets Violent Gang Task Force, and this is my partner, Laurie Cruz of the FBI." The women turned to look where Nora had gestured. She continued, "We're investigating a murder here in Kingsessing, and the victim was last seen here at this mosque."

Voices erupted in fearful murmuring.

"Who? Who was it?"

"A young woman who taught here, Hafsa al-Tanukhi."

This set off more murmuring, and Nora fought the instinct to question all of the women in the room. But with time weighing on them, she had to focus herself on the leads from Imam Anwar's wife.

"She was killed here, in Kingsessing?" a voice asked from the group.

Nora replied, "Her body was found not far from here."

"My cousin's body was found not far from here," a woman said, pointedly. "No fancy task force came asking around."

Bitter words followed this statement, with more snatches of personal stories. Nora raised her voice slightly over the grumblings. "If you have unsolved issues, please call me and I will do what I can," she said, as she passed business cards to each of the women, looking each one in the eye. "But right now, right here, it's my job to find out what happened to this woman who came and taught among you, and to try to make sure this sort of thing doesn't happen to anyone else here."

Seven women held the cream-colored card with the navy-blue embossed seal, and each one of them studied Nora's name.

The older woman said, "Well, you can imagine that we're a little nervous over here. The imam's house was burned down last night."

"I know, and I've been to the hospital and seen the imam. The task force is working very hard to return a sense of security to this neighborhood."

The woman looked at her incredulously. "And when was there ever a sense of security in *this* neighborhood?" A woman behind her laughed softly. "Listen, I know my Muslim obligation to provide trustworthy witness. I do have Basheera's number, and all of you are my witnesses before Allah, that it's my desire to please Him that's having me tell what I know. I could just as easily walk out the door." The women behind her were nodding. "I've never known Karima's contact information; she only comes every once in a while. But Basheera is usually here every day, doing this or that, helping out—this place is like a home to her. Now she hasn't come to the masjid all week, and won't return our calls. We've been worried about her."

Nora said, "She's not—listen, she's not in any trouble, please understand. I just want to speak with her as part of an investigation of this crime."

The older woman nodded, then pulled out an iPhone. "I guess that's okay. Allah forgive me otherwise." She called up Basheera Johnson's number and showed Nora the screen. Nora hastily scrawled the numbers onto her notepad, then she handed her a card. "Thank you, sister."

The women began exiting in twos and threes, leaving Nora with the two Arab women. Fatma al-Bakry had lifted her niqab again,

revealing her chestnut complexion and high cheekbones. The little girl with the headband clung to Fatma's abaya.

Nora looked at the woman whose hand she had shaken. "Are you,
by chance, Marwa Abd al-Hamid?"

The woman inhaled deeply, trying to steady herself. "I'm Marwa."
Her fear was palpable.

Nora sat down cross-legged on the carpet, and the women seated
themselves next to her. "Thank you for talking to me. I know it must
be scary. But it's much scarier thinking that there's a—" she glanced
at Fatma's little girl "—criminal out on the streets, isn't it?"

Neither woman responded, and the girl began circling the trio,
humming the theme song to "My Little Pony."

Nora swallowed, then looked to Laurie for help, who understood
her look immediately. "Could I—Madame Fatma, would you mind
if my partner entertained your little girl? Just for a few moments?"

Fatma nodded slowly, reluctant. She turned to her daughter. "Can
you sit with the nice lady while I talk to the sister here?" The girl
protested in a soft voice, but her mother insisted, as Laurie sank
down onto the floor. She had pulled out her notebook, and she
started folding paper airplanes, a move that seemed to bridge the
language gap. Nora felt a wave of relief.

"What is it you have to ask us?" Marwa asked. Her dialect was
Palestinian.

"How well did you know Hafsa al-Tanukhi?"

Both women looked reticent. Fatma finally said, "She began coming here about six months ago. She began teaching a class. Some
of us came to it to learn English. Some black sisters came also to
learn to read better. Sometimes she came to the imam's lessons."

"What happened at the last lesson the imam gave you?"

The women exchanged glances.

"He gave the lesson. We listened. We all left. Nothing happened
unusual," said Fatma.

One of Laurie's small paper airplanes sailed into their small circle. Fatma's daughter dashed over to retrieve it, then returned to Laurie.

"Hafsa left without speaking to the imam?"

Both women nodded.

"And you all left at the same time?"

They nodded again.

"Do you understand that this is the last place she was seen alive?"

Fatma said, "This is a tragedy. But it doesn't surprise me about this neighborhood. This neighborhood is hell on Earth. The worst back alley in Boulaq is paradise next to this place, all these blacks killing each other for the drugs and more drugs."

Marwa Abd al-Hamid nodded. "It is worse than anyone can imagine. God curse the day my husband brought us here trying to save a few dollars on the rent, may God take him and free me!"

Nora listened, concentrating hard as she followed the nuances of Marwa's Palestinian dialect. Finally she asked, "Do you have anything else you want to tell me? Anything at all?"

They stared at her with blank expressions, save for the occasional twitch from Marwa's eyelid. Reluctant to end the conversation, Nora handed them each her card. "Please, please call me if you remember anything that can help us find whoever killed Hafsa."

They assured her that they would call. When they didn't move to leave, however, Nora asked if there was something else. Fatma replied, "We will wait for you to leave. We don't want anyone to see us walking out of the mosque with you."

"Why?" asked Nora.

Fatma looked at her as though it were obvious. "Someone burned down the imam's house. Someone is watching."

Nora and Laurie walked gratefully into the cool November sunshine.

"What do you think?" Laurie asked.

"Did you get it?"

"Yes," Laurie said, turning the screen of her phone to display the long voice memo she had recorded as the women spoke.

"Okay, e-mail it to me, will you? I'm gonna compare it with the statement I got from the imam's wife. But I'm pretty sure those women were given a script."

"Meaning?"

"Meaning I heard nearly identical vocabulary used to describe that last lesson with the imam."

Laurie nodded. She tapped the Blackberry's screen a few times and the voice memo whooshed through cyberspace. Then she turned the key in the ignition, carefully backing the Buick out of the cramped space.

"Something bad is going on here," Nora said. "Some kind of creepy cover-up. We need to track down this Basheera Johnson woman right away." She was about to call up the number she had taken from the woman in the mosque, when a bearded face appeared at the passenger side window.

Nora let out a yelp of surprise. "What?" Laurie demanded, slamming on the brakes, her right hand sliding into her jacket for her Glock.

Nora struggled to catch her breath as she looked into the face of Rashid Baker. Cautiously, she lowered the window of the Buick.

"*As-salaam alaykum,*" she said, her heart pounding.

"*Wa alaykum as-salaam,*" he answered.

"You surprised me. Is this your mosque?" she asked.

"Sometimes," he answered slowly. "Are you worshipping here now?" she caught a thread of sarcasm in his tone, and saw his eyes skate over Laurie's hand on her weapon.

"Working," she said simply.

"You've already solved my sister's murder?" he asked, the calm eyes looking steely. "So now you have another case you're pursuing?"

"How is your mother?" Nora asked, ignoring his implications. She knew she could not possibly tell him about their latest case or the possible links with Kylie's murder, or that he was now perhaps himself one of those links. "Did she find any bullets from the drive-by in her home?"

Rashid shook his head. "And your partner?"

"*Al-hamdu lillah*," said Nora. *Thank God.* "He's alive."

"*Al-hamdu lillah*," echoed Rashid. He paused to give in to a deep cough, then said, "We are still waiting, Officer Khalil, to bury my sister. I hope that your time on other business is well-spent. Because, for my mother and me, every day we cannot put my sister to rest is another day of hell."

Nora nodded. "We are working as fast as we can."

He regarded her steadily, and then dropped his gaze. He mumbled the parting words of peace and walked off into the neighborhood.

Laurie exhaled as he walked away. "I didn't see him coming at all," she said, as something of an apology.

Nora said, "Me neither, don't worry . . . "

"Don't worry? If he had had bad intentions, he could have killed us both in an instant. I'm sorry, Nora, I let you down."

Nora grinned at her. "Laurie, you had your hand on your gun before I could even get out a word. I knew you had my back." She thought for a moment. It hadn't occurred to her to try to figure out in what mosque Rashid worshipped. She could have kicked herself. If nothing else, he might have insights into the imam's behavior. Her mind began manufacturing a long list of questions for him, and she had to prevent herself from pursuing him through the streets. But she wanted Wansbrough with her when she approached Rashid, not Laurie, who—though sharp—still didn't have enough background on the case yet.

Laurie pulled onto the street and aimed the car back toward

Center City. With a sigh, Nora gripped her phone and again tried calling Basheera's number.

There was no answer.

Laurie glanced over at her when she heard her exhale in irritation. "Gonna leave a message?"

Nora nodded. "I hope it's the right number." This doubt was dispelled when the voice mail message said, *As-salaam alaykum, you've reached Basheera. Leave me a message and in sha Allah I will call you back.* Nora left her name, title, and number, asking as directly and urgently as possible for the woman to call her immediately.

Laurie asked, "Why do you think those women in the mosque would lie about what they know?"

"No idea. But the imam has something to do with it. He was really scared before we talked to him and his wife. Now—"

"Yeah, well, didn't you get his house burned down?" Laurie asked.

"I did indeed," Nora admitted, regret surging through her. "And now he's not talking at all."

It was then that Nora's cell phone vibrated. She rushed to answer it, but realized it was just a text from John. She looked at it. "Something's up. We need to get back to the office." For Laurie this was an invitation to drive even more recklessly, and she started weaving in and out of traffic, with Nora almost wishing she'd kept her mouth shut.

When they walked back into the office, Wansbrough, Calder, and Burton were deep in conversation. "What'd we miss?" Nora asked.

John's expression was grave. "We've found Kevin Baker."

Kevin Baker's face was a raw and swollen mess.

Nora stared, shocked, at the haggard-looking figure splayed across the hospital bed. She looked at Ben, then whispered, "They really just dumped him on the sidewalk outside the William J. Green?"

He nodded, his eyes still reflecting the astonishment they all felt. "It was like someone was handing us a gift." He, Nora, and Laurie were perched in a row on the wide windowsill, as far from Kevin as they could be and still be in the room.

Nora tried to ignore the radiating warmth where her thigh touched Ben's. She whispered again, "And the security cameras picked up nothing?"

Ben shrugged. "It was a roll-by. Nondescript sedan. Door opens, Kevin's pushed out, car continues down Sixth Street. The best Libby could show us from the camera feed were a couple of baseball caps and some dark glasses."

Wansbrough and Burton entered the room. Wansbrough greeted Kevin's attorney. She was a thin woman named Catherine Zucco, whose carefully coiffed blond hair betrayed the money and time spent on it and did little to distract from the fact that she was at least fifty. It had taken her a very long time to get to the hospital, and the team was worried Kevin would lose consciousness again.

Burton began, "Welcome home, Kevin."

Kevin gazed numbly at him from the one eye he could still open.

"Ms. Zucco, thank you for joining us at last," he said.

She feigned regret. "Held up in court," she said.

"Of course," answered Burton.

"A court at the Racquet Club, maybe," Laurie whispered to Nora.

"At this point, we just need Kevin to give his opinion on some things . . . " Burton was saying.

"His opinion?" Catherine Zucco interrupted. "You are clearly interfering in his medical treatment by insisting on this meeting. He needs pain medication."

Wansbrough responded in measured tones. "He is getting everything he needs. We have some quick questions and we'll be on our way." He did not wait for her assent, but directed himself to

Kevin. "Who did this, Kevin? Who were your attackers? Dewayne's crew?"

Kevin's speech was soft and labored. "I don't know. When they spoke to each other, I couldn't understand them at all."

Nora leaned forward, surprised.

"Los Zetas?" Burton was asking. "Were they speaking Spanish?"

Kevin shook his head with effort. "They'd kill me before they gave me to you."

Both Laurie and Ben were nodding confirmation of that. Laurie murmured, "He can expose their supply lines now to cut a deal. He's like a ticking bomb for their organization."

Wansbrough said, "So you were just taken off the street? You didn't even see the face of the person who grabbed the great Kevin Baker?" The skepticism in his tone was thick.

He answered hoarsely. "We had just gotten to the parking lot. They jumped me and Big G from behind. They put some kind of bags or hoods over our heads. Shot the brother and left him there."

"And then what?"

"Drove for a while, I think back into West Philly. Took me into a house, man, I don't know where. They never took the hood off. And they just . . . "

His voice trailed off.

Catherine Zucco interjected. "That's enough now—You have to let him rest."

But Kevin continued, looking at the ceiling. "They just kept hurting me, man. Real bad. Didn't ask me about shit. Next thing I know I was on the sidewalk in Center City." He fell silent, and his right eyelid fluttered shut.

His lawyer spoke again. "With what is this young man going to be charged?"

Wansbrough and Burton both stared at her. Calmly, Wansbrough cleared his throat before rattling off the list. "Premeditated murder, discharging a firearm at federal officers, attempted murder of a federal officer, interstate trafficking in controlled substances, operating an organized crime ring . . . "

Kevin opened his good eye, registering a frown. "What federal officer? What are you talking about??"

Wansbrough raised his arm from within its sling. "*Me*."

"That's preposterous," Catherine Zucco interjected.

"Your car, Kevin. Your Escalade. Drive-by shooting three days ago right in front of your house."

Kevin searched for words, then said, almost whispering, "My Escalade was *stolen*. Last week."

John Wansbrough glared at him. "Before or after you used it in a drive-by shooting that took out Shane Dillard, a.k.a. Benzo, of the Junior Black Mafia?"

Kevin tried to shake his head. "I didn't have nothin' to do with that!"

"That's not the word on the street," John countered. "Word is, you killed Benzo. And that's why Dewayne Fulton killed your sister."

Kevin grimaced. "I didn't kill Benzo. And I didn't drive the car. It was already missing by then."

"So why would Dewayne kill Kylie?"

"I don't know!" Kevin murmured. "But when I find him—"

"That's enough, Kevin," Catherine Zucco warned.

John cut him off. "There's *already* been another killing. Right in JBM territory, just like Kylie's was right in the middle of yours. What can you tell us about it?"

"I can't tell you what I don't know, man."

"Well who *does* know, Kevin?" Burton interjected.

Kevin swallowed as he tried to form a response. "*I. Don't. Know.*"

John Wansbrough rose and took a measured stroll around the room. He stopped at the foot of the hospital bed.

"Have you ever been to Unity Masjid?"

"You don't have to answer, Kevin," said his attorney.

"What?" Kevin asked softly.

"A Kingsessing mosque. Ever been there?"

Kevin seemed to be trying to process this sudden shift in the questioning. "No."

"Ever heard of it?"

"No."

"Your brother Rashid was spotted there—"

He groaned softly. "I got *nothin'* to do with Rashid."

Burton and Wansbrough exchanged glances.

"Kevin," Catherine said, "You are to say nothing else."

His good eye fell shut again as Catherine Zucco glared at them. "You are going to need to issue a formal set of charges so I can request evidence disclosure. This is all backward. And you better see to it that my client gets the proper care." And with that, she exited the room and headed for the nurse's stand.

As soon as the team had gathered in the hall, Burton said, "That can't be a coincidence. Rashid and that mosque. Something's up."

Nora nodded, glancing down the hall to where Catherine Zucco was still conferring with the duty nurse. Nora ignored the vibration of her phone as she said, "Yes, Laurie and I just saw Rashid at Unity Masjid. It didn't seem out of the ordinary until now."

But John was shaking his head, "If I could find any link to Rashid and the A&As, maybe. But none of the kids we're bringing in even knows him. It's like he just materialized out of nowhere. There's nothing to indicate he has any role at all. And clearly there's some serious issue with Kevin."

"I think we should ask him to come in," Burton said.

John replied, "Bring him in. In the meantime, Nora, you had better call your friends at PD and make sure they located Kevin's fallen bodyguard."

She reached for her phone to call Mike Cook and then realized she'd forgotten about the incoming call she'd received. To her surprise, it had been from Basheera Johnson.

She would not allow Nora to come to her home, but suggested a Lebanese café on Walnut Street called Manakeesh. Nora and Laurie Cruz left the rest of Nora's team awaiting the arrival of Rashid Baker. When the two women entered the café, they found Basheera sitting in subdued silence at one of the small tables. She looked frightened, and her hands shook slightly as she spoke.

"Thank you for calling me back," Nora began. "I know this must be—"

"Please, sister," Basheera interrupted. "You really don't know anything of what I'm feeling about all this, so please don't say you know or don't know anything."

Nora swallowed and glanced at Laurie. "Okay, can you tell us, then? We're here to listen."

Basheera took a deep breath. "I . . . look, the Arab ladies might be able to live with themselves, but I can't. I saw that girl. I saw what happened. That girl . . . she could have been me."

Nora leaned forward. "Do you mean Hafsa?" she asked quietly.

Basheera shook her head, her eyes brimming. "Hafsa . . . Hafsa was my friend."

Nora said, "I know. I'm very sorry."

Basheera looked away. "She was only trying to help that little girl . . . that's how she was. Good, and strong—she could stand up for people who needed it. She wouldn't—couldn't—be quiet when something was clearly wrong." She looked around the café uncomfortably. "Maybe . . ." Nora fastened her eyes on her, trying to assess her unspoken signals. "Maybe we could take a walk?"

Nora hesitated, eager for Basheera to just finish a few sentences. But she rose and followed the woman out onto the street; Laurie kept a few paces behind as Nora spoke. "What little girl are you talking about? Hafsa's brother seemed to think the two of you wanted to talk to the imam that day."

Basheera nodded. "We knew what was happening, right here in the neighborhood under our very noses. We knew they had asked him for protection, and we decided we had to at least talk to him about it, protest his decision."

"I'm lost, Basheera," said Nora. "Who's 'they'?"

"There are things that are happening in Kingsessing . . . well, they are not . . . "

Nora supplied, "Islamic?"

Basheera nodded. "Not Islamic. Not correct . . . " her voice trailed off as she searched for words. When she spoke again, she sounded deeply angry. "There's people moving in that expect community protection when they—they aren't Muslims at all. That's what Hafsa and I were going to talk to the imam about. To tell him what we had found out—he needed to know so he could warn the community and keep us safe—because these people just aren't Muslims."

"In what way?" Nora pressed.

Basheera went on, as though not really hearing Nora. " . . . I think it must be because of the wars there, because of the poverty, they just don't have . . . ethics."

"What do you mean?" asked Nora.

"But then again," she seemed to answer herself, without paying attention to Nora's question, "there were some nice ladies from there comin' to the mosque, not two years ago—nicest ladies you ever saw . . . Good Muslim ladies, loved Allah, loved their neighbors . . . "

Nora couldn't keep from reaching out to grasp Basheera's arm. "Please."

Basheera slowed her pace, then looked at Nora and said, almost in a whisper. "The Somalis."

Nora looked at her. "Explain."

"Look, I'll tell you what you want to know, about that day, about

Hafsa . . . They were speaking in Arabic, so I didn't understand them, but I could tell Hafsa was trying to help before . . . " Her voice trailed off, then she gathered herself again, "You need to know I'm part of a neighborhood, a community, see? People are talkin' . . . about this new gang—people are scared, maybe more scared than they normally would be, because the other crews have always been local, see? Local crews know there's consequences. You can't just cut out somebody's eyes . . . " Basheera noticed Nora's frown. "Yeah, people saw that body. News travels in my neighborhood."

She paused and cast darting gazes about her. She seemed to visibly relax when a cluster of college kids with backpacks swept past them, making their way into Manakeesh. A plump woman in a tightly cinched trench coat and leopard-print leggings pushed a stroller past them going the opposite direction, and Basheera remained silent until the woman was several yards off.

Nora's heart began to race. "Please, Basheera, time is so short. You have to be direct with me."

"They began moving here maybe a month ago. Some were coming over from New Jersey, I heard, but some came straight, running from Somalia, coming into the port on the container ships. They have . . . There are . . . " Basheera twisted her hands together, her knuckles white.

Laurie Cruz noticed the increased tension and gave Nora a look. Nora shook her head slightly, waiting, desperate for some useful information.

Basheera swallowed; her face had gone quite gray. She began to walk again, taking quick, nervous steps. "Girls. They got young girls from Somalia, and they make them do terrible things. Sexual things," she added in a hoarse whisper.

"A prostitution ring?"

"No, no," Basheera said. "These girls ain't whores. They're so young. They don't wanna do these things, but they're drugged, forced. They're *slaves*. I heard . . . I heard that the gang wants to get more into drugs, that they're lookin' for a way to get in on the business, buy their way in usin' what they know about bringin' over girls . . . We had only heard the talk, but that day, the day they took Hafsa, there was a girl . . . "

Suddenly Laurie was shouting—"Down, get down!"

Nora saw him, first as a blur, and then as a swift reality, bearing down on them. She was just reaching for her Glock when his gun went off, a rapid popping sound; Laurie crashed into Basheera, slamming her onto the grass, as Nora was hurtled backward by the force of two bullets against her Kevlar vest. A bullet struck the huge plate-glass window of the café behind them, and the place erupted in screams as the window rained glass onto the tile and polished wooden tables within.

As quickly as he'd appeared, he vanished into the row of parallel-parked cars; it was all over in an instant.

"Basheera!" Nora cried.

Basheera lay limp on the ground, her scarf spread out against the thin stretch of grass. Laurie tore at the abaya, revealing a spreading stain across the woman's chest. Nora looked wildly around for the shooter. She saw a flash of navy-blue hoodie darting around the corner of a tidy twin. "Get an ambulance and backup," she cried, springing up from her crouching position and tearing headlong across the street.

She heard Laurie shouting into her phone, "We've got a shooter, navy hoodie, black ski mask, on foot . . . "

Nora pounded across the lawn, and saw the gate to the backyard still swinging on its hinges. He had scaled the chain-link fence at the far end of the yard. The matrix of twisted wires still shuddered from his touch. He had already dashed deeper into the alley by the time Nora shoved her gun into the holster at her back and began scaling the fence. The pain of the bruised rib made her cry out as she ascended, but the shooter was still in sight when she dropped into the alley.

Sirens and squealing tires signaled that backup was far quicker than she'd expected. *If I can just get him out onto the street,* was all she could think of, *get him out of this alley.* She pulled out her gun again and sprinted down the alley.

He disappeared around the bend; from the sound of the sirens, she calculated they would be racing out onto the street just as the squad cars were passing. She gritted her teeth and mustered up a final burst of speed just as she was rounding the corner.

The roundhouse kick thundered into her abdomen and she almost flipped completely from the impact of it, thudding onto the ground. The shooter leapt on top of her, shoving the gun deep into the soft flesh between her jawbone and neck. His accent was thick, his voice menacing. "Bulletproof vest, eh, cop? It won't help you now, will it?" he hissed. As she peered back at the ski mask, a cold panic gripped her as she realized there was only scarred flesh where one of his eyes should have been.

He pulled the trigger, and was rewarded with the unsatisfying *click* of an empty magazine.

He let out a frustrated moan as the air reverberated with screaming sirens. *Bint al-wiskha!* he shouted, enraged, and then pulled back his fist and slammed it against Nora's jaw. The last thing she heard before falling into blackness was the skittering of gravel as the shooter raced away.

PART **THREE**

CHAPTER 8

There was a rap on the door, and Nora struggled to sit upright. "Come in."

The door opened slightly, and Ben Calder stuck his head in. "Am I allowed in?"

Nora smiled. "I think 'come in' has a general sense. I didn't say, 'come in unless you're Ben.'"

"Okay." He came all the way in, exposing an armful of . . .

"Mint?!"

His green eyes danced. "I figured they might not have the real thing here at the venerable Hospital of the University of Pennsylvania."

Nora laughed. "Ben, I'm impressed."

"You should be. I almost bought basil. The checkout lady at Whole Foods helped me out."

"What are you, some kind of city boy?"

He drew up a chair and sat down next to her bed. "Guilty." He looked for a long while at her face. "I'm really sorry about all this."

"Do I look that bad?" she asked.

"Let's just say I'm less inclined to ask you out today."

"That's too bad. In my weakened condition I might have said 'yes' this time."

"Why, Nora Khalil—are you flirting with me?"

She bit her lip, trying to suppress a smile. "Something about the near-death situation, maybe. I'll get a hold of myself shortly."

He grinned at her. "Please don't." He placed an elbow on the bed's side rail, leaning closer. "Wansbrough told me you wouldn't let him call your family."

"God, no. My dad would lose his mind if he saw me this way. I called him, told him I had to go out of town for a few days. Then I called my brother and told him to keep Baba busy." She tapped her phone where it lay charging on the roller table next to the fat Styrofoam cup of water with the bendy straw. "If my dad calls I can answer and let him know I'm good. But Ahmad actually thinks you and I are . . . together, so I know he'll make a convincing case."

"Does he, now?" asked Ben, looking intrigued.

Nora nodded.

"And why would he think a thing like that?"

She was silent, eyes drifting to the television screen. She finally said, "I—don't get a lot of phone calls. You got noticed."

Ben seemed to want to say something, but he changed course. "Nora, talk to me. Let me get to know you. I came here; I brought mint. What more can I do?"

She sniffed the air thoughtfully. "It does smell good."

"Your . . . hair is down, and it's really . . . " he stretched his hand to pull a long strand away from her face.

Nora struggled to breathe normally.

"So relax a little and . . . tell me something."

"Like what, Ben?" she whispered.

"Tell me you like me."

When her breath came, it was uneven and hot. She opened her mouth as if to speak, and then closed her lips. "Ask me something else," she said softly.

He didn't drop her gaze, but he shook his head slightly. "Okay . . . " his voice trailed off, and he tried to find a neutral topic. "Tell me about running."

Nora blinked, trying to focus, feeling like her heartbeats were audible in the cramped hospital room. "Running?"

He nodded.

"Okay, well, I . . . starting when I was about twelve, I used to get bullied at school."

Ben leaned in, listening.

She took a breath, continuing, "*Sand nigger. Towel head. Osama.* The kids knew all about me because of what happened to my dad."

Ben looked slightly guilty. "Burton told me he had been arrested. Accused of plotting to bomb some buildings. Never charged. But it was pretty public."

Nora nodded. "I wasn't very strong. The one time I decided to stand my ground I got a pretty bad beating."

Ben took a sharp breath, unblinking.

"The *next* time," Nora continued, "I decided to run. And I found out that I was fast. I was *really* fast. I just took off, I dropped my backpack and ran. And from then on that's what I did, even if it was the middle of the day."

Ben was watching her speak, transfixed.

"The teachers were really great, you know, they didn't want to see me get hurt. One day, after this one kid had been on my case, saying a lot of—well, the gym teacher had heard the shouting and was just coming out when she saw me take off. She tried to catch me and she couldn't. I didn't even hear her when she called out my name, because I was just . . . " Nora flattened her hand and slid it across the top of the blanket, " . . . gone. So she came over after school and had a talk with my parents. She said they really needed me on the track team."

Ben's face relaxed into a smile. "I'm sorry that's what it took."

Nora looked down. "It helped me get hired as a cop, I think, the running. And this is what I'm supposed to do."

"Why? I mean, I'm glad, but why?"

"Because, Ben, my mom asked me to take care of my brother," Nora said. And she told him how she had promised to take care of Ahmad and sworn to keep him safe. She told him how Ahmad had cried so long and so hard after his mother's death, that he actually ended up needing glasses. And how Nora had become his mother in every way. All through her high school years and throughout college, she kept Ahmad close, determined that he would never be bullied as she had been. She would read to him, study with him, and cook for him any meals he did not take from the restaurant. She waited for him after school almost every day, and he would ride his bike alongside her as she ran. He had come with the team to track meets, and even traveled with her to the NCAA regionals, bundled into her red sweatshirt and hunkered over a book as he waited for her races. Nora called him her luck charm as her feet flew ever faster. Knowing nothing of biology and chemistry, she held endless flash cards for him as he fought his way into the right high school that would lead to the right college that would get him into medical school.

"And because of what happened to my dad, and because of who we are, I will always be scared that some anonymous tipper can make my brother disappear. But I figured if I'm here, if I'm part of the system, then I won't have to just stand on the sidelines and watch, hoping that the *process* will work itself out."

Ben listened in silence.

Nora continued, "So now you know. I don't have some big noble goal like you—In the end it's just selfish. I want to take care of him the best I can, because I need him so much, because I can't lose him. If I can do some good along the way, well . . . that's good, too." She studied his face. "Do you . . . you know, think less of me?"

Ben leaned closer, "I have never thought more of you, Nora Khalil."

She closed her eyes, feeling the warmth radiating off his skin, inhaling the scent of his aftershave; she wanted more than anything for him to lean even closer and brush his lips against hers.

A rapid knock sounded against the door, and John Wansbrough walked in with a stack of papers, followed by Burton, who held his own stack. Both halted abruptly, taking in Ben's proximity to Nora's bruised face. Wansbrough cleared his throat slightly, then asked, "Nora, how are you?"

She felt a blush enflame her face. "I'm good, fine. Better," she said, feeling slightly confused, fighting for clarity. "Well, come on, guys, gather round. I see you haven't come empty-handed."

"Our version of Arab hospitality," John said. She saw he had brought from her desk the file of photographs of the crime scene that she had compiled. "We can do this later, if you want. I don't want to push you too hard. But we know that time is of the essence here."

She answered him by reaching for the file. "John, I'm fine. It looks way worse than it is." She shifted herself slightly in the bed, spreading some of the pictures out across her blankets.

"A one-eyed Somali with an empty magazine, huh?" John said, leaning over her from the opposite side as Ben in order to investigate the nasty bruise on her cheek. "I had one of those in my third year."

"A one-eyed Somali?" Ben asked, winking at Nora.

"Empty magazine. Gun pressed to my chest. Trigger pulled. Scary as hell," he said, and he patted Nora's shoulder before seating himself in the chair next to her bedside.

Nora winced, remembering the stain on Basheera's chest.

"You okay, Nora?" John asked.

She shook her head slightly. "I—I don't know what I should have done differently, guys."

Ben said, "Nora, you did everything you could. You pursued an assailant across tough terrain—with what turns out to have been a bruised rib from the other day. You got shot—twice, and your face is totally messed up!"

"I got a witness killed. I should have taken her directly into custody."

"*You* are not the problem, here," John said.

Burton offered, "The slugs they pulled out of your vest were .22 caliber."

Nora looked at him blankly.

"They match the bullets that hit John's car."

"And the one that hit John," Ben added.

Nora shook her head. "I'm not following. Kevin Baker was behind the drive-by that got John shot. This wasn't Kevin Baker."

John said, "Kevin Baker's official story is that his car was stolen and used in the drive-by."

"Well, if Kevin didn't kill the JBM kid, and Dewayne didn't kill Kylie, then what's going on?"

Burton nodded at his pile of papers. "This new direction with the Somalis is a good one. While you were with Basheera, Rashid Baker answered the invitation to come in."

"And?" Nora asked, sitting up a little higher in the bed.

John answered, "That whole line about Kevin being a victim of the neighborhood fell through. Rashid admitted he's angry with Kevin because he's involved with the drugs and the sex and the money and yet ignoring his mom's health, not taking care of his own. I guess while Rashid was in jail, they had a hard time, days when they went hungry. Rashid is working part-time in a grocery at Forty-fifth and Walnut, reporting to his probation officer, and trying to stay away from his brother—which is easy because Kevin moved out while Rashid was still locked up."

"And the mosque? What was he doing there?"

Eric Burton answered, "He said that it's an obligation to pray in the closest mosque. When he's nearby, he prays there. When he's not, he doesn't."

Nora was nodding. "Sure, okay. You checked the grocery thing?"

"Yes. And Rita Ross's characterization of Kevin Baker matches what Rashid said about him. So it seems a dead end there—but these Somalis . . . based on what you told us over the phone, I compiled some information on Somali gangs. It's the first time we've found any in Philly, but they've been really active in the Midwest, especially Minnesota, and also in Jersey. The sex trafficking isn't new, either. There was a case in the Twin Cities and Ohio where they were shipping girls across state lines . . . "

"Little girls? Minors?"

"Some as young as thirteen," he confirmed.

Nora shifted in the bed, thinking. "I was up close and personal with this guy. He had a really heavy accent."

"He spoke English to you?" asked Eric.

She nodded. "Yes. But when he swore at me, he swore in Arabic. Sounded kind of like Yemeni Arabic to me."

Burton confirmed, "Arabic is spoken in northern and coastal areas of Somalia. The rest of the country speaks Somali—some Swahili in the south."

"Basheera said Hafsa was trying to help someone."

"You think there's a girl involved?"

"According to Basheera there are multiple girls right here in the city, right now, a group. But it was clear from our conversation that Hafsa had some sort of interaction with one of them. At the mosque."

"And Hafsa's intervention might be what got her killed?"

"Maybe?"

John nodded. "It's as plausible an explanation as any so far."

"And maybe her body was meant as a lesson? To keep the girls from running away?" Nora's stomach was twisting as she leafed through the pictures again. "John, we have to look at these houses more closely—especially the abandoned ones. We have to get inside. What if there's some kind of brothel prison right under our nose?"

John nodded. "Yes. Yes, we'll take another look. But we need to talk about one more thing. You had said something about drugs?"

Nora inhaled, remembering the flash drive and Jane Doe in her hospital bed. She tried unsuccessfully to still the urgency she felt about finding the young girl Hafsa had tried to help. "Yeah, Basheera said the Somalis were aiming to get more into drugs, somehow use the girls to leverage them in or something."

Her three colleagues exchanged glances. "You have to have territory to do that," Ben said.

Burton stood suddenly and began to pace. "Of course. Classic, really. They're playing both groups off against each other. And we've been helping, rounding up all the gangsters from both sides, leaving the playing field open for the new guys."

The other three sat in silence, soaking this in.

Nora felt a chill take hold of her. "All they would have needed was Kevin Baker's Escalade . . . What if—" Nora found herself meeting Eric Burton's gaze, and they both seemed to arrive at the same conclusion simultaneously. "If the Somalis gave us Kevin Baker, it would eliminate a huge chunk of the competition."

"Why didn't they just kill him?" Wansbrough asked.

"So he can lead you to Los Zetas, eliminating them as suppliers as well," Burton answered, a note of respect entering his tone. "If this gang has their own suppliers then they are positioned to take the whole pie."

After they left, she tentatively stood, gripping the bed rails, and found her legs. Slowly, cautiously, she crossed to the small bathroom.

Flicking on the over-bright light, she came to stand at the wide mirror over the sink. She peered at the bruises on her cheeks and jaw. She had never been struck before. She played the whole scene back in her mind, over and over again, until she could hear the *click* of the empty chamber without flinching and recall the way his fist connected with her flesh without recoiling physically. She pulled the hospital gown away from her chest and stared at the marks where the bullets had tried to penetrate the vest—one contusion lay above her right breast, the other nearer her left shoulder. She envisioned the way his finger would have depressed the trigger as he aimed for Basheera, silencing her forever. She constructed his every step, and how the intent to harm them had settled in his mind.

"I'll find you," she whispered into the mirror, tracing the bruises on her cheek with her fingertips. "I will never stop looking until I find you."

As she walked back to the bed, her eyes came to rest on one of the pictures now littering her nightstand. She seized it, then pulled a picture out of the file and studied them both intently. Then she grabbed her BlackBerry. "John," she said urgently as soon as she heard his voice. "Remember when we stopped back at the crime scene—after talking to the hairdresser?"

He replied slowly, "Yes, what?"

"There was an upstairs window in one of the houses that's supposed to be abandoned."

John was silent, waiting for her point.

"In one of my pictures, the window is broken!" Nora's voice was rising excitedly.

John asked drily, "Isn't that typical for an abandoned home?"

Nora waved the other photo in the air, as though he could see it. "When we went the next day it was boarded up. The next day! Someone's in that house!"

It was barely two hours later that the call came. "No one's in the house," John was saying through the phone.

Nora wilted. "Nothing at all?"

"Oh, plenty. But no people. Someone had a home generator up and running. It was hooked up wrong; any longer, and whoever was here could have died of carbon monoxide poisoning. It was also used as a storage facility; dust patterns in the basement show there were a lot of bottles, boxes, that have recently been moved. We have a tech crew trying to pull prints—the place is wiped down, but I'm sure they'll find something. I mean, it's wiped down but these people moved out very, very fast. Someone had to have made a mistake somewhere. Some faucet, some banister. . . ."

Nora was nodding to herself, clinging to this hope, but devastated all the same. She clutched the phone in silence.

John's voice went on. "We have some powder, too, traces on the bed in one room. Ben is thinking probably some form of heroin."

Nora had swung her legs over the side of the hospital bed and was listening intently.

John continued, "I think it was just the sort of prison we were worried about. Four bedrooms, and it looked like the dining room was converted for that use, too, there was a mattress on the floor—same goes for the living room. In each area there were hair and bodily fluid traces. And . . . signs of struggle."

"Don't let them out of there until they find a solid lead, John. We have to find those girls."

"Nora—don't worry. We're close. You just get your rest so you can get back out here."

Everything ached, her *limbs, her soft, secret parts, even her jaw from struggling to keep it closed as he would yank it open to shove in his pills.*

She had begged him to leave her alone, but he kept saying she was his now, his property, to do with as he pleased.

And now that he was done, now that he was satisfied, all she could think of was to slip away, to run away, to get away, anywhere, anywhere. He slept on his right side, his back to her. He was snoring deep, ugly snores, and she moved carefully, slowly, slowly, slowly, not breathing, not making a sound,

no sound,

no sound,

no sound . . .

She dropped her bare feet to the floor, fearing the floor, hating the floor that seemed to be mined with tools and cans and small, creeping bugs. He had constructed a makeshift bedroom in that cold, dark basement. Only the palest filtered light found its way into that tomb. The door to the upper floor seemed beyond reach, for it lay on the other side of the heavy, creaking door; she knew there was someone up there—could hear the footfalls even when her captor was with her below.

If only she could reach that upper floor, but it was far,

so far,

so far . . .

She gathered the abaya from the chair and wrapped it around herself as she took each timid, terrified step, not breathing, not making a sound,

no sound,

no sound,

no sound . . .

Her body ached, how it ached now even more with the effort of walking so carefully, all of her muscles tensed and knotted and coiled in fear. If he hadn't made her swallow the pill she would be steady on her feet, confident that what she saw on the floor was where she saw it. Her pointed toes gingerly explored the freezing cement before taking each step, putting a little weight, just a little, and then more, a little more, and then stepping and feeling out the next step, and the next,

careful . . .

careful . . .

But with nothing to hold onto, she could not keep her body from swaying. A false step sent an aluminum container skittering across the floor, and in an instant he had turned, and seen her, and he was on her in two strides, his arm encircling her and slinging her across *the room, back onto the bed, sweat-stained, as he cursed her in a furious but hushed tone, cursed the plotting of women, cursed and cursed as he pinned her, forcing open her already-bruised thighs and plunging into her again and again; one rough hand clamped against her lips, as the floorboards creaked overhead.*

CHAPTER **9**

Nora awoke, startled to find Ahmad staring down at her.

"What is that on your face?"

She put her hand to her cheek, squinting against the light of the desk lamp he'd turned on. "What time is it?" she asked, her voice low to match his.

"Three o'clock. I saw your shoes on the rack, so I knew you were home. I was expecting to find you with a hickey or something, not bruises—"

Forty-eight hours in the hospital had been more than Nora could handle. When her doctor had made his rounds on the second night, she badgered him until she and her internal and external contusions ended up with a prescription for plump ibuprofen and her release papers. Now she sat up, adjusting the pillows behind her, eyes narrowed. "What do you know about hickeys, boy?"

"Enough to know I'd prefer you have one to what you've got there. Tell me Special Agent Colleague didn't do that to you," he said. His brown eyes were wide and filled with concern.

She smiled. "Special Agent Colleague didn't do that to me."

"Then what, Nora? Were you even with him?"

"His name is Ben, Ahmad. And no, I wasn't with Ben. I was in the hospital."

Ahmad clapped his palm to his forehead, his eyes wide, but Nora raised a hand. "It's okay, *habibi*. Really it is."

"Can you talk about it with me?"

She wanted to more than anything else in the world. She missed talking to Ahmad. It used to be that she told him everything—well, almost everything. He had known more gossip about her four by 400-meter relay team than the team itself. But something had changed. There was too much, now. Where could she start? The details about Hafsa's death? The drive-by and her bruised rib? The leads that brought them to Basheera and her story about the Somalis? Could she really tell him about the exploding window at Manakeesh and Basheera lying dead on Walnut Street? Or how she'd pursued the man on foot, and the sound of that trigger clicking—? She realized with a pang that she really wasn't a rookie anymore. Too much had happened. And she could no longer take her work stories to her little brother for processing. She needed a friend.

She needed Ben.

Nora shrugged. "You know what, *habibi*? It's not a very good story. We were training up in Bucks County, and they were trying to toughen us up. I was riding a zip line, and didn't get out of the way of a tree. It was so humiliating!"

Ahmad stared at her. "Seriously? You want me to believe that you were that stupid?"

She smiled, for the first time grateful that Ahmad avoided looking at anything resembling news on the Internet. "That's my story and I'm sticking to it."

Her brother frowned. "I think you're not telling me so you don't worry me."

He'd seen right through her. He always did. "Well, if that were the case, then I guess you'd have to realize I am an *awesome* sister."

He shook his head, and reached out a hand to gently touch her swollen cheek. "I don't know what I'd do without you, Nora," he said.

"Look at me, *ya Ahmad*. If you end up having to find that out, I will have failed you altogether, okay?" she said, leaning forward to kiss the top of his head.

He stood to leave, and then Nora remembered she needed to talk to him about Baba.

"Hammudi, there's one more thing."

"What is it?" he asked.

"I'm thinking about moving out. How would you feel about that?"

He sat down again on the edge of her bed. "What happened?"

She swallowed, choosing her words carefully. "Baba is . . . Well, I don't want to live under Baba's rule anymore. And I think it's time for me to go."

"What about Baba?"

"Well, he and I just . . . " She groped for words in the dimness that would express how much she loved her father and how badly he had let her down.

He leaned down, searching her face. "You know, don't you?"

She frowned, alarmed. "What are you talking about?"

"You tell me, then I'll tell you."

"No, you first," she insisted, her heart thumping in her chest.

"About Baba and the woman, the dentist or something."

Nora shifted onto her knees, her breath becoming shallow. "How do you know about this?" she demanded.

Ahmad was laughing. "I've always known. I caught him on the phone with her in the basement of the restaurant—I heard stuff that made me wanna puke. It's like my earliest, clearest memory of Baba."

"And you didn't tell me?" Nora was furious.

"I didn't want to upset you, *ya Nora, wallahi*. And then Mama got sick, and then when she died, it was like, well, there's no point in bringing it up now . . . "

Nora shook her head. "I've been going crazy since I found out, not wanting to tell you, but wanting to tell you, and being so angry with Baba that I just didn't know what to do! And you knew all along! That must have been killing you." She threw her arms around him. "What a terrible thing to have to deal with all alone . . ."

But he was disentangling himself from her arms and wiping at her tears. "Nora, it was okay, I swear. Easy, easy . . . come on. It's okay. Plus, you know, I was storing up. I figured I'd play that card one day and at least get a decent car out of it. Maybe a Nissan Xterra, right? But now that you know all about it, I've got no more leverage." He shook his head in disgust, then added, "Way to mess up my life, Nora."

She hit him, hard. "*I'll* buy you a car, *in sha Allah*. Just get that scholarship. Now go to sleep, it's late."

Now it was Ahmad who kissed her on the head. "And you don't move too far away. I gotta be able to get to you to protect you from trees."

Ragab sat smoking and reading his paper, his chef's jacket hanging open to expose a plaid button-down shirt.

Nora knew she wasn't ready to have this conversation. But she also knew that she was sick of carrying it around with her. Besides, Ahmad had given her an idea.

"*Sabah al-khayr, ya Baba.*" Good morning . . .

"*Sabah al-nuur, habibti. Hamdellah ala-l-salama!*" Thank God you're home safely. He stubbed out his cigarette quickly. "You look thin, *habibti*. Let me make you a foule sandwich. Maybe some helawa?"

Nora shook her head. "Not right now. Baba, I want to talk to you."

"*Khayr, habibti*, what is it?" Then he saw her face. "Nora! What happened?" He reached across the table, trying to touch her, but she pulled away. "Do you—Do you need some ice? Did you fall?"

She nodded. "I ran into a tree while at the training retreat . . ." she said slowly.

Ragab was shaking his head, peering across the table at her cheek.

"I don't think this task force job is right for you, *ya Noora*. This traveling now, and now you are getting hurt. How can you make 'safe streets' if you yourself aren't safe? It just isn't right."

She worked her still-aching jaw back and forth, regarding him with irritation. "So . . . I should quit?"

"Or you should make sure that they put you just in the computers, you know?"

"This is my job. I like it. I won't change one thing about it."

He tilted his head, trying to figure out what was behind the sharp tone in her voice.

Nora ran a finger along the dinner fork at the place where she was sitting. She rested her finger on the tines. Her father regarded her, found her looking very serious, and closed his newspaper. "Is this because you are still angry that I talked to you about the doctor from Dallas and the young man you were riding with?"

"Yes, I'm still angry, but no, it's not about all that."

He continued, as though he hadn't heard her at all, "Because it's not wrong for me to want to protect you. You have to take the possible bridegrooms in your future into consideration . . . "

"Baba," her voice was sharp.

"*Eih, ya Noora*—what's wrong?"

She regarded him steadily, tapping the fork she was holding against the table as she spoke. "We won't be talking about bridegrooms anymore."

Ragab stared at her, the seriousness in her voice setting him on edge.

She continued, "I found something out at work. Something about . . . about what happened to you."

He swallowed, and she watched his features grow increasingly concerned. "What? What did you find?"

"There was a woman. You—"

He held up a hand. "*Bas, ya Noora*, let's not talk about this."

"We will talk about it. Right now. Mama, Ahmad, and I, *we* were the victims, then. Not you. You brought what happened on your-self."

His face looked at turns both angry and pain-stricken. Finally he rubbed his open palms across his face, saying, "All of this is— Who will benefit from talking about this *now*?" She knew he was really asking her if she was going to tell Ahmad.

"You and Ahmad will have to talk about this one day. But, for now, I need you to know that I know. And you have *nothing* to say to me anymore about men or marriage . . . It's all been nothing but lies and hypocrisy."

"What do you mean, what do you mean I have nothing to say?" he demanded, suddenly on high alert. "I am still your father!"

"You weren't my father when you went to that woman's apart-ment. You weren't my father when you cheated on my mother."

"That had nothing to do with you!" he sputtered.

"That had *everything* to do with me. You broke *all* the rules, *all* of them."

"I am different. I am a man—"

"Yes, you are different. Different than what I thought. And your rules don't apply to me anymore."

"Nora, these are not just my rules—this is our religion . . . "

"Not the way I understand it. And I matter. *My opinion matters.*"

He was shaking his head, not looking at her, tsk-tsking.

She stared at him fiercely. "There's something else . . . I'm mov-ing out. I'm getting my own place."

"*What?* What are you talking about?" He stood up, unable to contain himself any longer, gesturing with his hands. "How are these things even related?"

"My mother didn't leave you. For me, for my sake. Now I'm leav-ing you. For her . . . *And* for me." She stood up, then headed for the door. She felt his shocked eyes following her as he struggled to find the right response. Finally, uncharacteristically, he fell silent.

When she reached the sidewalk, she stopped to relace her shoes. Two days in recovery would have to be plenty. Carefully, she shouldered her drawstring backpack and broke into a slow jog that seemed to make her whole body groan in protest.

As she tucked the earbuds into her ears, she realized that at no time in their conversation had her father tried to apologize.

The 12th District of the Philadelphia Police Department was housed in a squat, nondescript structure located at 65th and Woodland Streets. The building was utterly unremarkable save for the bold mural painted onto the tan bricks. As she descended from the creaking trolley, Nora paused a moment, staring at the massive blue angels, their wings sheltering the city. She took a deep breath, then entered.

Mike Cook had been swiveling in his desk chair, and he sprang to his feet as soon as he saw her. He came to stand in front of her, wordlessly studying her with a frown.

"It looks worse than it actually is," she said, reassuring him.

He tilted his head, thinking, then said, "I'm not sure this gig with the feds is all it's cracked up to be."

"You know, you're the second person to tell me that just this morning," she confessed.

"I heard about it. I'm sorry I wasn't on duty when that call came in."

Nora shrugged. "Thanks, Mike."

"One more good story for the bar. Or in your case, the tea house." He led her to his desk. "You're here about Kevin Baker's bodyguard, right?"

"Yeah," she said. She carefully picked up the pile of files that occupied the rickety folding chair. Mike reached for them and added them to another pile on the corner of his desk as Nora sank into the chair. She was happy to be sitting. Everything ached.

Mike thought for a moment, then said, "There's not too much to tell on this."

"Any forensics yet?"

Cook chuckled. "This murder was night before last. Don't get confused about the address here now. On this side of the Schuylkill things take some time."

Nora smiled. "You got an estimate?"

He rolled his gray eyes, then said, simply, "No."

"Can I see the report?"

Mike rearranged still more file folders before handing her a slim one. "I can give you the summary, though."

Nora glanced up, then back at the file. "Listening," she said as she skimmed through it.

"Bullet to the back of the head. Execution. The hooded body was found in the parking lot not far from the Kingsessing Recreation Center."

"Hole look .22 caliber to you? We're having a special this week."

Mike Cook sighed. "I try not to look."

"Can you send him to Monty?"

Mike shrugged. "I'll see what I can do."

Nora traced her finger along the dense text on the page for a while in silence. When her finger reached the bottom edge of the page she looked up. "Where are his things?"

"Sorry?"

"His stuff. What he was wearing."

"What are you after?" Mike asked.

"The hood. They put one on Kevin Baker too. I guess it'd be the one thing they left behind, right?"

Mike blinked, then abruptly rose. He gestured for her to follow him, then stopped and regarded her with renewed interest. "I guess when the feds aren't letting you get mauled, they must be teaching you a few solid tricks."

Nora grinned. "One or two."

When her phone rang, she had just handed Monty Watt what looked like a coarse burlap sack, so bloodstained that only a few portions of it still appeared tan. Monty promised to examine it and figure out what it had contained before it had covered the head of Big G, whose actual name Nora realized that she did not know. John Wansbrough got to the point. "Nora, we've been trying to find you, where are you?"

"John, I found something important at the twelfth District . . . "

"Well, it's going to have to wait. You have a visitor."

She frowned into the BlackBerry. "Me? Personally?"

"Yes, well, it took her a while to explain who she needed. But we were pretty sure where it was all going as soon as she walked in."

Nora rode the elevator to the eighth floor, then followed John to the interview room and peered through the glass. There was a figure in full niqab swiveling back and forth nervously in the roller chair. "I assume she had to give a name to get in here?"

John checked the stub from her visitor's pass. "Fatma al-Bakry."

Nora nodded slowly, summoning her energies, hoping for a break. She pulled her notebook from her backpack and handed the pack to John, then smoothed her button-down shirt. "You'll need to tape it, of course. She doesn't speak English."

John said, "Already set up."

"Madame Fatma?" Nora asked, entering the room.

The veiled woman looked up.

"*As-salaam alaykum*," Nora said, pulling the other chair around to join Fatma al-Bakry on her side of the table.

"*Wa alaykum as-salaam*," came the response, and Nora recognized the Egyptian woman's voice, remembered her as one of the women who had initially gone to Hafsa's classes to learn some English.

"What can I get you to drink?" Nora asked in Arabic. "Tea? Tea with milk?"

But Fatma al-Bakry was shaking her head vigorously. "No, no, nothing."

Nora tried to insist, falling into the prescribed patter of hospitality, but the visitor would not be persuaded. "I'm so glad you came to see me, Madame Fatma," Nora said finally. "I know how difficult it must be—it took great courage for you to come here."

"I wish I didn't have to," came the answer. "But I . . . they buried Basheera yesterday. All of the women were too frightened to attend the funeral service. It was . . . it was my husband, actually, who insisted I come, he—we rode the bus here together. Because giving false witness is a deadly sin, he reminded me. And because I am the mother of a little girl."

Nora looked deeply into the woman's wide brown eyes. They were red-rimmed, the lids swollen. "Please, Madame Fatma. Can you—will you uncover your face?"

"There are—I know there are cameras . . . "

Nora related the knowledge she'd gleaned from her mother about the face veil and witnessing.

Fatma al-Bakry was silent for a moment. "You sound like Hafsa, may God have mercy on her."

"I think we would have been good friends," Nora said earnestly, holding Fatma's gaze.

The woman extended two small, gloved hands and pulled back the long strip of cloth, letting it rest atop her head to expose her caramel skin. Her nose was slightly pink. It looked as though she'd been crying for the better part of the week.

"Thank you," Nora said sincerely. "Can you please talk to me about what happened on the last day that Hafsa came to the mosque?"

Fatma nodded. "We were sitting with Hafsa in the women's section, reading Qur'an together, waiting for the imam to begin the lesson, when the door swung open, and this skinny girl came in, dressed so . . . inappropriately—"

"How?" Nora asked, perfectly able to guess what that meant.

"Just a thin slip, so see-through it showed her skin. She was very black. We all just stared at her for the longest time, not knowing really what to do." Fatma stopped for a moment, remembering. "She crossed over to us, stumbling a little, and then she just sank down, just laid down with her head on the carpet."

"And then?"

"Hafsa went to her, talked to her. She spoke to her in English, nothing—she knew nothing. The girl was black, but Somali—she could speak Arabic, not very well, but enough . . . "

"What did she want?"

Fatma looked at the ground. "She was running away. I guess she saw the mosque and thought—She thought that she would be safe there. She said her name was Rahma. She had . . . she had gotten away from a man."

"A man who was hurting her?"

She nodded. "Who was . . . having sex with her. For money. She was . . . she was part of a group. Not like a prostitute, more like . . . " Fatma's voice trailed off, and she kneaded her hands in frustration.

"A slave?" Nora suggested.

"Yes, yes. More like a slave. There was a group, a gang, that kept them all in a house. And used them, let men visit them, and then kept the money."

"All? How many?"

She trembled, "She said six. Her and five others. She said she was the oldest." Tears collected in her eyes, threatening to spill over. "And then, even as the girl was still talking to Hafsa, two men—" Fatma al-Bakry shook her head, then took a deep breath, trying to master the shaking of her voice. "We heard the squeal of brakes and doors slamming, like a car had been driven right up to the entrance of the women's section. Then two men burst in—right into the women's prayer area, no shame, nothing. They had . . . they had guns. They had come for the girl and they wanted her back."

Fatma continued, her voice low. "The girl was weeping, begging, hiding behind Hafsa, clinging to her, and Hafsa was determined not to give her up. We—the rest of us women were terrified, cowering, but the men told us that no one was to move—their Arabic was harsh, ugly, but we understood. Even the black women understood what they wanted, all it took was for them to wave their guns."

Now the Egyptian woman gave up and began to sob, tears careening down her face. "Only Hafsa stood up for the girl, talked back to those men. She started to call the police on her cell phone, and one man—the tall one, the one with the sunglasses—he was on her right away. He bent her arm backward, and took the phone and crushed it with his boot, but then she swung at him with her other arm and hit him in the face." Fatma shivered. "That is when things got very, very bad . . . "

"What, Fatma? What happened next?" Nora felt her own heart thumping, and her breathing was hard coming.

"So many, many things happened at once." Fatma mopped at her eyes with the edge of her scarf. "The imam, he heard the shouting, and he ran in, and one man caught him and held him. The imam was yelling at them that it was a mosque, that there could be no guns, no violence there. That they had to leave right away. And then he saw the one with the sunglasses, and he got very scared. And that man started talking to the imam, very fast, very serious, telling him that he had already threatened him, and that he knew what he could do to him and his wife if he defied their gang."

"Already threatened him? So the imam knew what was going on?" choked Nora, furious.

"I only know that the imam was very scared, terrified . . . in a way that surprised us all. And although he begged them to stop what they were doing, he . . . did not attack them, did not threaten to call the police, did not do anything. And the one man said to him, *I guess you will know how to control this lot*—and he gestured to us. *No one here saw anything. Nothing happened here*, the man said. And then the imam just watched as the men took both of them."

"Took them?"

"The one holding Hafsa yanked her scarf off her head and tied it in her mouth as a gag. He held her by her hair, and was telling her that she would learn what it means to strike one of them. She would learn some respect. And the girl, the little girl . . . the other man told her . . . he told her . . . "

Fatma looked as though she would collapse, and for a moment she held her face in her hands. Then she looked up at Nora, her face filled with self-loathing. *"He said that if the man they'd sold her to wasn't still waiting, he would make her watch as he killed her 'protector'."*

Nora stared at her, unable to move or speak.

"When they had gone, the imam came to us, and he told us what to say if someone came, rehearsed it with us, drilled us on it, made us swear never to tell any version but that one. He told us that these men had guns, that they had threatened him and his wife—that he lived in terror. They knew where he lived and every move he made. That they had settled in the area and would not be leaving—and that the best thing to do would be for us to help them and live in peace, or to leave, to find somewhere else to live, because they were trained killers."

Fatma sighed, brushing away her tears with her gloved fingers. "These men are demons. But our fear has made us demons, too, may God forgive us."

CHAPTER **10**

"You gonna handle it?" Nora was asking again.

John Wansbrough nodded. "I already said I can handle it."

"Because you know how upset I am right now."

John glared at her, then waited for an elderly couple to exit the elevator on the hospital's fourth floor. When they were alone, he said, "I'm sure that you will be handling yourself with utmost professionalism. Use your Arabic, but don't threaten him with crazy stuff that no one's gonna be followin' through on."

Nora couldn't keep from smiling. "You've figured out my MO, Agent Wansbrough. It only took six months, too."

They exited the elevator at floor six, and walked side by side down the long corridor with its overpolished floors. "Speaking of figuring you out, how are things with your dad?"

"I told him this morning I was moving out."

That stopped John in his tracks. "Seriously?"

She nodded, continuing on toward Anwar al-Islahi's room. "Yep."

John followed after her. "He angry?"

"Well, of course he's angry. But also confused, because he's embarrassed. And I'm the victim here—me and Ahmad, not him. So I think he's still sorting through how to handle it."

John said, "Will you be okay?"

"Of course, Agent Wansbrough. *I* have a gun!" She rapped on the door to room 407, then pushed it open without awaiting an answer.

The shaykh was lying on his back, the IV hooked up to an arm that was otherwise entirely bandaged. He turned his head to see who had entered, then turned it away again.

"*As-salaam alaykum*," Nora said pleasantly.

"*Wa alaykum as-salaam*," the shaykh answered automatically.

"We were wondering if you would like to revise your story about Hafsa al-Tanukhi," Nora said.

"Why?" he asked, immediately on guard. "What has happened?"

Nora opened her mouth and then closed it again, as John stepped forward. To handle it. As they had agreed, he spoke about the women's statements: "After listening to the statements of the women at Unity Masjid, their similarity on certain points gives us reason to believe they were scripted, and we believe that you are the one who scripted them." As the imam made to protest, John continued. "We have received testimony that you knew exactly what happened to Hafsa al-Tanukhi on the day she disappeared, and that you knew exactly who took her away, and that you knew about the sex and drug trafficking activities of a certain group of natives of Somalia."

The shaykh was already pale, but now he blanched. At last he said, "What do you want from me?"

"Information," John said. "Aiding and abetting criminals is a crime in this country. You said you hadn't come here to die, but you should know that we can see to it that you go to prison for a long, long time for attempting to cover up a crime, for perpetrating a conspiracy, and, of course, let's not forget *lying to federal investigators.*"

"I'm a dead man anyway if they find out I've talked to you."

Nora felt her nostrils flare in anger. John gave her another look that said, *Give me a chance first.*

"Imam Anwar. Who took Hafsa al-Tanukhi?"

He swallowed, then turned his face to stare out of the gray window. His silence was prolonged, and John was about to repeat his question, when the imam began to speak.

"His name is Asad. Despite his injury, he couldn't get refugee status because of a criminal record in Somalia. He eventually got himself smuggled in on a container ship. He lived for a while somewhere else, not Philadelphia, I think with some cousins, some friends. He came to the mosque three weeks ago. He came to my office after the last prayer to speak with me in private—it was just as I was about to lock up the mosque for the night. He was very tall. Wearing sunglasses . . . dark lenses, dark rims, even though it was night. He said he was a businessman new to the area. He said he wanted to make some connections that could help his business grow."

"What did you say to that?" John asked.

"What anyone would say. It's a tough time in the whole country. But that I wished him well and welcomed him to the mosque."

"And then what?"

"Well, he laughed. He said he wondered what America would do if it really saw a tough time; he said he had seen tough times and he knew how to survive them. And then he was more specific. He said he wanted to get into a particular business. And that he had collateral. He had contacted some business leaders in his field and was finding their cooperation to be—minimal. So he was pursuing other avenues."

Nora could be silent no more. "What business? What collateral?"

Imam Anwar kept his gaze focused on John Wansbrough. "He wanted to know what I knew about some of the worshippers at the masjid maybe being involved in drugs. He knew it was a rough part of town, and that even the Muslims were sometimes involved in . . . illegal activities."

"Do you know of people in your mosque who are involved in the drug trade?"

The imam nodded. "Of course. Many of the young men come to Islam in prison. Their intentions are good, but sometimes the roots of their previous lives cannot be pulled out. I encourage them to stop, but there's only so much one voice can do. And life in our neighborhood is not easy . . . "

"What was this Asad's angle exactly?" John wondered aloud.

The imam gave a mirthless smile. "He said that the most lucrative business in this country was selling drugs, and that he would only sell them to the *kuffar*. Because they would then destroy themselves. This is how he asked for my aid."

"*Kuffar?*" John asked, glancing at Nora.

"Non-Muslims," Nora said, feeling nauseous.

"He said that everything is war, every day, and that the fools who can't fight every front—even in the smallest way—are the ones who will die. And he called me a fool."

The agents looked at each other, wondering how far the Somali was willing to take his warfare.

"What was this collateral he talked about?" John asked.

"Girls," the imam answered. "He was trading in young girls, sluts, he said, from situations so desperate they would do anything for pennies. And he knew how to get many, many more."

John leaned forward, his eyes flashing. "So what did you tell him?"

"I tried to throw him out, of course."

John surmised, "But he wouldn't be thrown out?"

The shaykh shook his head.

Nora asked softly, "What did he threaten you with?"

"Everything. He told me what he would do to me, to my family. My honor. My future children. I told him . . . I told him I feared only Allah."

Nora realized that tears were streaking his cheeks.

"Asad said that was unfortunate. He said that at home, in the war, he had learned for certain that there was no God. And then he pulled off the sunglasses and showed me that one of his eyes had been dug out. He said he feared nothing and no one. And so, he said, I should fear *him* much, much more than I feared Allah," the imam said, unable to hold back a sob.

Nora looked from him to John and back again, as John said, "Did he assault you? Physically?"

The man's voice was faint. "In a way that . . . he knew that I could never bear to tell. Could never bear to explain."

Both Nora and John were staring at the shaykh in stunned silence.

"And so, I gave him a name."

The door crashed open as the agents streamed in, guns at the ready.

Lenora Baker struggled to pull herself to a standing position, as she sputtered, "What the hell—" just barely louder than the television. Agent Jacobs crossed to her and began escorting her out of the house, reading her her rights. Little by little her voice escalated, the disbelief compounding until she began to shriek, "Rashid, Rashid!"

By then, however, Nora and John were racing down the stairs into the dank basement, with Ben and Laurie on their heels. Burton had drawn backyard duty with Agent Lin.

Ben Calder stopped short at the bottom of the stairs. "Oh my God. Nobody shoot anything. We'll all go up in a ball of flame," he said, staring at the giant bottles of acetone and phosphine. "It's an entire meth lab, right here in the basement."

They were all scanning the musty basement for Rashid. Lin and Jacobs had been staking out the house after the imam's tip, and had been certain that Rashid was there. But the basement was a labyrinth of equipment and makeshift work surfaces, jugs and glass bottles. Small, grubby windows let in a choked light, and Nora's eyes fought to adjust to the dimness. The floor was hopelessly littered with tools and trash.

"Coal cellar!" John murmured, nodding behind them, and they followed him deeper into the dark, fanning out. The coal cellar was in the northern corner of the basement, and Calder approached the heavy door slowly, but then suddenly shoved it open. It swung open with a loud groan. Nora crossed to it, and her gaze fell on a makeshift bedroom with a filthy mattress, a metal desk and a folding chair. A single lightbulb in a lamp with no shade cast a dull light; it was rigged with an extension cord from the main area of the basement.

In the center of the coal cellar, a thin girl shivered, eyes wide, wrists bound, a dirty bandanna tied around her mouth. She wore a gray, stained camisole. The room reeked of sweat and urine. Nora nearly rushed in, but John held up a hand, determined to make certain that no alternate exit or entrance existed for the tiny room. He had just stepped inside when they heard a voice.

"Y'all find what you lookin' for?"

All four agents froze. Rashid Baker's voice was coming from very near the stairs they had descended. He emerged from behind a set of shelves that were laden with fat jars of chemicals.

Laurie Cruz was closest, and she raised her gun automatically, training it on Rashid.

"Whatcha gonna do with *that*?" Rashid asked, laughing softly.

"I'm a very good shot," Laurie said fiercely.

"You would need to be. Go ahead."

Calder said firmly, "Come out of there with your hands up. It's over, Rashid."

Rashid laughed again. "That would be too easy, wouldn't it?"

"Come on, Rashid," said Nora. "You know this isn't how it should be. "

He looked at her, and she could see the loathing even from the distance between them. "You're right. It's not how it should be at all." In a flash, he pulled out a gun, and shot the bottle nearest to him.

CHAPTER 11

The first thing that Nora saw was Laurie thrown backward against the stairs from the force of the explosion. Then Rashid Baker's body arced up into the air, only to be caught and tossed back and forth by the string of explosions that ensued. Nora felt strong hands grab her collar, dragging her over the threshold of the coal cellar, and the slam of the coal cellar door as John and Ben threw themselves against it.

"Cover your face, cover your face!" Ben was shouting, but the poison in the air had already begun penetrating the tiny room.

"Laurie," Nora cried, trying to pull Ben out of the way.

"There's nothing you can do for her now!"

Chest heaving, Nora tried to force her brain to function. Her eyes fell on the girl, and she scrambled to the mattress and tugged the girl's bandanna up and over her nose, then yanked off the ties that bound her wrists.

The heat in the room was unbearable, and Nora began to feel dizzy. She yanked off her jacket and was tying it around her own head as Wansbrough began to yell, "Find the coal chute!"

Nora was the first to spy it—"There, John!" She pointed to the small trapdoor in the ceiling that once had received wheelbarrows full of coal, poured in from the backyard.

Calder shoved the huge desk under the trapdoor. John was the tallest, but he couldn't reach the trapdoor. He jumped, stretching, to no avail. They all scanned the room for an object to shove upward, but found nothing at all.

"Lift Nora!" Ben croaked out; he was gasping for air as his eyes watered from the powerful gasses. The sound of sirens penetrated their prison from outside.

Eyes streaming, Nora scrambled up onto the desk and into John's powerful arms. He held her aloft, and her fingertips just brushed the rusty trapdoor. "Stand on my shoulders," he coughed.

As he held tightly to her legs, Nora thrust herself upward, pounding against the door. Rust cascaded into her eyes, but she kept pushing and pushing. "John," gasped Nora—"Squat down and thrust yourself up—I can't get enough force—"

"Hold on," and she felt her partner lower himself slightly, and then, with a loud grunt, he pushed up hard with his legs. Nora put every ounce of force she had into her open palms, and was relieved to feel the trapdoor fly open, ushering in a shaft of cool air. She began screaming with all the sound she could muster, and had never imagined she could be so happy to see Eric Burton's face.

Burton immediately flopped onto his stomach and extended her his arm—

"The girl—" Nora gasped, looking down into the cellar.

"Just *go*!" Wansbrough choked out. "I'll lift her up next!"

Nora scrambled through the trapdoor, and up onto the cool, wet grass of the Bakers' backyard, gasping for air. An emergency worker appeared almost immediately, handing her a gas mask, then forcing one onto Burton's face even as he remained on his stomach attempting to catch the thin girl's wrists.

"We need a ladder!" Nora screamed, and was stumbling across the yard in search of one when she finally passed out.

She awakened in the back of an ambulance some distance from the Bakers' house.

The girl, Rahma, was next to her, unconscious on a stretcher, a fat oxygen mask strapped to her face. Nora tugged at her own mask, and the EMT worker tending them held up his hand. "Hold on, there, ma'am."

Nora shook her head. "My team—where's my team?"

"Next ambulance over. They're gonna be fine."

Nora was just struggling, trying to rise from her own stretcher, when Ben Calder appeared at the ambulance's open door. He had a portable oxygen tank, with a tube hooked up to his nose.

Nora gazed at him, her eyes brimming. "Laurie?"

He shook his head. "They're still putting out the flames. They won't be able to bring her out for a while yet."

Hot tears streaked Nora's face as she looked beyond him to the still-blazing fire. "John's okay?"

Ben nodded. "Bleeding a lot after using a wounded arm to push you through a ceiling. But okay."

Burton appeared at Ben's side. "Hey, Nora," he said, his face concerned.

"Eric," she said, holding his gaze. "Thanks, man."

He shook his head. "That was a close one. I'm glad you guys made it out okay."

"I'm glad you were there," she said. She let her gaze fall on the little girl at her side. But then a dark realization crept across her still-reeling brain. "With Rashid dead, how are we going to find the Somalis?"

CHAPTER 12

They were all struggling with respiratory problems, but all refused to be admitted to the hospital. For Nora, it was the loss of Laurie Cruz that made it hardest to breathe. She walked slowly to work the next morning, the downtown streets blurry as she blinked back tears. Armies of strangers brushed by her as Nora fought the urge to sit down on the curb and walk no further. Laurie's body crashing against the stairs replayed in her head with every step. Nora had missed something along the way, she was sure, and she could not shake the feeling that she was to blame.

It was as she stood numbly in the jammed elevator, slumped against the wood paneling, that she found the piece that had eluded her. She emerged on the eighth floor in a haze. A few agents intercepted her in the hall to offer condolences and ask about her health, but Nora only gave curt responses. She swallowed hard and walked into the office. "This was my fault," she said softly, and all three agents looked up from their computer screens.

"What was?" John asked.

Nora clenched her eyes shut, seeing it all again. When she spoke at last, she said, "Class D larceny."

"Come again?" said Burton.

"I should have seen it earlier," Nora murmured.

John frowned. "Class D—oh. You mean, Rashid?"

"He was working for a warehouse in South Philly. He filled up a U-Haul with merchandise from several of the companies storing their stuff there. Among them, a beauty supply distributor." Nora's eyes were full of regret.

Ben Calder understood immediately. "Acetone," he said.

"He ended up with a lot of shampoo and hair extensions. But, also enough acetone to last him for a long, long time," she said. "It's not like they made him turn it in when they sent him off to prison. He hadn't been on anyone's radar. No one knew he could cook."

"But by the time Rashid got out of jail and was ready to start up again, his brother was getting his meth from Mexico," Burton said.

"And that's not a relationship you sever," said Ben. "Unless you want to end up wearing your own entrails."

Wansbrough said, "But Nora, all of us missed something. Rashid and his mother were always coughing, classic sign of having a meth lab on premises. It never occurred to me. Hell, we were in the house together, and I found it hard to breathe. Why didn't we search the basement that day we went into Kylie's room?"

"If the part of the story was true that he was angry with Kevin over how he neglected the mom and sister, then leading the Somalis to take Kevin's car would make a certain amount of sense," John said, adding that line to the report he was working on.

"So Rashid can implicate Kevin in the killing that starts a gang war," Nora said.

"But what about Kylie? Would he have led the Somalis to her as well?" Ben asked. "Even if he was trying to help the Somalis start a gang war, why would Rashid have consented to Kylie being one of the victims?" Ben asked.

Eric Burton met Nora's eyes. She read his gaze, while appreciating his silence. Not dropping her eyes, she said softly, "Honor killing?"

The other two agents contemplated this theory in silence. Then John said, "We have to find Asad . . . and that car. If Monty Watt's right, and Kylie was killed in a vehicle, it might have been that one. And Hafsa's body probably took a ride in it before being dumped."

Nora checked her watch. "Catherine Zucco should almost be there by now," she said.

"It being a half an hour after we agreed to meet," Wansbrough said irritably. "She'd sure as hell better be there by now."

All four stood, gathering files from their desks, and made the short trip to Hahnemann Hospital. Soon they found themselves once again crowding into Kevin Baker's room. This time Laurie hadn't joined them, and only Nora and Eric Burton sat on the wide windowsill. Unlike their past visit, Kevin Baker was lucid and angry. "You take my mama into custody? Old lady like that?"

"First, if we hadn't removed her from the house, she'd be dead now," John Wansbrough answered. "Second, are you suggesting she *didn't* know what your brother Rashid was up to? That it wasn't part of his plan to have the sweet old lady feeding us all that information?"

Although he could still only really open one eye, Kevin regarded Wansbrough steadily. "What do you know about it?"

Ben interjected, "What do *you* know about it?"

Ever-poised, Catherine Zucco was saying, "I advise you not to answer that."

Kevin listened, cocked his head slightly, and remained mute.

John Wansbrough was irritated. "You do understand the concept of sentence reduction, right? It implies you will share *information* with us in exchange for a lighter sentence. In your case we are going to be hearing from you all about your contacts in Los Zetas. But first, we want to know when you last saw Rashid?"

Kevin glanced at his lawyer who nodded assent that he answer. "Last week."

"Before the drive-by in which Benzo was shot?"

"Same day."

"Did he have a spare key to your car?" John asked.

Kevin shifted uncomfortably in the bed as he considered this. "Maybe. I had left a valet key in the house somewhere . . . "

"Did Rashid want to participate in your business?"

Kevin nodded.

"And you kept him out?"

His bruised face darkened slightly, in fear, in remembrance. "I'd made a deal with Los Zetas. They had ways of being sure I carried through with my part." Kevin glanced at his lawyer, who hesitated, but nodded again. He chose his words carefully. "It turned out to be the right decision, keeping him out, though. He was too much of a risk."

"How?"

"I knew he'd be on probation a long time. But I also figured, you know, with the beard, him comin' home from jail all Muslim . . . that the FBI'd be watchin' him anyway. To see if he'd gone sand nigger or somethin' . . . "

From her perch on the windowsill, Nora flinched.

"Tell me about your relationship with Rashid," Ben was saying.

The lawyer leaned in. "Irrelevant, don't answer personal questions."

"Relevant," responded John Wansbrough loudly. "We believe that Rashid might have set Kevin up."

That got Kevin's attention. He said, "The last time I saw him, he was angry. He'd been approached by one of Dewayne's crew, asking him to cook for them. His cooking was top secret, see. Even when he was supplying the A&As back in the day, nobody was supposed to know it was him. That's how he played it safe."

"He thought you'd let his secret out?"

Kevin nodded.

"And did you?" John asked.

"Hell no!" Kevin said, indignantly. "Naw, man. I didn't want no trouble from him."

Ben studied him, then asked, "You were scared of your brother, Kevin?"

Kevin looked from Calder to Wansbrough, his gaze heavy with ugly memories. "My brother been through shit nobody should go through. Saw Mama get beat up all the time. Saw his daddy killed right in front of him. Gangbanger stab the man, right in front of him. Right in front of him, and walk right off. Police don't do nothing. It made him hard, made him, like, dead inside."

The two agents were silent a moment, waiting to see if he would add anything. Finally, John Wansbrough said, "What was the last thing he said to you?"

"He said I'd betrayed him, sold him out. That all along I hadn't done right by the family, not by Mama or Kylie, and not by him . . . so he had new friends now, new brothers. He said . . . He said they were running from war just like him—that life in Kingsessing is war every day, in every way. And so they understand each other just fine. And that they would be taking over my business, and that he would help them. That more war was brewing, and I was next to die."

"So he thought you had exposed him, put him in danger," John said. "What did he say when you told him it wasn't you who had 'sold him out'?"

Kevin Baker's voice became soft. "He wanted to know who it was, then."

"And you said?"

Kevin looked at his hands, then raised his eyes. Even Nora and Eric could see the remorse there. "I told him he should ask Kylie, cuz word was . . . word was she was . . . with Dewayne."

Eric Burton was talking very fast as the cluster of agents bent together outside the interview room. "So it wasn't supposed to be Kylie. They were going to start the war by killing Kevin first."

"But Rashid found out about Kylie," Ben said.

"And either volunteered her to be their next victim, or killed her himself," Eric surmised.

"In the Escalade," Nora said.

"In a car, Monty Watt told us. That probably was the Escalade.

The same Escalade that likely delivered Hafsa to the alley. Goddam, I want that car," John said, frustrated.

Suddenly Ben Calder looked up, eyes bright.

"It's a miracle she hadn't died already, though, right? Isn't that what you said, John?"

The rest of the agents looked at each other in sudden, confused silence. "What?" Burton demanded.

"From a sexual disease. It's a miracle she hadn't died already," Ben repeated.

John, Nora, and Eric all stared at him, confused.

He started to laugh. "I think I know where the flash drive is," he said excitedly.

"What? Where?" John demanded.

Still laughing, he grabbed Nora by the arm. "Give us an hour!"

"Where are you going?" Burton called after them.

"Medical examiner!" Ben called over his shoulder, pulling Nora by the arm through the hall. He almost bumped her into six different agents as he hurried her to the elevator and punched the down button.

"Have you lost your mind?" she asked, yanking her arm back and rubbing it.

"What was weird about the scene in the loft?" he said excitedly.

Nora shrugged. "Everything about that scene was weird."

"The bathroom?" he prompted, clearly expecting her to know the answer.

Nora reflected as he pulled her by the other arm into the elevator and punched "B." The car was already half-full of employees from the ninth and tenth floors. "There was a laptop in the bathroom?"

"Yes, but what else?" he pressed.

"Ummm, toiletries?" She scanned her memory. "Condom wrappers?"

He snapped loudly, startling his fellow passengers. "Not condom wrappers! *A* condom wrapper. One."

Nora shrugged. "So?"

"The whole reason we have Dewayne in custody at all is that he has left his semen *all over the city.*"

The woman next to Nora wore a dark gray suit and a pile of pearls. She eyed them both with distaste, then appeared grateful when the doors whooshed open at the lobby.

Ben continued undaunted as he and Nora waited for the car to continue to the basement. "Reality is a gangster, and a player, and he does *not* wear condoms."

Nora frowned. "What are you saying?"

"I'm saying," he said, green eyes flashing, "that the easiest way to smuggle something—say, in my field, drugs—out of a tricky situation is to *swallow it in a condom.*"

"Eww . . . " Nora winced. "Are you telling me . . . ?"

Ben laughed out loud as he ushered her into his car. " . . . that the hooker I shot had just eaten her flash drive!"

The Philadelphia medical examiner hadn't even touched Lisa Halston's mostly headless corpse until Nora and Ben stormed in. The flash drive that the M.E. pulled out of the dead hooker's stomach was indeed a moneypot. Libby and Jonas had taken only a few hours to decrypt it. One level of decryption allowed them to see what the Internet clients would see: girls, some as young as nine, in a variety of poses, sometimes completely naked, sometimes scantily clad, sometimes alone, sometimes with adult men or women touching them, displaying them. The second level of decryption exposed Lisa Halston's files on each child. Her name, how much she was bringing in, how many clients she could service per day (the average was five). Tameka Cooper was among them, and so was Jane Doe, whose picture appeared next to the name Susan.

There was a list of security guards at local motels who would keep their mouths shut, and for how much . . . There was a list of clients with cell phone numbers or e-mail addresses for each name. And most damning, an accounts receivable page listing Dewayne's cut and hers. Lisa Halston had been organized, thorough, and utterly soulless. Had Ben Calder not shot her in the head, the seventy-six girls on that flash drive would have netted her and Dewayne no less than twelve million dollars a year.

It was only a few hours after John Wansbrough had signed the evidence disclosure statement when Dewayne's lawyer called to let them know he would cut a deal.

The lawyer, whose name was Jenkins, twisted his Rolex back and forth on his arm. "I'm here to ensure that my client's rights are not violated during the process of helping the state with its case."

Nora did not disguise her disgust. "Such a noble public servant."

Dewayne laughed out loud at that—"Aww, the sister dissed you, Jenk . . . "

Before he got any further, Nora rounded on him. "I want to know about gang pimping."

"You would make a nice addition," Dewayne answered, letting his eyes travel slowly over her entire body. "Kinda skinny, maybe, but you smell real good . . . "

Nora let her rage smolder, looking to Ben who was standing next to the table. "Why minor girls, Dewayne?" he asked.

Dewayne shrugged. "Customers pay more. Just business. The younger ones is fresh, sweet. You know. *Softer.*"

Nora bit back her fury as Dewayne spoke. She accepted a steadying look from Calder, then said, with great deliberation, "But there's something more, right? They're easier to scare."

Dewayne thought this over. "It's a business. I can't take them home to mama each night for cocoa and bedtime stories. They have to believe that it's life or death."

"They perform for you or someone gets hurt."

Dewayne glanced at his lawyer who shook his head.

"And Kylie?" Nora demanded.

"Kylie was different, she came to me. But she did it. She was good at it, didn't complain like the others."

Nora recalled the doodling in the girl's biology textbook. "Because she loved you?" Nora asked, suddenly peering curiously into Dewayne's icy eyes.

Dewayne didn't answer. Nora knew she hadn't expected him to.

"Did you kill her?"

"I keep telling you people, I didn't kill her. Why would I kill her?"

"To mess with Kevin Baker?"

Jenkins interjected, "All of this is hypothetical, you needn't answer at all, Dewayne."

But Dewayne ignored him. "Naw, man. Kylie made me a lot of money, see. It woulda been stupid."

"Do you think Kevin Baker killed her? Because she was sleeping with you, his biggest rival?"

Dewayne shook his head. "I don't know, man . . . "

"Or perhaps it was Rashid Baker? Different brother, same reason?"

Nora saw Dewayne glance at his lawyer, and she pounced. "You know something about Rashid Baker."

Dewayne shrugged, frowning.

Ben sighed in frustration. "Come on, Dewayne. Were Rashid and Kylie close—did he know about the two of you?"

Dewayne rapped his knuckles against the tabletop, a deep frown still furrowing his brow. Then he looked up and said, "Kylie hated him. He was always up in her face, askin' where she goin', what she doin', who she doin' it with . . . Didn't like her clothes, didn't like her attitude. She start comin' to me after he got out. He made her crazy, so it was like she wanted to get away, you know . . . "

"Did he threaten her?"

"Every day, man," Dewayne answered.

"Did he know about the two of you?" Ben repeated. "Or that you were pimping Kylie?"

Dewayne shrugged. "I don't know, man. I know Kylie was too scared to tell him—about me. Or about the tricks."

Nora asked, "Did you know he could cook?"

Dewayne nodded slowly. "It was Kylie said he was starting to bring all these bottles and shit into the basement, made her swear never to go down there. Her mama don't go down there anyways, what with her knees, right—but Rashid started tellin' Kylie don't go down in there. I understood, then. Even sent a runner to talk to him, see about supplementing our current suppliers with some homegrown product."

Ben and Nora shared a glance. Then Ben asked, "Did you hear anything about Kevin Baker's Escalade being stolen?"

"The Escalade they used to take down Benzo?"

"The same."

Dewayne narrowed his eyes. "A&As sayin' they didn't do it?"

"Kevin Baker says he didn't do it, that his car had been stolen. What do you think?"

Dewayne seemed to be thinking. He glanced at Jenkins, who said again, "You only have to answer direct questions—you're not here for conjecture."

Ben glared at the lawyer. "He's asking for a deal in exchange for volunteering useful information. He can engage in a little conjecture." He turned his gaze back to Dewayne. "Come on, Dewayne. You have to have a theory. Same Escalade was used in a drive-by against federal agents. Lot of arrests happened after that. Could it be that someone's trying to play the JBM and the A&As off against each other, trying to punk you?"

Dewayne worked his jaw back and forth. Then he said finally, "There's some Africans on the scene."

Nora sat up straighter in her chair. "Go on," she said, hoping to keep her tone measured and calm.

"New in town, you know. Mean motherfuckers."

"How did you hear about them?" asked Nora.

Dewayne tapped his finger meditatively on the smooth tabletop. "They was offering deals to get into the business. To get hooked up, you know. So they could be sellin'."

Ben leaned forward. "What kind of deals?"

"They had some girls who was off the grid, see? No one lookin' for them. No papers. No missing persons databases." He said this last as though there were no greater irritation in the life of a gangster. "These girls were guaranteed ready to go all day every day, if you know what I mean—little meth, little H, and they was . . . cool. For the right info, the right connections, you could get a couple. For keeps. After that, they could make it regular, you know. Start bringin' 'em in whenever."

Nora looked at Ben, then looked away. Ben sensed her rage, and asked for her: "They were *selling* the girls?"

Dewayne nodded. "Offering a couple samples, like I said, in exchange for information. If we liked, we could make some investments."

"Did you take any?" Nora demanded.

He held her gaze. "Not this week." He held up his cuffed wrists. "Been busy."

"Did he say where the girls came from?" Nora asked.

"Nah. But the brother was definitely from Africa."

"Who was it that approached you?" Ben asked.

"Not me," Dewayne answered. "He went to one of my crew. My boys tried to follow them, but they disappeared. Said they'd contact us to follow up. That was that."

Nora and Ben exchanged glances, then stood to go. When Nora

arrived at the door, however, she turned and crossed back to Dewayne. "There's only one thing that makes me feel better about all this," she said softly.

Dewayne smirked. "What's that, beautiful?"

"Your cellmates will be so irate over contracting that sweet case of gonorrhea you have that they'll probably kill you themselves."

She was gratified to see her words had wiped the smirk right off his face.

It was late afternoon when Nora walked into the psych ward. Nurse Bedford gave her the look. "Six to eight," she said.

Nora stared her down. "I need to see her now. Let me in *or I will take you in*."

That got the woman's attention. She muttered all sorts of unfriendly remarks as she led Nora down the hall, but Nora was no longer interested in popularity contests.

When the nurse had left, Nora stood by the bedside, immobilized for a moment, watching the girl as she clutched tightly to the teddy bear. "I'm sorry," she said, her voice a whisper. "*Susan.* I'm sorry, Susan."

At the sound of her name, the girl looked up, but then looked away once more.

"It's going to be easier now to find your family and get you home, I promise." She groped for words, feeling that something trite like *It's going to be okay* would be a vicious lie. Finally, she just knelt on the floor next to the bed and placed her hand on Susan's thin arm. "I'm so sorry for what they did to you, what they made you do. I'm sorry."

Susan Jackson held her bear tighter, pushing her chin against its soft head, as tears welled up in her wide, brown eyes.

———

On the practice range the next afternoon, Nora was angry. "John, I've never been so frustrated. Ever. They're like ghosts. I mean, look, even Dewayne and his crew couldn't track them. How could they move so fast into an area and be able to blend in, and begin operations, not even scared of reprisals?"

John nodded, reloading, and realigning his body to compensate for the arm injury. "They had to have help, Nora. Facilitators. You heard Dewayne: their MO is to take existing structures and build on them. That's why they wanted to key into the JBM supply lines instead of trying to start their own. It's smart. Like a corporate takeover. Dumping Kevin Baker on our sidewalk was actually brilliant, I have to admit."

Nora considered this. "Brilliant," she conceded. "But just, like . . . satanic, right? Every time I think about those girls, that prison you found . . . " her voice trailed off, and her anger flowed out of her trigger finger. She was gratified to see the target with almost as many holes through its head as the one John was reeling in.

He pulled his ear protection off, peering at her work. "Looks good, Nora."

"The thing is, John, we're talking about sex slavery. Homegrown. Our own gangsters are doing it right under our noses."

John sighed. "Slaves used to run to Philadelphia to *gain* their freedom."

"Well, then, I guess we have something to work toward. In the meantime, I found Susan's parents in Albany and had to call and ask them to drive down to pick up their very sick ex-slave daughter."

Their eyes met, and he nodded, and she could see him imagining what that must have been like for the parents. "Any word on—who was the girl?"

"Tameka. Our agents located her at the motel Dewayne was using in Camden. Tameka was supposed to have been picked up after servicing a client. But then all hell broke loose, Dewayne was arrested, the crew scattered, and her ride never showed. The security guard had been getting fat kickbacks from Dewayne, so he'd locked Tameka in a closet this whole time. He'd been scared she'd get away and Dewayne would come back and kill him."

John winced. "How was she?"

"Starved and crazy for meth by that point. She went straight to the hospital. Her mother is with her now."

John sighed. "At least . . . she's going home."

"Yeah, except now she's gonna have years of rehab ahead of her for the meth they got her hooked on."

John shook his head. "I don't have any answers, Nora. I wish to God I did, but I don't."

She sighed. "We got a lotta work to do." She had just unclipped the poster when her BlackBerry shuddered with a new text message. She glanced at the phone. Monty Watt had sent the words *Teff flour.*

She and Wansbrough made their way through the basement from the range to Watt's lab. "What's going on? What's teff flour?" she asked.

Monty looked up. "The hood used on the shooting victim was actually more like part of a burlap sack containing teff flour."

"Which is—?" John pressed.

"An Ethiopian flour used in injera bread . . . and general baking."

John and Nora looked at each other pensively, then back at Monty.

Monty shrugged wearily. "Look, I don't make the information. I *relay* it."

They found Ben and Eric Burton at their desks and shared Monty's latest discovery.

"Okay, but what's teff flour?" Ben was saying as they sank into their desk chairs in the cubicle.

"Don't you know anything, man?" Wansbrough asked, throwing up his arms in mock frustration.

Nora suppressed a smile and felt a surge of gratitude that Wansbrough was back to lightening the mood again.

Ben wasn't quite there yet, though. He rejoined irritably, "Apparently not, *man*. What does it have to do with anything?"

Eric Burton gave Nora a wink so surreptitious she at first questioned whether she'd actually seen it. Then he piped up, "Well, Benjamin, given the 'investigators' moniker, we're optimistic we'll figure it out."

Ben raised his eyebrows at all of them, then laughed out loud. "Okay, let's ask the Google Oracle." He scanned the screen, and Nora rolled her chair over to his desk. "Also known as 'lovegrass,'" he read. "Imported from Ethiopian highlands . . . What's injera bread?" He Googled that too, and all three of them stared at the images of flat bread on the screen.

"'Popular in Ethiopia, Eritrea, Djibouti and Somalia . . .'" Nora read aloud.

"What does a fifty-pound bag of teff flour cost in this country?" asked John.

Ben typed it in, wondering aloud what had gotten done at the Federal Bureau of Investigation prior to the emergence of the Internet. "More than two hundred dollars," he responded finally.

John harrumphed. "Then that's not just something average people are buying."

All three men suddenly looked at Nora, who exhaled sharply and then murmured, "*Restaurant.*"

The Suburban skidded around a corner, then swerved to miss an elderly woman pushing a grocery cart full of plump trash bags. Ben and Eric followed not far behind in Ben's car. The SWAT van was barreling through the tangled streets of West Philly and deep into

Kingsessing. It had taken all of an hour to get surveillance on the small detached garage behind the neighborhood's one Ethiopian restaurant. The confirmation was quick in coming: One Cadillac Escalade.

"How many gang members?" Nora was asking.

"Our guys put the count at eight," Wansbrough responded.

Nora cast a quick glance at him. "Vest?"

He nodded, patting his chest and smiling at her.

The vehicles converged on the small building, so close to the site where they had found Hafsa's body. As Nora anchored her Black-Berry in the dash holder and opened the line with Ben and Eric, she stared at the tiny restaurant. Its bright plastic sign gave homage to the Ethiopian flag, the colors striking a contrast with the gray day and grayer surroundings. A curling metal railing sprawled wildly to the side of rickety cement steps, an entryway that did not appear to beckon to customers.

Now the black-swathed men poured out of the van with swift efficiency, with half the team crouching as they raced for the back entrance, and the other half assembling at the front door. Nora watched breathlessly as they entered the restaurant; despite herself, she checked her watch. She noted that it was two o'clock, and wondered if such a restaurant drew late lunchers. Everything in the neighborhood seemed to slow to a standstill as the sound of shouting spilled out onto the street; they heard the shattering of glass within, and the discharge of a weapon, followed by more shouting that escalated to a fever pitch.

Nora was just going to ask John what their next move should be when the garage door exploded outward in an angry shower of splintered wood, and the Escalade barreled out onto the street with a banshee shriek of its spinning tires. Behind the wheel they saw a tall, lean Somali wearing black wayfarer sunglasses. Just as the imam had described him.

John stared for a split second at the empty SWAT van, its team ensconced within the restaurant, and without further hesitation slammed the Suburban's gearshift into drive. Nora leaned over and flipped on the siren and flashing lights, then fumbled with her seat belt as the SUV devoured the uneven pavement of Kingsessing.

Suddenly, a bullet slammed against the front window; the glass held, but exploded into an intricate web that crackled across the surface. "Jesus, how can he drive and shoot that well?" John protested, craning his neck to look through a clear spot in the glass.

Nora heard Ben's voice—"Are you guys all right?"

"We're fine," she shouted. "Do I return fire, John?" Nora pulled the Glock from the elastic holster at the small of her back.

"I want you to shoot out his tires, Nora, but only when you have a clear shot—we can't risk striking a pedestrian!"

She rolled down the window and took aim.

"Ha!" John was yelling. "Trolley! That should slow you down, bastard!"

The snail-like Chester Street trolley was just ahead, with a line of traffic approaching from the opposite direction, and Nora watched in terror as the Escalade jockeyed for position, nearly flattening a mother pushing a stroller across the street. The woman screamed and thrust the stroller between two parked cars, then leapt after it. Unable to pass, the Escalade suddenly tore across the oncoming lane and into the grass of Clark Park. It jolted down the steep hill, past a dog walker who dropped all six leashes in his charge; the dogs scattered. John had to wait for two oncoming cars to pass, but then he followed suit, almost striking a galloping yellow Lab. The Suburban bumped across the grass, as Nora clutched her weapon, still hoping for a shot. The Escalade was out of range now and had just tumbled onto Baltimore Avenue and continued its flight.

She cast a backward glance and was relieved to see that Ben wasn't behind them—his car would never have made it through the park. John grimaced as he steered with his bad arm, downshifting with his right to help the Suburban up the hill onto Baltimore; the intersection was hopelessly congested, but he added a honking horn to the scream of the siren, and most of the cars parted.

"Did he stay on Baltimore or cut through?" John was shouting.

"Baltimore, Baltimore! Go, go, go!" Nora cried, leaning slightly out of her window for a better view. Then they heard the sickening sound of careening vehicles and the crunch of metal smashing into metal. In a moment, they saw what had caused the noise. Two cars had swerved to miss the Escalade and crashed into each other, spinning into the middle of the intersection and coming to rest perpendicular to the flow of traffic, effectively sealing off the road. John couldn't get the wide Suburban through the fissure between the wreckage and the parked cars lining the sidewalk.

"Mother*fucker*!" John swore, as he jammed on the brakes. Nora flopped forward against the iron embrace of the seat belt. The Escalade whipped out of sight, turning the corner onto 38th Street.

But both agents immediately heard a screech of tires, and Nora was shocked to see Ben's Ford barrel past them on the sidewalk, and then bump down gracelessly just beyond the accident.

"Alright, Calder!" John yelled.

Ben's response was clear through Nora's cell, "We gotta keep him off Seventy-six!"

At almost any other time of day they would have been able to count on the Schuylkill River Expressway being impassable and hopelessly clogged. But at two o'clock in the afternoon it would be clear; at higher speeds on the expressway, the pursuit could potentially become far more deadly.

John yanked the gearshift into reverse and spun the car around to rocket the wrong way up 40th Street, up to Spruce and into the heart of the campus of the University of Pennsylvania. "He's heading up to Market," Nora heard Eric Burton shouting.

Nora holstered her weapon in order to cling better to the handle above her window. John's entire concern now was to keep from plowing the Suburban into a group of backpack-toting students, and his knuckles gleamed beige on the steering wheel. Nora saw he was gritting his teeth through the pain in his injured arm. He cut up to Market Street, desperately trying to catch up.

"Where's that backup?" Just as Nora asked, a counterpoint to their siren reverberated through the air. They heard Eric Burton hollering orders that the police should seal off the entrances to the expressway. Nora spotted the Escalade careening past the 30th Street Station, but veering sharply right onto JFK when Asad spied the roadblocks. John sped up, weaving in and out of the traffic. Nora heard gunshots and saw that Eric Burton was leaning out the window of Ben's car, trying to shoot out the Escalade's tires. The Escalade returned fire, and Ben's front window exploded.

"Ben!" Nora screamed.

"Goddammit!" he was shouting. Then, "We're okay!" he shouted.

All three cars were rocketing up 20th Street now, and the sound of sirens bearing down from behind them filled the air. Traffic was getting congested again, and a taxi and a minivan slid into each other as the Escalade shot through the red light at the Benjamin Franklin Parkway. "I can't get a shot—" Eric was yelling, even though he didn't have to hang out the side window anymore.

Nora watched the Escalade and the Ford swing left onto the parkway. "Where is he going?"

John was shaking his head. "He's just desperate now—maybe he's trying for the expressway access from the Spring Garden Bridge."

But Nora could see the flash of red and blue lights blocking that route as well.

"What the—!" John exclaimed.

The Escalade had changed directions again and was heading up 23rd and then inexplicably turned left, vanishing into the tunnel that traveled one way under the parkway, beneath the Museum of Art's east entrance and the seventy-two steps where Nora so often ran. It emptied out on the other side of the museum by the Spring

Garden Bridge. From there the Escalade could easily enter the expressway.

"Gotcha now," Nora heard Ben yell, and she heard the squeal of his tires as he turned hard left to pursue the Escalade.

"No, Ben—" John shouted. "Don't follow him into the tunnel!"

Nora looked from John to the still distant entrance to the tunnel in terror. "Oh, *shit!*" she heard Ben yell. "He's shifted into reverse . . . "

That was when a deafening crash filled the Suburban. From the open windows, from the BlackBerry on the dashboard—to Nora it seemed that the sound tumbled down upon them like an avalanche. The Suburban half-skidded, half-spun to a stop at the mouth of the tunnel, bringing into view the remnants of Ben's car.

No sound would come, even though Nora's mouth was open, and in her head she was screaming Ben's name over and over and over.

John Wansbrough's door was closest to the tunnel, and he opened it and crouched down, his gun drawn, with the door between him and the scene. He peered into the smoky opening, glanced at Nora, and began to shout Ben's and Eric's names.

Nora opened her door, but he motioned to her not to descend from the car yet.

"Something's going on," he hissed.

Then, as the smoke was clearing, Nora saw John's eyes widen. Midway through the tunnel, they could see that Asad had pulled an unconscious Ben out of his car and was holding a gun to his neck. The Somali's sunglasses were nowhere to be seen, and Nora could just make out the hollow, shrunken space where his left eye had been.

"I want safe passage!" he was shouting, and Nora knew the voice immediately, had heard it every night in every dream she'd had since the same gun had been held against her own neck. Hearing that voice made her see the bright red stain on Basheera's chest all over again. She stared desperately at Ben's limp form.

"Your man is *alive*, see—he is still breathing! I am going to put this man in my car, and I will drive away. If anyone comes near me, I will kill this man! If anyone cuts me off, I will kill this man! If I see flashing lights or hear even one siren, I will kill this man!"

John repeated these things into the radio on his dashboard, then glanced at Nora, who was blinking rapidly. She wondered with a sinking feeling if Eric had survived the crash at all. John began shouting, trying to stall the tall Somali by any means—"Now, wait, now . . . we can talk about this. You know, if you kill a federal agent it will be much, much worse for you! We can cut you a deal . . . "

Nora stared at Ben's helpless body, dangling from the crook of the tall man's elbow. She glanced at the traffic jams piling up behind the Suburban, making it impossible for the police cars bearing down on them to get through. Uniformed officers were beginning to approach on foot, weapons drawn, but John was furiously waving them off in an effort to protect Ben. The man called Asad would surely hear the sirens and brakes of any cars approaching from the tunnel's other end. The Somali was dragging Ben backward, step by step, his eyes riveted on John Wansbrough. Twenty paces behind them was the waiting Escalade, the back of which was severely dented, the massive window destroyed, but which otherwise appeared intact.

She stared into the tunnel, then gazed up at the museum. Suddenly she bent and double-knotted her shoelaces. Then she patted the holster at the small of her back, making sure her gun was secure.

"Talk to him, John. Whatever you do, don't stop talking. Promise him anything and everything, but do not let him leave." Instead of sitting up again, she remained hunched over and slipped out of the car.

John's eyes darted her way, then he gave her a brief nod, understanding. He yelled into the tunnel, "I can get you a helicopter, man. Don't be hasty. A car will only get you so far . . . "

This was the last thing Nora heard as she held her low crouch and slipped into the crowd of cars jamming Pennsylvania Avenue. She circled out, beyond the Somali's field of vision, then began racing for the parkway. Her feet flew beneath her as she maneuvered through the already snarled pack of cars in Eakins Oval at the Benjamin Franklin Parkway's northwest end. The ripple effect from the crash in the tunnel had halted traffic and brought angry honking from motorists. Nora sprinted along the foot of the museum steps, then dashed into the bicycle lane and up toward the Spring Garden Bridge. She couldn't tell if the pounding in her ears was from her heartbeat or the thump of her sneakers against the pavement. Finally, she gained the opposite end of the tunnel.

She had to walk several paces in before she could see the Escalade. Asad had not yet reached the SUV, but was still little by little dragging the limp body of Ben Calder. Nora couldn't see John Wansbrough, but she heard his deep bass voice resounding through the tunnel as he pleaded with the Somali: "Come on, man—You've got a decorated agent there. You walk outta here with him and the whole government will be on your ass. But leave him safely here and we can get you a jet to wherever you want to go. You pick the island, man. You can *pick* it!"

She prayed John's voice was loud enough to cover the soft tread of her Pumas. She pulled her gun and then crouched low, gluing herself to the shadows on the side of the tunnel closest to Asad. If he turned, he could perhaps see her moving through the dimness. But the far side was on a lower grade, and filled with remnants of autumn leaves that would have given away her position immediately.

Am I close enough? She wondered, weighing the gun in her hand, squinting.

One shot.

Just one shot.

She heard Ben's voice in her head. *There is no other way to deal with him than to shoot him dead* . . .

Asad had reached the car and was reaching for the door handle. Nora inhaled, relaxing her neck muscles, and rose to a full standing position to square her stance.

For a moment her mind brimmed with images of Ben and Basheera and six missing girls.

And then she knew perfect clarity.

And she pulled the trigger.

CHAPTER 13

"**I knew I** hated coffee, but hospital coffee is impossibly bad," Nora said. "I can't believe how bad this tastes, and I've dumped in three packs of sugar and all this fake creamer . . . "

John looked at his own cup of hospital coffee and shrugged. "It's called taking one for the team, Nora. You don't want to be out prowling around for tea when Ben wakes up, do you?"

She looked back at where Ben Calder lay, his face covered with cuts and several sets of stitches. John had been down in intensive care checking on Eric Burton. Until John had walked in, she'd been holding Ben's hand. Now she sat feigning calm in the taut blue vinyl recliner, trying to drink the coffee the nurse had brought her.

John had pulled a straight chair over so they could talk softly. "The men the SWAT team arrested told us how to find the rest of the girls," he said. "They're with Rahma at Children's Hospital now—they've practically got their own floor."

"What's next for them, John?"

He shook his head. "Well, as victims of trafficking they can get T-Visas so they can testify, and eventually they can apply for permanent resident status. But it will take a while. They'll be in limbo for a long time . . . "

"And what they really need is counseling and care," Nora pointed out.

"We don't yet have services in place for this kind of thing," John said.

Nora considered this, then said, "I'm going to have a pull-out couch. IKEA's finest."

John looked thoughtful. "You're a good egg, Nora Khalil. But that's not even an eighth of an answer for what they really need." Then he tilted his head, his eyes searching hers. "Your dad's cool with you moving out? You two okay?"

Nora frowned, recalling the scene. Ragab was emphatically not cool with her moving out. But she shrugged. "He'll find a way to laugh about it—save face. He knows I love him, and I know all the fuss is because he loves me. Plus, you know . . . "

"Yeah, I know, you got the gun." He glanced at his vibrating phone. "Watt," he said to Nora before answering it. He listened intently, nodded a few times, then thanked Monty and hung up.

Nora looked a question at him.

"That hunting knife that killed Kylie. They just pulled it out of the ashes of Rashid's workshop."

Nora sipped unhappily at the now-cold coffee. "Honor killing? Or vengeance for exposing family secrets?"

John had no answer. He had already told her about the traces of blood they'd found in the Escalade—a combination of Windex and peroxide had been used to try to wipe them away, but the blood was clearly Kylie's. As for Hafsa, several strands of curly black hair had been pulled out of the SUV; some from the passenger backseat, suggesting she had ridden there alive when she was taken from the mosque; other hairs were found in the rear storage area.

John said, "Well, add that to the blood-soaked carpet that was pulled out of the restaurant's Dumpster, and a restaurant basement that matches the shards of lime and lye under her toenails . . . " The SWAT team had found the Ethiopian family who ran the restaurant living as prisoners. Their primary role had been to shelter and feed the Somali gang. Nora was relieved that it would not be her job to prosecute the group of seven for their crimes against the family and for the murder and human trafficking charges.

"So . . . we're done . . . " John said.

"And busier than ever," Nora said thoughtfully.

"Who's done?" came a whisper, and both agents turned to see Ben looking at them.

They jumped to their feet and went to stand at his bedside.

"You okay, Ben?" John asked. "You scared the hell out of us."

Nora searched for her voice but couldn't find it. She contented herself with resting her hand on Ben's and squeezing it repeatedly, unconcerned that John saw.

"Eric?" he asked.

John answered, "Eric's gonna need a lot of physical therapy, but he's gonna be okay. Two broken legs. He's downstairs until they can get the internal bleeding under control."

Ben swallowed and looked down at his own body. "How about me? Everything make it through?"

"Broken arm, lotta stitches. Pretty face ain't so pretty anymore."

"What happened? Did we get him?"

John Wansbrough looked at Ben with a wide smile. "Well, he almost abducted you to use you as his ticket to freedom. But . . . my rookie blew his head off."

"No way," Ben said, gazing at Nora with shining eyes.

"Way," Nora said softly, unable to prevent the tears from spilling down her cheeks.

John Wansbrough said, "I think I'll go get us a little more coffee."

EPILOGUE

The light pouring through the living room window was warm and bright. Nora sat on a nubby blue area rug, surrounded by open IKEA boxes and a scattering of screws, bolts, and plywood.

When the doorbell rang, her chin jerked up, and she frowned, alert. She brushed her fingertips over her Glock, which hung from her shoulder holster on the coat stand, as she peered through the peephole. When she saw who it was, her shoulders relaxed, and a slow smile worked its way across her features.

"Hi, Ben," she said, pulling open the door.

"Officer Khalil," he said. "Although I did just hear a rumor you have an application in to the FBI . . . So maybe it will be Agent Khalil soon?"

She grinned. "Well, I heard that federal officers were . . . what was it? 'A breed apart'? 'More sensitive'?"

Ben laughed. "It's true, I swear!"

"We'll see. Schacht said if I really want to work on human trafficking cases that's the best way to go. And now that I'm out on my own, the decisions are mine. So if I get in, the apartment may be pretty temporary. But it's perfect for now." She looked him over. "Would you like to come in?"

He nodded. "That would make it easier to give you this housewarming present," he said.

Nora grinned as Ben took a rolled poster tied with a bow from his arm with the cast and handed it to her using his good arm. "For me?"

"I knew you'd be suffering from bare walls."

She looked from the gift to Ben. "Should I open it now?"

"Well, you could offer me weed tea or something. So much for Arab hospitality."

She laughed. "My bad. But since I've already breached etiquette, I'll just be opening this first." She tugged at the bow and unrolled a vintage poster of Umm Kulthoum. Nora gasped.

He tapped the poster with a smile. "You don't know how hard it was to find that."

Nora shook her head, laughing. "eBay?"

"Amazon.com."

"And the hard part was?"

He looked sheepish. "Figuring out how to spell her name."

She grinned. "Typical."

"But, once I did, I ordered CDs, too. And I've been listening. I have."

"You need a coach, silly. Someone to translate the words. The poetry is the magic."

He tilted his head. "So you'll translate for me, then?"

She nodded. "I would consider that a noble use of my skills."

"Deal." He took in the light-filled room. "I like your place," he said.

"Me too," she answered, looking around again as though seeing the small Chinatown apartment for the first time.

"I hope I get to see a lot of it."

"Well . . . I guess that depends on how many posters you're willing to give for the cause."

"As many as it takes," he said, holding her gaze.

Nora smiled, feeling heat rising in her cheeks despite her best efforts.

"Does this mean you're gonna give us a chance, Nora?"

She swallowed, not answering.

"Nora?" he said softly, taking a step closer and slipping his good arm around her waist.

"I guess I decided that putting labels on you is as wrong as accepting them on myself."

He leaned in. "I like that decision," he said, his breath warm against her skin.

She looked away, then back at him, allowing herself to be pulled into his eyes.

"So what now?" he asked, his voice almost a whisper.

Nora inhaled his scent, her eyes fluttering closed, then she met his gaze with a smile. "Well . . . I know this cute little café that now serves halal cheesesteaks . . . "

POSTSCRIPT

Half the Sky, by Nicholas Kristof and Sheryl WuDunn, details the obstacles that women and girls across the globe face in their daily struggles for survival. Sex trafficking and sexual slavery exist as far away as Cambodia and as nearby as L.A. and Nashville and St. Paul, while honor killing and female genital mutilation compete in the intensity of their tragedy with the aborting of female fetuses or the starvation of female children in order to privilege their brothers. The number of "missing women" on the planet today ranges between 60–107 million, with two million *vanishing* as a result of gender discrimination each year.

The authors call for real leadership in the global fight against slavery generally and sexual slavery and forced prostitution in particular, as well as sustained international focus on educating the planet's women and girls and granting them economic opportunities that can lead to the advancement of entire communities. Because the book is geared toward answering the question, "What can I do to make a difference?," the appendix to *Half the Sky* lists many organizations and websites where we can transform our energies into tangible change. In that spirit, please explore the following:

- *Polaris* seeks to eradicate modern slavery networks and raise awareness worldwide.
  www.polarisproject.org
- *Apne Aap* battles sex slavery in India, including in remote areas in Bihar that get little attention. Apne Aap welcomes American volunteers.
  www.apneaap.org

- *Campaign for Female Education* (CAMFED) supports schooling for girls in Africa.
  www.camfed.org
- *ECPAT* is a network of groups fighting child prostitution, particularly in Southeast Asia.
  www.ecpat.net
- *Equality Now* lobbies against the sex trade and gender oppression around the world.
  www.equalitynow.org
- *International Justice Mission* works tirelessly against human trafficking by focusing on victim relief, perpetrator accountability, survivor aftercare, and structural transformation.
  www.ijm.org
- *Made by Survivors* seeks to empower women by giving them job training skills and also sponsors individual children at risk for being trafficked.
  www.madebysurvivors.com
- *Shared Hope International* fights sex trafficking around the world.
  www.sharedhope.org

ABOUT THE AUTHOR

Dr. Carolyn Baugh holds both a master's (2008) and a doctorate (2011) from the University of Pennsylvania in Arabic and Islamic Studies. She is an assistant professor of History at Gannon University in Erie, Pennsylvania, where she teaches courses in Middle East and world history and also directs the Women's Studies Program. Her graduate research focused on minor marriage in early Islamic law, while her translation work includes the Sufi treatise of the celebrated fourteenth-century jurist and scholar Ibn Khaldun.

Dr. Baugh codirects the *Erie Voices* refugee oral history project geared at collecting the stories of Erie's diverse refugee community for purposes of increasing tolerance and understanding between cultures. She is faculty advisor for Students United Against Human Trafficking and the Muslim Students Association.

She is a failed concert pianist, a psychotic soccer mom to two indomitable girls, and the only one in the house who feeds Oreo the Cat.

www.carolynbaugh.com